A LOUD CRACK SENT LANAKILA SKYWARD—

Sarena screamed in agony, as fire ripped through her shoulder and into her back, dropping her flat onto her chin.

Something had her. She turned and kicked desperately with claws extended, but the vicious jaws did not flinch. She snarled and grabbed with her teeth, but they met with a hard, painful clink. She kicked again, making the pain even worse.

Lanakila landed and instantly began jabbing at the assailant. He struck it twice with his beak, then recoiled in pain. He hopped all around it with his wings spread as Sarena dropped her legs and stopped kicking.

"Help me!" Sarena cried.

"It's a trap!" squawked Lanakila. "A man trap. . . ."

CATAMOUNT

Michael Peak

A ROC BOOK

ROC
Published by the Penguin Group
Penguin Books USA Inc., 375 Hudson Street,
New York, New York 10014, U.S.A.
Penguin Books Ltd, 27 Wrights Lane,
London W8 5TZ, England
Penguin Books Australia Ltd, Ringwood,
Victoria, Australia
Penguin Books Canada Ltd, 10 Alcorn Avenue,
Toronto, Ontario, Canada M4V 3B2
Penguin Books (N.Z.) Ltd, 182–190 Wairau Road,
Auckland 10, New Zealand

Penguin Books Ltd, Registered Offices:
Harmondsworth, Middlesex, England

First published by Roc, an imprint of New American Library,
a division of Penguin Books USA Inc.

First Printing, March, 1992
10 9 8 7 6 5 4 3 2

 Roc is a trademark of New American Library,
a division of Penguin Books USA Inc.

Printed in Canada

For Karen Shapiro,
my friend across the lifetimes.

ACKNOWLEDGMENTS

I believe it was Kaibab, one of the beautiful mountain lions at the San Diego Zoo, who first gave me the idea to write about *Felis concolor californica*. I'd like to thank my friends at the zoo, Jeff Jouett and Georgeanne Irvine, who made my meetings with Kaibab possible, and Gary Priest, who was much more patient than I might have been.

Without a doubt, it was Sheba from Bob Farner's Wildlife Rescue who let me know firsthand just how awesome and powerful these great animals truly are. Thank you, Sheba. I will never forget you.

PROLOGUE

"In closing . . ."

The voice of the Creator drifted like the edge of a dreamy whisper, flowing majestically with knowledge and compassion, on the last day before Time. They were all there, the lords and ladies of every animal destined to walk the earth. They sat in a huge circle around the Creator, and stretched their ears like flowers reaching for every golden ray of sunlight.

Lady Farri began to fidget nervously as she stared in disbelief at the Creator. It was over. In all of their schooling they had ascertained so much, yet so little. Now he was sending them on their way.

She had not learned enough. She would never be able to guide every species of cats through such a violent world, with the scant information offered by the Creator. Yet there He stood, ready to give his final remarks.

"All of you are worried," said the Creator. "Some of you more than others. And so you should be. You have been given the charge of millions of animals. It's not a charge to be taken lightly."

"What if we fail?" asked Farri, voicing the concern of them all. Fortunately she was the Creator's favorite, and could speak up when others were too frightened.

"If you are very lucky, 'if' is all you will be concerned with," said the Creator. " 'When' is more likely. And each time a line disappears, you'll pay a visit to Me."

"Each time?" asked Farri, confused.

"Even you, my dear Farri, will suffer the loss of your lines," the Creator said. "Not all of them, but several, if not most. Each loss will be more painful than their languages can express. And each loss will be painful to all of us, not just to the individual lords and ladies. Each death of a line will be mourned for the life of the planet."

"Why will so many perish?" Farri asked with despair. She looked around at the others. There were so many of them, but the world was a large place. Large enough for them all, if they would cooperate.

"Look not at the others, my Farri," said the Creator. "They are not the ones. Look at yourself—all of you—and see the rigidness of your natures. It is this rigidness that will bring you down, for only those who can adapt to constant change will survive.

"Some will simply tire of the world and wish to move on," continued the Creator. "No blame will be cast for this, since they will have spent an enormous amount of time on the planet, and they will certainly deserve a rest. Others will simply vanish as a result of their stupidity."

Farri nodded, but was certain there was more. At least she hoped there was. The others seemed satisfied, but as far as she was concerned the Creator could never furnish her with enough information.

"You are not content, Farri," He said.

"It still sounds easier than Your implication," said Farri. "We could all agree to coexist as best as possible, within the cycles of life we've learned about, without killing ourselves off. What am I missing?"

"It does sound easy," the Creator answered. "It sounds easy because you have yet to meet the most ferocious and destructive animal in Creation. He will never hear your words, and will rarely hear his own."

"Why isn't he here?" asked Farri. "We could reason with him now."

"He won't arrive until all of you hold your places on the earth. He is My great experiment, and I suggest you learn to live with him, or avoid him to the fullest of your abilities."

"How will we recognize him, then, if he's not here?" asked Farri.

"He will be the only one to walk on two legs."

CHAPTER 1

Laura Kay would rather eat glass than cover governmental meetings. They were always felony-boring, and in Southern California no one really cared what local governments did anyway.

It had been just over a year since she had landed the job with the *San Diego Union*. After working on smaller papers for nearly five years, she had finally made what amounted to The Big Time in newspaper reporting. In her year of general assignment reporting in The Big Time, she had managed to escape the dreaded task of covering meetings. Today her perfect record had come to an end.

Laura sat in the dimly lit basement auditorium of the State Building in downtown San Diego. The Board of Commissioners of the California Department of Fish and Game was having the first of the two semiannual meetings it would conduct in San Diego. The Board met in a different city each month.

Most of the time no one cared what Fish and Game did, so the *Union* rarely gave them any coverage. Today was different, and since covering animal stories was part of Laura's beat this meeting was all hers.

The meeting was fifteen minutes from starting and already the auditorium was packed with a standing-room crowd of the most bizarre mix of people Laura had ever seen. There were men in ultraconservative business suits sitting amidst people who looked like dropouts from the 1960s. Dressed twenty years out of date, they held protest signs and wore cutout masks shaped like the faces of mountain lions. Laura decided to approach them first.

"Hi, I'm Laura Kay from the *Union*," she said to a

man in a rainbow-colored T-shirt with long, stringy brown hair. "Are you all part of an organized group?"

"Yeah, we're from Mountain Lions Forever," he said. "The guy you want to talk to is standing over there, leaning over and talking to that lady. He's our spokesperson, Brad Berglund."

"Thank you," said Laura. She looked down at his sign, which read, WE KNOW YOU'RE LYIN'. SAVE OUR LIONS!, then she turned and walked away. Certain no one was looking, she rolled her eyes and smiled. At least this would get interesting.

In his jacket and tie, Brad Berglund looked like a man completely out of place. He might have been able to pull it off if everything at least had matched, but the disastrous color combination coupled with his over-casual demeanor gave him away. Laura walked up and introduced herself.

"Hi, I guess I'm the guy you need to talk to," said Brad. He sported shoulder-length, straight blond hair and a brown beard, which actually went well with his John Lennon-style glasses. Laura finally noticed the running shoes he wore with his suit. He handed Laura a large press packet.

"Tell me a little bit about your organization and why you're here today," Laura said. With her left hand she held up a tiny cassette recorder and her reporter's notebook. She scribbled notes with the other.

"Mountain Lions Forever is here to protest the Department's proposed issuance of two hundred and fifty permits for trophy-hunting mountain lions in the upcoming season," said Brad. "They are scheduled to hold three public meetings to hear testimony on whether it's correct to do so, but all seven of the commissioners are hunters and they've already made up their minds to go ahead with the hunt."

"Two hundred and fifty permits statewide doesn't seem like so many," said Laura, who always took the other side when interviewing.

"If they had supporting data to back it up, then no," said Brad. "But there is no accepted estimate by *anyone* of how many mountain lions there are left in California. Even the commissioners admit that no one knows. There could be one, or ten, or ten million. No one knows.

Confirmed sightings are so rare that it's impossible to tell how many there might be."

Laura nodded and scribbled some notes. She knew this could not be completely true. The Department of Fish and Game wouldn't allow a hunt if they didn't have at least their own estimate of how many were out there.

"This is their third attempt to have a season," said Brad. "The past two years they've been stopped by a court order in San Francisco. The Commission has appealed both times but lost. So each year they try new wording on their proposal, and each year we have to take them to court again."

Laura looked toward the front of the auditorium and saw the commissioners taking their seats. There were three armed, uniformed Fish and Game officers standing near the front of the stage. Apparently they expected trouble.

"We plan to get arrested," said Brad. "We'll give our testimony, and then when they start talking about how the hunt is appropriate we'll disrupt the meeting."

"You came here all the way from Sacramento?" Laura asked, when Brad handed her his card.

"Yes," he said, finally straightening his shoulders and throwing out his chest. "Mountain lions are worth it."

Laura stood along the left side of the room as the meeting started. She decided to put some distance between herself and Brad's group, who were seated on the right. Laura wanted to appear as neutral as possible.

She could have sat up in the front at the press table, but most of those seats were taken up by TV people. She wanted to keep her distance from them as well, since it was for their benefit that the folks from Mountain Lions Forever would get themselves arrested. It always made great video in otherwise boring meeting footage.

Laura studied the commissioners. All of them were middle-aged white men, perhaps in their fifties. They looked more like a group of retired marines than they did state officials. Each one seemed bored and irritated with the public testimony, no matter which side the speaker took. They didn't look at all friendly, nor did they look like people who would be interested in protecting wildlife, which was their job. Laura knew looks could be deceiving, but at least the members of Mountain

Lions Forever were sincere in their objectives, and they looked the part. The commissioners did not.

Only two speakers were in favor of the hunt. One of them was a Fish and Game staff member who gave a report on the current increase of livestock lost to mountain lions. The other was from the National Rifle Association, who talked about the people's constitutional right to bear arms and how the anti-hunters were trying to take that right away.

Over fifty people wished to speak in opposition, but the chairman limited each side to a certain amount of time so only group representatives were permitted to speak. Conservationists, biologists, and various other groups were all represented. They were all very professional and well mannered in their deliveries. The commissioners were not impressed.

Laura was. Not as much by the delivery, as by what they said and the commissioners' response. Apparently Brad Berglund had told her the truth: There was no accepted estimate of the number of mountain lions in California. No one knew, and no one, not even the Fish and Game staff, dared to guess.

The presentations began to get repetitious, and after an hour Laura began to lose interest. She had already picked out the quotes she would use from the public testimony and from Brad Berglund. She would have left already, but she needed to stick around and try to get an interview with a commissioner after the meeting. The old rule of two sides to every story obviously had been made up by someone who had never gone out to cover one. As with this story, there were usually several sides.

She began to scan the crowd. The Mountain Lion Forever people were getting restless. They were scheduled to be the last speakers in the public testimony. All of them, which Laura estimated to mean about forty, held lion masks over their faces. The only exception was Brad Berglund, their representative who would speak.

Toward the back of the room Laura was stunned to see Keith Gallatin, one of San Diego's premier celebrities. He was looking so conservative, dressed in a blue pin-striped suit and wearing his dark brown hair combed back, she barely recognized him. He sat beside his tall blond bodyguard, who also was well dressed.

Keith Gallatin and his twin sister, Danielle, had built an empire making music together. Their highly commercial, mainstream records, put out simply under the name of "Gallatin," had sold in phenomenal numbers. Keith and Danielle, both twenty-eight, had first hit the pop charts when they were thirteen years old. Their remarkable string of hits then put them in the category of rock's most successful stars.

It didn't take Laura long to figure out why Keith was here. He and his sister had used their rock-and-roll dollars to purchase an FM radio station, a TV station, and a professional basketball franchise. All three of these ventures were located in town, and the basketball team was called "The San Diego Pumas."

Laura decided she would try to get a reaction from Keith as soon as the meeting had ended, then worry about the commissioners later. She wondered what he would say. He was the more public relations-conscious of the twins. He was always willing to talk to the media, but he had a reputation for never taking any kind of strong stance. He was an expert at dodging tough questions, which had come frequently in the early days of the Pumas, but he had become an institution in San Diego, and popular enough to be elected king if ever there were an opening.

Laura glanced across the room again just to make sure she hadn't missed anyone else important. There was no one. She looked back at Gallatin and their eyes met, but he looked away instantly. He was used to being stared at.

It was Brad Berglund's turn at the podium. A slight, barely noticeable buzz went through the room, as everyone expected a far more colorful speech than had been given by his predecessors at the microphone. He was allowed three minutes, but he barely took one.

"Mr. Chairman, and honorary commissioners," Brad began. "You all know me, and I won't take up any more of your time with facts you are all fully aware of. After all we've been through, I will only say one thing: Please . . . don't do this."

Brad's followers cheered as he turned and walked away from the podium. Laura looked over to get Gallatin's reaction, but his expression was exactly the same as it had been when the biologist was speaking.

"Silence, please!" requested the chairman, but this brought on the exact opposite of his request. The Mountain Lions Forever people stood up and began to chant in unison.

"Save our lions! Save our lions!"

The chairman did his best to ignore the protesters, but eventually he acknowledged them by pounding his gavel in anger. All three of the TV crews, including Gallatin's, had gone portable, and were beside the protesters, blasting them with light and rolling tape to capture their outburst. Berglund was leading the shouts.

The shouting continued for almost three minutes, until finally two of the uniformed Fish and Game officers approached the noisemakers and arrested the three loudest. Berglund and his two associates allowed themselves to be handcuffed without the slightest resistance.

The officers escorted the three prisoners out the back door of the auditorium, and they were followed by a parade of TV cameras and other media, including the photographer working with Laura. She decided to follow, just to see where they would be taken. They were all led outside to a Fish and Game vehicle, where the prisoners were put in the back. One of the officers looked at Laura, then rolled his eyes and shook his head. Another well-staged media event.

Laura went back inside and saw all of the Mountain Lions Forever people walking into the hallway outside the auditorium. Their job was done for the day. Laura went inside, where the commissioners were discussing their views of the hunt.

She immediately looked around for Keith Gallatin. He was gone.

CHAPTER 2

Sarena crept forward in a low, calculated crouch, nearly dragging her belly on the rocky ground. There was just enough breeze to rustle the chaparral and cover the almost inaudible sound of her paws. Her breathing was careful and slow, emitting not even the tiniest hiss.

She loved this part of the hunt. Even after four full years of hunting as an adult, the suspense of a stalk was always exhilarating. Every hair on her body tingled as the rivers of information surged with intensity through her heightened senses. Individual muscles throughout her shoulders and back flexed and shivered with anticipation.

Sarena carefully placed her front paws on a large, smooth rock and peered above the high sage for a quick assessment of the situation. The doe was in a large open space, quite a distance from the nearest cover of thick brush. She was bent over, carelessly nibbling at the long grass at her feet. She was nearly at the bottom of the ravine, so Sarena would have the advantage of momentum from a downhill run.

The thick growth of dry, brown foliage ended abruptly at the edge of green where the doe was eating. Sarena knew instantly that her attack would start from there. If she kept low she would be able to risk a cautious jog to that point. In addition to the risk of alerting her prey, high acceleration would be too much for her limited lung capacity. She needed to conserve her strength for the actual attack.

Sarena stopped suddenly just before reaching the edge of the brush. In her efforts to remain hidden and keep the wind at her face while approaching the attack sight, she had lost sight of the doe for several minutes. It had

17

walked uphill toward her and was much closer than Sarena could have hoped for. Although only a few strides away, the doe was still unaware of the puma in the sage.

Immediately dropping to a crouch, Sarena quickly scanned the area, trying to predict the alleen's escape route. It didn't matter. At this range Sarena might have it down before it had taken two strides.

Extending her claws slightly as she always did before a strike, Sarena crouched as low as she could and took a deep breath. Suddenly there was movement to her left. She glanced over and was stunned by the sight of a huge buck, apparently the doe's mate. It was perhaps five strides past the closer alleen.

The buck was enormous. He was nearly twice the size of his mate, with a respectable rack of antlers. He peered over at the doe, then bent over for some grass. Sarena couldn't believe she hadn't spotted him earlier. She was also amazed that, as close as she was, they hadn't yet spotted her. She silently thanked Lady Farri, queen of all cats, for the wind at her face.

The buck would be quite a prize, but he was simply out of the question. His sheer magnitude and speed might make a lone takedown almost impossible, even for a puma of Sarena's size, which was close to one hundred and twenty pounds and quite large for a female. The added prospect of dealing with the buck's menacing antlers made Sarena look back to the doe.

For a painful moment Sarena lost her concentration. The tall, strong buck, and Sarena's inability to chase it, was yet another reminder of how badly she wanted and needed a mate. As a team they could catch even the largest of alleen with relative ease.

They could do other things as well. Although Sarena wasn't quite sure what all of those other things were, she did know that she wanted to find out.

A strange smell snapped her back to reality. It was sweet and somewhat familiar, but Sarena couldn't place it. The two alleen had their noses to the air as well, but they seemed unconcerned.

The buck began to walk toward her. With each step Sarena's eyes opened wider. She could not believe the two alleen did not smell her. She could certainly smell them. The wind and the strange odor it carried were

apparently acting as her shield. The buck turned somewhat and stopped next to the doe.

Now was the time. Sarena crouched as low as she could
get, positioning herself for maximum spring off of her
powerful hind legs. She could feel her heart, rapidly
pounding inside. Her tail twitched the slightest bit with
excitement. She took a deep breath.

Balance was critical. She took one final glance at the
ground between her hiding place and the spot where the
doe stood. They were ten long strides apart now, but it
would take as many as ten more to reach the doe, since
the alleen immediately would bolt. Sarena carefully
picked the spots where she wanted to land.

Trembling slightly with excitement, Sarena began to
exhale. She would take one more breath, and then
launch.

Suddenly the buck screamed in agony and began to fall
toward Sarena. A tremendous clap of thunder crashed
through the canyon just as the alleen hit the ground.
Sarena, now standing straight up, saw a huge smear of
blood gushing from the left side of the buck's neck.

The doe charged straight for Sarena, but stopped hard
and almost fell over when she picked up the puma's
scent. Sarena was completely confused, but stood
motionless despite her desire to chase the doe. The doe
was equally confused, but only over which direction to
run in. She stood four strides away, looking frantically
for an escape through terrified eyes.

The ground erupted in a cloud of dirt only inches from
the doe's feet, followed by another boom of thunder.
The alleen charged for the brush to Sarena's right and
crashed through without looking back.

Sarena was stunned. Every instinct in her body was
screaming for her to run. She involuntarily shook with a
terror she did not understand. She looked over at the
buck, who only a moment ago had been a tall, beautiful
animal. He was now a dead, bloody mess. His head
rested on white granite, with the mouth open and the
tongue dangling out. His open, unseeing eyes gazed
almost directly at the bushes where Sarena hid.

Where had the thunder come from? She looked into
the sky but saw no clouds. It sounded as if it had come

from across the ravine. What had caused the dirt to fly? The doe had known. Of this Sarena had no doubt.

Sarena still did not understand. A puma was the unquestioned master of the Canyon and always walked proudly and without fear, but Sarena was shivering all the way down her spine. Something large and noisy was making its way through the brush toward her, and the strange, sweet smell was getting stronger.

CHAPTER 3

It was a very risky move for broad daylight, but morale in the tribe was high and Grash was in a mood for adventure. Since their escape nearly three weeks ago the members of the tribe, with Grash as their leader, had gone from a loose-knit, unorganized pack of stray kribas to a highly efficient and structured gang of assassins.

Maybe "assassins" wasn't the appropriate word, yet, but Grash had no doubt the tribe eventually would be working on that level. They were already capable killers, attacking in the night with systematic effectiveness. So far they had only killed for food, but changes would be coming soon. There were many, many debts to be settled.

Grash was one of two German shepherds in the tribe. Telsh, his brother, had also gotten out on the night of escape. With them were six others: three Dobermans, a pit bull, and two others who both looked like shepherds mixed with something black.

As a group the tribe was remarkably smart. Kroth, the Doberman who stood as the tribe's second-in-command, was cunning beyond even Grash's comprehension. His strategies for ambush were nothing short of genius. Grash would follow Kroth's plans down to the minutest detail, and be assured success every time without the slightest flaw.

Broed was always the key in every attack. With those powerful jaws the stout pit bull could bring down anything. He was always positioned perfectly when the tribe moved in, sending the intended prey directly into Broed's waiting grasp.

Every kriba in the tribe had a specialty. Grash made

sure each one of them was performing exactly what he did best and therefore living up to his individual potential, which was why Grash was the leader. His specialties were insight and doling out authority. The others recognized this, appointed him leader, and followed his orders without question. Grash was the first to admit that some of them were smarter, but none could match him for administrative abilities.

The target this afternoon was a large ram penned up in the backyard of a house near the edge of the Canyon. Kroth had planned the attack well, leaving little room for error. There was sufficient cover for most of them to reach the yard undetected. The maneuver would be very quick and very quiet.

Only a minor physical effort would be needed to take the ram, so Kroth had provided for extra security. Grash and Telsh would stay in the street, ready to sound the alarm at the first hint of unforeseen trouble. This would be in addition to the other two Dobermans, Bruether and Krayde, who watched the backs of the assault team. As the fiercest-looking of the tribe, it was their responsibility to simulate an attack on anything coming to the aid of the target. They were to indicate aggression, but strike only if absolutely necessary.

The two black shepherds, Grallus and Roashas, were the youngest, with the most energy. If necessary they would chase the terrified ram into the waiting jaws of Broed. There was a good chance they would actually run down the ram themselves. Broed was simply the last stop.

Kroth had gone on to plan their next raid, so the seven of them moved in silence toward the house. When they reached the last cover of thick red shank they stopped for a moment and took a breath. Grash was panting with nervous excitement. Their first daytime operation was about to begin.

Grash nodded and the tribe moved. They ran as a pack half the distance to the house, then split instantly into their assigned directions when Grash uttered a low growl. He ran with his brother to the street, secretly wishing to be in on the action but knowing it was not his place this time.

When they reached the street there was no sign of

movement, so Grash and Telsh stopped and turned to witness the chase. Grash watched the others race to their positions with professional precision. He smiled, proud at how proficient they had become in such a short period of time.

The ram began to scream the instant it smelled the tribe's approach. It began to run hysterically in circles. It cried and pranced, trying to make as much noise as it possibly could. Grash bit down hard, hoping the tribe could shut the beast up and drag it into the Canyon before it alerted the entire neighborhood.

When the attack team hit the yard after jumping a low section of fence, the ram bolted in the opposite direction. Grallus and Roashas split immediately, trying to cut the ram off and chase it back toward Broed, who was hiding back where they had entered the yard.

Grallus ran to the right, sending dirt into the air as his feet hit the ground. Roashas charged to the left with his head down and teeth clenched. He passed the ram quickly, then turned back toward center to meet it.

The ram knew its legs were no match for the two charging kribas. It turned even before they had a chance to intercept it, screaming as loud as it could. Grallus turned abruptly to follow, but slipped and fell on the soft dirt. Roashas had better luck. His feet held, enabling him not only to turn, but to gain ground as well. He was within three strides and closing.

Suddenly the ram tripped and fell hard on its face. Roashas had no time to recover and toppled right over the goat. Grallus, who had resumed the chase, pounced on the prey before it had a chance to get back up. He grabbed it by the throat while Roashas, who had somehow rolled underneath it, yanked at its belly. The ram was dead before Broed arrived to assist.

"Come on!" said Grash, jumping into a run with Telsh a step behind him.

The commotion started the instant Grash left the street. The Dobermans erupted into a frenzy of barking as a woman ran out into the yard from the back door of the house. She ran in a screaming frenzy, waving a large stick over her head. The Dobermans, snarling wildly with teeth bared for attack, stopped her cold. She continued to scream and wave the stick, but she slowly began to retreat.

"You help the others!" Grash yelled at Telsh, as he raced to help the Dobermans. The other three were trying to force the dead ram through a space in the fence.

"Don't touch her!" Grash ordered the Dobermans, who continued to force the woman back toward her house. She was almost there, still screaming with fury. Grash could see fear and hatred in her eyes, as they darted back and forth between her assailants and the work being done with her dead ram.

Finally the woman threw the stick at Krayde, who was the closest to her, barely missing his head. She turned around and ran for the door, which was only a few feet away. She bolted inside, slamming it behind her as she passed. The Dobermans continued to bark crazily as the woman looked out through a window.

Footsteps. Grash could feel them, even over his snarling companions. More men coming. What to do?

Grash turned around to check on the status of the others. They had torn the ram into enough small pieces to get it through the fence. Within moments they would break for the Canyon without looking back.

"More men are coming," said Grash to the Dobermans. "Let's go distract them so they don't see the others."

The Dobermans turned immediately. The three of them ran in the direction of the street, where they smelled the other men. There were two of them running around the side of the house toward the backyard. The men froze when they saw the three charging kribas.

One of them yelled and started waving his arms. This might have spooked a normal kriba, but for members of the tribe it was an invitation. Grash had to scream at the others to keep them from ripping the man's throat out. The kribas stopped dangerously close to the men and continued to bark with everything they had.

Realizing the kribas would not back down, the two men turned and ran. The Dobermans trotted beside them, snarling viciously with every step. Grash stayed one step behind, making sure they didn't reverse their course.

When they reached the street, the two men jumped on

top of a car. They stared down at the growling kribas, eyes bulging with horror. They were gasping for air, even though they had run only a few strides. They looked pathetic, the way they shook with fear. Grash knew both of them were thanking the Creator for letting them continue to live, when in fact they should be thanking *him* instead.

"Okay, let's go," said Grash.

The three of them turned around and dashed for the Canyon. The men would see, but they had no choice. Anyway, the Canyon was big enough to give them plenty of places to hide. The tribe would just have to be a little more careful for a while.

CHAPTER 4

Sarena decided to roll over and let the left side of her tawny coat feel the warm, clear sun of a Southern California autumn. After discovering a wonderful bed of long, soft grass, she had slept most of the afternoon away. She indulged in a luxurious stretch as she turned, then lazily sniffed the air with her delicate, crimson nose for any nearby neighbors who might be about. Possibly some hina, the common-speech word for rabbits, but nothing more. So, after finding a comfortable niche, Sarena closed her bright, golden eyes and decided more sleep in the sun was in order.

It was easier when she slept. Sometimes the loneliness haunted her dreams, but usually she was left in peace.

Pumas walked with other pumas, or else they walked alone. All other animals were either prey or enemies. Occasionally Sarena had found it possible to do business with lynxes, but they were far too untrustworthy to associate with at any length. Lynxes were only friendly if a nasty pack of krahstas, the common-speech term for coyotes, needed chasing out of the area.

Krahstas could be a problem, but only if grouped together in a large pack. They almost always avoided pumas unless they happened to catch one asleep, which was impossible, since krahstas, when roaming in packs, made enough noise to wake the entire Canyon. In Southern California krahstas were the only Canyon animals capable of harming a puma, but their threat was minuscule compared to damage continually being done to pumas by the world's deadliest animal.

The only animal on earth who walked exclusively on two legs was the puma's most ruinous enemy. By the relentless expansion of the human environment, the habitat of pumas was nearly gone. So, too, were most of the pumas.

Sarena opened her eyes again. As comfortable as she was, she knew she would have to hunt again, soon. It was about time to move on, anyway. It seemed like she was always moving on. She would move into a new area and stay a few weeks; looking, smelling, hoping. There was new hope with each new area, but when the new hope faded she would move on again. Always moving, but never any closer to wherever it was she was going.

There had to be more pumas, somewhere. She could remember seeing only one other adult puma, shortly before it died of the crazy sickness. It had been over a year, and she had not seen one, or smelled one, or found any sign of one since. Sarena closed her eyes. It was time to move on.

A sudden noise and shadow snapped her to her feet. She looked up just in time to see a huge bird landing on a mass of stone a few strides to her right. It took a quick breath, then cocked its head to the right and began to look her over.

Sarena had never seen a bird as large as this. His feathers were dark brown going all the way up to the bottom of his neck, where they abruptly turned to white and covered his entire head. He had a yellow beak and piercing golden eyes, which cast a scrutinizing gaze upon Sarena. He did not appear threatening, only curious.

The bird stood with his back straight and his head high. His face bore a visage of wisdom and intellect Sarena had never before seen in the Canyon. Up on the rock with the cloudless sky behind him, Sarena thought he looked majestic. He and Sarena stared at each other for quite some time before either of them spoke.

"I think we can be friends," said the stranger finally. He nodded his head in satisfaction, as if his words were something he had known all along but only needed to confirm.

"Such a bold statement," said Sarena. "And we haven't even met."

"No, but I feel as though I know you quite well, Lady

Puma," said the bird. "I have been watching you for some time."

Sarena opened her mouth to speak, but then stopped. She tilted her head to the right while assessing his words. She wondered how he could have watched her at all without her knowledge.

"Your eyes, my friend, are not fixed to the sky, as mine are to the ground," said the bird, as if reading Sarena's thoughts. "I see all who walk the Canyon, and someone as grand as you is hard to miss. I, however, am hardly ever noticed . . . at least until it's too late."

Sarena nodded. If ever there was a bird designed to be a predator, this one was it. She had seen hawks and owls hunting uncountable times, but compared to this bird the others were puny weaklings.

"My name is Lanakila," said the bird. "You sure are quiet for such a big girl."

"Yes . . . well, I must say . . . I have never been approached by a bird before," said Sarena. "And I have never even seen a bird such as you."

"Nor have I seen an animal such as you," said Lanakila.

Sarena looked down at her paws, then slowly closed her eyes. The slow, nagging ache inside that she had been carrying around with her for months suddenly exploded into every part of her body. Her forepaws began to tremble and she immediately sat down. She began to get dizzy and started to pant.

Lanakila had never seen another puma. If ever there was anyone who might have, it would be this bird. This bird saw everyone who walked the Canyon.

"Never?" choked Sarena.

"I'm sorry, my friend," said Lanakila. "I wish I could say I had. I know how you feel. Your words are as devastating to me as mine are to you. You see, I've never seen another bird such as me, either."

"I am an ahila," said Lanakila. He had jumped off the rock, and now sat beside Sarena in the tall grass. "I can't say I'm the only one, because I do remember my mother and my sister. It has been countless seasons since I left their nest to seek a mate and rule my own territory. I have not seen them since, nor would I remember how to find them. Since I left them I have never seen another ahila."

"I have heard the word before," said Sarena.

"As I have heard the word 'puma,' " said Lanakila. "It is a feared word, I must say, but to me you look like nothing more than an overgrown ball of fur."

Sarena's eyes opened wide. Her conversations over the past year had been sparse, but she could not recall ever having spoken with someone so bold. She usually spoke with animals who were terrified of her, but Lanakila clearly was not. Sarena might have been offended, had it not been for the slight trace of mischief in his eyes.

She was beginning to like him already. He obviously did not want to dwell on their loneliness but wanted to move on with the process of getting to know each other. His voice was low, strong, and clear, with an exotic accent of the common speech. He possessed a wit not unlike her own. He would take getting used to, but otherwise his assessment of their ability to be friends was correct.

"In fact I think I'll just call you 'Fur Ball'," said Lanakila.

"And I shall call you 'Lunch'," said Sarena.

"You'll have to catch me first!" said Lanakila. He suddenly jabbed at Sarena's tail with his beak, then launched himself skyward.

Startled by the attack, Sarena instinctively jumped to her feet and swiped at the ascending bird, only to strike air. Lanakila squawked with laughter and circled just out of reach of the confused puma.

"My little ball of fur has forgotten how to play!" cried Lanakila laughing. "We're not getting old, are we?"

Sarena watched the huge bird circle. His wingspan was almost as long as she was. Lanakila grinned down at her with delight. He was a prankster who was going to take a lot of getting used to.

"Old is something you might never live to be," said Sarena.

Lanakila pulled in his wings and began to drop. He broke into a hover directly above Sarena then landed on her back, just behind the shoulders. Sarena was again surprised by his boldness, but decided to go along with it. She didn't want to be called "old" again. She leaned her head back as the ahila leaned his head forward. Their eyes met, their faces only inches apart, and at that moment Sarena knew they would get along just fine.

CHAPTER 5

Laura still needed to get a response from one of the commissioners before she could leave. She waited until the lunch break, when everyone stood and began to mill about. She had never dealt with any of the commissioners before, so she approached the closest one.

Jack Dwyer had been a commissioner for six years. He wore a plain brown suit, with a yellow shirt sticking out over his immense belly. He had the jowls of a bulldog and a huge, pockmarked nose. His thinning gray hair looked as if at one time it had been black.

Laura introduced herself. Dwyer nodded with resignation, then motioned for her to follow him back over to the desk where he had been seated during the meeting. Laura sat down next to him up on the stage, away from the crowd. Laura reached into her purse and pulled out her recorder and note pad.

"Commissioner, first of all, your reaction to the demonstration in here by the Mountain Lions Forever people," said Laura.

"It's a shame they have to carry on like that," said Dwyer. "We try to conduct nice, orderly meetings and let everyone have their say, but these people don't want to play by the rules like everyone else. We sat quietly while they were speaking. I wish they had given us the same courtesy."

"What's your position on the proposed mountain lion season?" Laura asked.

"I'm on record as being for it," said Dwyer.

"How can you support a hunt when your own staff admits they don't even have an accurate estimate of how many lions are out there?" asked Laura, taking the oppo-

31

sition's side, just as she had done when interviewing Brad Berglund.

"It's true we don't know down to the specific cat how many there are out there, but we know they've grown substantially in numbers. Reports of attacks on livestock have skyrocketed in the past few years. Confirmed sightings are up three hundred percent. There have even been instances where humans have been attacked, including one right here in this city. It can be pretty dangerous when you have hundred-and-ninety-pound animals coming up to the streets."

Laura nodded as she scribbled notes. She had covered the story in which a little boy was grabbed by a mountain lion right in front of his parents. That lion was later shot by an off-duty narcotics officer and turned out to have had rabies.

"But isn't two hundred and fifty an awful high number?" persisted Laura.

"That's the number of permits we're looking at," said Dwyer. "Not all of the hunters will be successful. We're estimating only one third that number will actually be taken."

"Thank you," said Laura, standing up. "Oh, by the way, what's going to happen to the people who were arrested in here?"

"Nothing," said Dwyer. "I'm sure they've already been let go. We just wanted to get control of our meeting, so we appeased them by taking their leaders outside. They weren't even taken anywhere."

"Okay, thanks," said Laura, then began to turn away.

"You know, there's a lot more to it than just mountain lions," said Dwyer, stopping Laura. "Those people are out their waving the mountain lion banner and saying it's an isolated case, but it's not. They're strictly anti-hunting and strictly anti-gun. This is only one step in their efforts to chip away at the right to bear arms. It's really irritating and insulting, and it's really sad. They don't know how good they have it in this country."

Laura nodded and turned away. She needed to get back to the office so she could start writing this story. She had all of the elements, so it would be simple enough. She would have liked to get a reaction from

Keith Gallatin, but could easily live without it. She decided she would try to track him down later anyway.

She walked out into the parking lot and got into her silver RX-7. She looked back down at her notebook before starting the car. As a story it was pretty straight-forward and easy to put together, but something was bothering her. Over the years it had gotten easy to leave her feelings out of stories, which was, as a journalist, what she was supposed to do. It was usually pretty easy, since she rarely covered stories she had any emotion for anyway. This one was different, although she wasn't exactly sure what sentiments were getting in the way.

Looking through the press packet from Mountain Lions Forever, she found two black-and-white photos. The first one was the close-up shot of a mountain lion's face. It was a beautiful animal, and Laura instinctively wanted to pet it. Then she rolled her eyes, since that was the exact reaction the people who had enclosed the photo had wanted. Nice kitty.

The second picture was equally effective. It was an historical photograph, dated 1932. There were two hunt-ers, standing ten yards apart between two trees. They held rifles in their arms and wore proud smiles. A rope was stretched tightly across from the two trees and from it, hanging by the feet, were six dead mountain lions.

Laura tossed the pictures onto the passenger seat then turned away and shook her head, fighting back an urge to gag. The Mountain Lions Forever people had done their homework.

CHAPTER 6

Sarena wondered what the rest of the Canyon would think when they saw *this* arrangement. She still wasn't sure what *she* thought about it. She imagined it was quite a sight; a full-grown puma walking openly on a dirt path with a full grown ahila perched on its back.

For convenience, this is how they would travel short distances. Lanakila's legs were too short to keep up with Sarena on the ground and Sarena couldn't fly, so for now this was how it would work. Sarena didn't mind at all. Despite his size Lanakila was very lightweight, and his company was more than welcome.

Sarena chose the smoothness of a dirt path to practice carrying Lanakila. The Canyon was quiet and still in the afternoon sun, save for the occasional movement of insects and a curious set of eyes belonging to a large, well-hidden animal in the brush on top of the ravine.

"I think we could work as a team," said Lanakila.

"I have been thinking the same," said Sarena. "There are several ways we can work together. What are some of your thoughts?"

"I have seen you hunt the alleen," said Lanakila. "I think we could do this together."

"Oh," said Sarena. It was still a bit unnerving to know she had been watched. She wondered exactly to what extent this had gone on.

"If we work together the alleen will become easier to catch," said Lanakila.

"If you were a puma they might," said Sarena, surprised the ahila would consider hunting first. "How can you help bring down the alleen?"

"By showing you where they are, my dear ball of fur,"

34

said Lanakila. "From the air, I can see everything in the Canyon. From here, at your perspective, I can see only sky. Unless I am mistaken, the alleen do not fly."

Sarena stopped. She had been so obsessed with Lanakila's ability to help search for other pumas she had completely overlooked the obvious. The day-to-day struggle for survival had just gotten a lot easier.

She again wondered about the strange bird riding on her shoulders. He was turning out to be far more intelligent than she would have guessed. He was proving to be imaginative, yet practical. It had been his idea to ride on Sarena's back, and as ridiculous as it probably looked it made sense. So did the plan to hunt the alleen. And while he was up there hunting, it didn't hurt to know he would be looking out for other pumas as well.

"I see the potential for great things," said Sarena. "For now, I suppose the alleen should be our first priority."

"Yes, yes. I am so tired of eating hina."

Sarena stepped off the dirt path and back into the cover of sage, which was a crumbly brown from several months without rain. The dry brush broke the outlines of the two companions and they became nearly invisible, their coats blending naturally with the terrain. They came into a small clearing where the brush had been choked out by a rock formation.

When Sarena stopped, Lanakila hopped onto a large chunk of granite. He spread out his wings and flapped them slightly, stretching out after the ride on Sarena's back. His wingspan was almost equal to the distance from Sarena's long whiskers to the tip of her thick, furry tail.

Sarena watched the magnificent bird in awe. She had never been able to understand how an animal could fly. He was surprisingly light for his size, but she knew there must be more to it. She had never seen a bird this close before so she examined his feathers, looking for clues, but could not tell.

She stepped closer to the rock, extending her nose to smell him over carefully. Lanakila kept his wings spread but did not flinch as she approached. He stood motionless with trusting composure while Sarena sniffed about the feathers of his breast. He carried the strong, spicy smell of a predator, but different from anything Sarena had ever encountered. She pushed her nose deeper into his feathers, but he stepped back and began to playfully bat at her face with his wings.

"You're tickling me, Fur Ball!" Lanakila laughed.

"I'm wondering how you'll taste," said Sarena.

"Worse than krahsta," said Lanakila.

"Probably. I must say, you are far braver than the krahstas."

Lanakila hissed and collapsed his wings.

"Are you complimenting me for having more courage than the howling cowards of the Canyon?" asked Lanakila. He darted his beak into his breast feathers and began to preen.

Sarena sat down and looked up at the bird with amazement. She had always considered krahstas to be cowards, but then, when faced with a puma, all animals were cowards. She had always assumed smaller animals would find the krahstas fearsome. It had never occurred to her that there might be others in the Canyon who regarded krahstas the same way she did.

"You are simply filled with wonders, my little friend," said Sarena.

"Who cares about wonders?" huffed Lanakila. "I just want to rule the Canyon."

"Yes, well, maybe together we will," smiled Sarena. "For now I am simply delighted to have your company. Pumas are not known for their friendships. Except for a few brief encounters with smaller cats, I have always been alone. I have longed for companionship. Especially someone to hunt with. In an odd way, I suppose some of my wishes have come true."

"Maybe, Fur Ball, but why don't we wait and see how successful we are as hunters before we talk about anything coming true."

"Agreed," said Sarena. "Now, before this day is too old, I must curl up and take a nap."

"I will rest beside you," said Lanakila.

Sarena walked back to the edge of the chaparral and found a comfortable patch of rye grass in which to lie down. Lanakila hopped off the rock and landed beside her. He sat down, then wedged his way into a comfortable position in the straw-colored grass. He blinked twice at Sarena, then tucked his head under his left wing.

Sarena closed her eyes. There was much to think about, but first she needed to rest. She tamped down the tall grass into just the right mold, then waited for the familiar twinge of pain to begin to creep into her stomach. After a longer period than usual it finally crept in, but without the fierce bite it normally carried with it. Sarena began to doze, without even realizing she had been purring for the first time in months.

The ram was quite good. Grash finished off his portion with delight. While chewing on the soft delicacy, he had almost forgotten about the near disaster involved in getting it to this point. He licked at a leg bone, then licked his lips with a growl of contentment.

"Maybe we should keep to the nights when we hold our raids," said Kroth. "I was not there, but it seems my timing estimates were slightly off."

"Who could have known, my friend?" Grash asked. "Your estimates have fed us well."

Kroth nodded, then began to gnaw on a shoulder bone. The other tribe members finished up with their shares of the feast as they hid in the cool shade of a holly tree.

"Still, we learned much today," said Grash. He was glad he had waited. They were all nervous and upset upon their return from the raid. The good food had soothed them, and now they were relaxed enough to speak rationally again.

The key flaw Grash had noticed in the tribe was its high-strung nature. Every one of them was a trained attack dog. This, coupled with the volatile nature of their breeds, left them very hot-tempered. They exploded quickly, but came back down to earth slowly. Grash knew their ultimate survival would depend upon how well he could prevent their natural instincts from spinning out of control.

"I have thought about looking in other directions," Grash began when the others all had finished. "While it's true we've been very successful to this point, the time may be upon us to lie low for a while."

Grash silently exhaled relief when every face reflected

agreement. This would be easier than he had expected. Still, he decided to continue to choose his words very carefully.

"None of us want to go back to where we were," Grash said to a chorus of growling agreements. "Now that the men have seen us, they know where we are. They may also figure out who has been doing the other raids in the past."

"Do we move on then?" asked Telsh. "Do we? I like it here like this."

"We will stay," Grash said affectionately. He loved his brother very much. Somehow they had always managed to remain close, even during the days of misery in the camp. Telsh's company was the only thing that had kept Grash sane through it all.

"Is it safe to stay?" asked Kroth.

"Yes, for now," said Grash. "I believe they will wait for us to strike again, then surprise us with an ambush. They will wait and wait, but we will not show up. In time they will forget about us."

"What now, then?" Broed asked. "How to hide and eat?"

"There are ways," said Grash, still baffled at how an intelligent kriba like Broed could have so much trouble with the common speech. "For now we will turn our eyes to the Canyon. There is enough prey out here to feed us forever, if we want."

"But how will we catch it?" asked Kroth. "Our talents are in ambush. We are not skilled in chasing hina like our cousins the krahstas."

"Maybe we can learn from them," said Grash. "It's not that hard, anyway. All of us have caught hina since our escape."

Grash knew he didn't sound very convincing. They were all starting to realize food might get scarce for a while. Grash looked across the vast open space of the Canyon and *knew* there had to be an answer out there. He could feel it as strongly as if the great Lord Kriba was standing right beside him and saying so.

CHAPTER 7

The Canyon was alive with the voices of countless birds, just as it was every evening at sunset. Returning to their places of roost for the night, they each sang out a verse of farewell to the disappearing sun. There was racket enough to awaken even the most determined of the Canyon's nappers. It even woke Sarena.

She slowly opened her eyes and began to stretch. She instinctively checked the air for predators or prey, but smelled nothing of interest. She began to close her eyes again but snapped them back and open and gasped. Lanakila was gone.

Sarena stood up and stretched again. She momentarily began to fear the encounter with the ahila had been part of a dream. She glanced over to where Lanakila had been resting when she had fallen asleep, and her anxiety began to melt as she saw the dry grass matted down. When she leaned over to sniff the area for confirmation a small feather got sucked in, causing her to sneeze twice.

Perplexed, she sat down on the grass and yawned, trying to clear her head. She wondered where her new friend had gone and hoped he would return soon. She didn't think Lanakila had tired of her company yet, since they'd only just met. Still, she noticed a slight twinge beginning to swell inside of her.

A sudden thud only inches from her flank jolted her airborne in surprise. Claws and teeth bared, she turned with a growl and landed not knowing what to expect. She instinctively crouched to strike but saw no movement. She quickly scanned the area but saw nothing unusual, until her eyes went back to the place where she had been sitting. There, motionless in the grass, was the carcass of a dead hina.

Sarena gasped her astonishment. Fur fluffed and ready for battle, her eyes darted across the surrounding manzanita, but she sensed no enemy. There was only the dead hina, and how it had gotten there she had no clue. Nothing had moved in the brush. It could only have fallen. . . .

"And I thought my Fur Ball was going to sleep her life away," Lanakila said from behind, startling Sarena into another jump. She turned around and saw the huge bird perched on the granite near the edge of the chaparral. She hissed at him slightly, then sat down in the dirt.

"The day is nearly gone," said Lanakila. "How can we hunt in the dark? I brought you a hina so you wouldn't starve."

"What do you mean, 'How can we hunt in the dark?' " Sarena huffed. She was very relieved to see him but feigned annoyance, since she was still a little bit rattled over the dropped hina incident, which had practically scared the fur right off of her.

"My Fur Ball will have to hunt by herself," said Lanakila, somewhat irritated.

"Why?" asked Sarena, confused. "I always hunt at night."

"Maybe you do, but ahilas do not. At least this ahila doesn't. Like most animals I sleep when I'm supposed to, after the sun sinks below the land."

"Well you'll just have to change that," said Sarena. "Hunting at night is the best time."

"How am I supposed to see the alleen after dark?" asked Lanakila. "Or *anything*? I cannot fly in the dark because I cannot see in the dark. I will only get lost and hurt myself."

Sarena was flabbergasted. She had always taken her spectacular night vision for granted. She knew the eyes of other animals were not as good as hers when the sun went down, but she had never dreamed it might render them blind.

"Then what do you do at night?" asked Sarena.

"Like all civilized animals, I sleep."

"All night?"

"All night."

"This is a dilemma," said Sarena. "I guess I could hunt

during the day, but I do love my morning and afternoon naps."

"From what I have seen, you are nothing but one *big* nap," said Lanakila. "I have never seen an animal sleep as much as you do."

Sarena looked at him suspiciously. How long had he been watching her before his initial introduction? This made her nervous.

"All of the cats sleep the day away," said Lanakila, as if reading her thoughts. "I have seen the lynxes sleep all day as well. Like you they romp a bit when the sun wakes up, but then they roll up and die for the rest of the day."

"It is the bane of all cats," said Sarena. "It's not just the day that we sleep, but also most of the night. It's never occurred to me before, but I guess the other animals *are* always awake at whatever time I'm up."

"So why do you sleep so much?"

"Some say it is a curse and others say a blessing," said Sarena. "It goes way back to the beginning, when the Creator of all things was instructing the lords and ladies of the races. They were all assembled in a great field, and the Creator told them all about the cycles of life and how to respect the earth.

"It had been a long day for them all," Sarena continued, "and Lady Farri, the queen of all cats, grew weary. She already knew the Creator's lessons for the day, since the Creator had blessed her line by making cats the smartest creatures on earth. . . ."

"Excuse me, but I think I'm going to be sick," said Lanakila. Sarena cast him a nasty glance and he said, "Okay, Fur Ball, I'll humor you. Go on."

"And obviously we know who the *dumbest* animals are," said Sarena sarcastically. "Anyway, since Lady Farri knew the Creator's teachings she curled up way in the back of all the other animals and took a nap. When the lesson was over, all of the lords and ladies went on to tell the lessons to their lines. All except Lady Farri, who was still asleep in the field."

"Figures," said Lanakila.

"The Creator knew she had slept through his speech," said Sarena, ignoring the interruption, "but said nothing about it until all of the others had left. When Lady Farri opened her eyes to see an empty field with only herself and the Creator, she jumped up immediately. She was quite embarrassed, but the Creator only smiled at her. It was fortunate that she was His favorite."

"Right, right right," said Lanakila, rolling his eyes. "Just get to the point."

"The point is, my little feather-brain, that I will have both you and the hina for dinner if you are not more polite."

"Yeah, yeah," chided Lanakila.

"Anyway, the Lady stood before the Creator, who said, 'My dearest Farri, I apologize for my boring monologue. I know it was truly beneath you.' Lady Farri only bowed her head low. She knew a feeble excuse would only make things worse. 'It's true your line is already blessed with intelligence and grace far exceeding all of the others, but still, listening ears will always learn.'

"As you can guess, Lady Farri was getting pretty nervous, wondering about what she had missed. 'I added a surprise to the lesson today,' the Creator told her. 'So there could be no secrets, I went around to each of the lords and ladies and had them tell everyone what they expected to be the single most important activity of their lines.' "

Lanakila burst out into laughter. "I guess she told them!"

"I guess she did," smiled Sarena. "When Lady Farri's turn came to speak, she slept right through it. The other lords and ladies took this as a statement of her line's most important activity. As a result I'm awake so little I don't even know how much I sleep."

"Huh?"

"Nothing. I'm still tired, I guess."

"Do you *like* to sleep so much?" asked Lanakila.

"I do enjoy it," said Sarena. "Especially when I get lonely. I don't have to think about it when I'm asleep."

"So how did you end up being able to see in the dark?" asked Lanakila, obviously trying to change the subject.

"The Creator took pity on Farri," said Sarena. "Since cats would be sleeping so much, they would be waking up at all hours. So the Creator blessed Farri's eyes and told her that her line would always have vision, no matter at what time they chose to awaken and prowl."

"Um, I have another question," said Lanakila. "About cats being the smartest animals? Besides ahilas, the man would obviously have to be considered smarter than cats and pumas."

"Since when does being the most belligerent have anything to do with being the smartest?" asked Sarena.

CHAPTER 8

The newsroom was unusually noisy for an early afternoon. Far more reporters than normal were at their desks, pounding out stories at their computer terminals. It was amazing that any of them could concentrate, with all of the loud conversations and unanswered phones.

Laura had six phone numbers for Keith Gallatin. Four were the office numbers of various businesses he owned and the other two had nothing attached to them. She had gotten them all from the computer file on everything the newsroom had ever done on the Gallatins. It was quite a file.

The most obvious number was his recording studio in La Jolla. She called there first but only got a runaround, and no straight answer as to whether he was even there or not. She left her number and hung up. She glanced at the two unlabeled numbers but decided against calling either of them yet, for fear of reaching some bimbo from a Keith Gallatin one-night-stand. On a hunch she called the Pumas' office at the Sports Arena.

Expecting another hassle, Laura was surprised when the switchboard transferred her straight back to Gallatin's office. She identified herself to the secretary who answered, and was immediately put on hold.

"Keith Gallatin," came the voice after about twenty seconds.

"Hello, my name's Laura Kay from the *San Diego Union*, and I'm calling in regard to the Fish and Game meeting you were at this afternoon."

"Ah, yes," said Gallatin. "You must be the pretty brunette in the purple blouse who was leaning up against the wall, off to the side."

"Well . . . I guess that could be me," stammered Laura, caught completely off-guard. "How did you know?"

"I never miss a pretty lady," said Gallatin. "Especially one who keeps looking over to check out my reaction every time something happens. I figured you'd be calling."

"I was that obvious?" Laura asked.

"Afraid so."

"Well, I was quite surprised to see you there," said Laura. "What brought you there in the first place?"

"Am I being interviewed?" asked Gallatin.

"I suppose so."

"Okay. Well, I went to see what was going on. As you know, my sister and I have an unusual stake in the fate of mountain lions. After all, you've reached me here at the Pumas' office. I wanted to find out if mountain lions are really going to be hunted."

"It's not completely certain yet," said Laura, scribbling notes on her reporter's pad.

"I know."

"Are you supporting the Mountain Lions Forever organization?" Laura asked.

"Absolutely not," said Gallatin.

"You're not? Why?" asked Laura, quite surprised. The owner of the Pumas, who happened to be not only a rock star but a well-known political liberal, didn't strike her as being the type who would support hunting mountain lions.

"I only went to see what was going on," said Gallatin. "I haven't formed an opinion yet."

"Oh, come on!" said Laura. "I don't believe you would support a hunting season on mountain lions."

Silence. Gallatin was choosing his next words very carefully. He was sufficiently well seasoned when it came to the media to know how dangerous every word could be.

"You've asked me two different questions," he finally said.

"What?"

"The first question, 'Do I support Mountain Lions Forever?', I answered no. The other question is, 'Do I support a hunting season on mountain lions?' The answer to that is also no."

"Don't they go hand-in-hand?"

"No. They are two separate issues."

Laura nodded to herself as she wrote down his words. He was turning out to be far smarter than she had given him credit for.

"Are you going to do anything to fight the Fish and Game Commission?" she asked.

"At this time, no."

"You're just full of 'noes,' aren't you?" quipped Laura.

"No."

"Why don't you support Mountain Lions Forever?"

"Their motives are noble, but their tactics are questionable," said Gallatin, sounding more like a politician than a rock star. "They did nothing today that will help their cause."

"Okay," said Laura. "Anything else I haven't asked you that you think is important?"

"The mountain lions are the real losers in all of this," said Gallatin. "You saw those people today. They looked like a bunch of bozos. And they're the only representation the mountain lions have. It's really a shame."

"Then why don't you do something about it?" Laura asked. She had no patience for idealists who never took action. "Maybe someone like you can make the difference."

"I can't right now," said Gallatin. "I'm up to my ass in alligators as it is. And besides, I don't want to get tagged with the label of being a special-interest monger."

Laura smiled, but only because she could relate to his dislike of special-interest groups. The rest of it sounded like a cop-out.

"Anything else?" she asked.

"No, not about mountain lions," said Gallatin.

"Call me if you decide to do anything?"

"You bet," said Gallatin, and hung up.

Laura returned the phone to its cradle and then stared at it for several minutes. She had not expected to get Gallatin and he had surprised her in many ways, even though what he'd actually said hadn't really amounted to much. She wanted to be angry at him for not getting involved, but realized she wanted him to do something she wouldn't even do herself. Journalists becoming part of a story was a no-no.

This story bothered her. There were too many problems. She had dealt with Fish and Game so many times and they had always been so careful—she couldn't believe they would want to go ahead with a hunt without an accurate estimate. No wonder they were taking so much flack.

The local officers were great. Laura had just done a story with them on an increase of deer poaching in the county. The officers suspected a group of as many as five men, who had preyed mercilessly on the local black-tailed deer population. In reality the officers had no idea who was involved, but they'd asked Laura to use quotes to the effect that they just might. Playing along for a good cause, Laura's article implied that the officers were hot on the trail, which had the hoped-for result of scaring the culprits into hiding. Poaching in the county had virtually stopped cold since the printing of the article.

She was not about to be as cooperative with the officers' bosses from Sacramento.

Laura flipped through her note pad, checking out all of the scratchings she had scribbled down for the entire story. After looking it over carefully, she closed it and tossed it onto her desk. She decided she would have to fit Gallatin in somehow, even though he wasn't really one of the players.

She opened a computer file and began to type out her story. When writing, she rarely referred to the countless notes she took, except to check exact quotes. She liked to say she wrote from feeling rather than structure.

"I have something you might be interested in," said Bill Sesma, interrupting her train of thought. He leaned over Laura's desk and handed her an assignment sheet.

Laura was used to writing with interruptions. They were part of the job description in every news operation in the country. It was absolutely impossible to get through an entire story without having someone disrupt your concentration.

Bill Sesma was good at tracking down stories for the staff. He had worked in news for eighteen years. He was short, with gray hair and the thick glasses he needed after countless hours of squinting over news copy. He smiled a lot but his hands were always clenched in tight fists, making Laura suspect he was not as happy as he let on.

"It seems a pack of wild dogs is running loose, terrorizing North County," said Sesma, as Laura began to look at the information typed out on the assignment sheet. "Big dogs. A couple of shepherds, a pit bull, and a Doberman. Some others, too, but those are the ones that stood out."

"I'll bet," said Laura. "Where'd you get this?"

"A couple of people called it in. Apparently the dogs have been tearing up the area for a few weeks now. They've been attacking other animals—people's pets—and making everyone in the area too afraid to let their kids outside."

"Great," said Laura. "I'll start making calls as soon as I'm done with the mountain lion story."

"Good," said Sesma. "I thought of you immediately when I saw this. It's got your name written all over it."

Laura smiled and put the assignment sheet on her desk next to the phone as Sesma walked away. It really was her type of story, and she was glad Sesma thought enough of her to have saved it for her.

"A pack of wild dogs," Laura murmured, laughing quietly to herself. "Sounds like most of the men I've gone out with, lately."

CHAPTER 9

"**I**s my Fur Ball going to sleep all day tomorrow as well?" Lanakila asked, only minutes before the Canyon would be completely dark.

"No, dearest," said Sarena. "We will hunt together in the morning."

"First light," said Lanakila. "If you are sleeping, I will lift you into the air by your tail!"

"Are you going to sleep here?" Sarena asked. She was still in the large, grassy open space where she had napped earlier. Lanakila remained perched on the large boulder near the sage.

"No. I always spend the night in a tree. It's safer. I'll be in that one over there," he said, pointing to a large eucalyptus.

"What could be safer than having a puma as your guardian?" Sarena asked. "You rested here this afternoon."

"My only defenses come with my ability to fly," said Lanakila. "If we were to be ambushed I would be a useless fighter, since I cannot fly well in the dark."

"Ambushed?" Sarena laughed. "Who would ambush a puma? Certainly not the krahstas. Even you called them 'the howling cowards of the Canyon.' "

Lanakila hopped off of the granite and landed beside Sarena. When standing, the two were of almost equal height. An expression of concern flashed across Lanakila's face, erasing the one of humor Sarena had grown accustomed to seeing in their few short hours together.

"I do not fear the krahstas," Lanakila said coolly.

Sarena sat down and tilted her head to the left. She

waited for him to continue but he looked around at the brush, as if contemplating his next words.

"You should hurry, my little friend," Sarena said, "or the light will be completely gone. Tell me what there is to be afraid of in this Canyon."

"It is the kribas I fear," said Lanakila.

"Kribas?" asked Sarena doubtfully. "There are no kribas in the Canyon. They stay close to the men."

"You don't know?" asked Lanakila, shocked. "You must have heard."

" 'Heard,' my little one?" Sarena asked. "No one speaks to pumas. Or have you forgotten?"

"It is no wonder," said Lanakila. "We will talk of this tomorrow after we hunt. It is dark. Good night."

The great bird spread his wings and launched into the early evening sky. Sarena watched him glide across the Canyon. He flew straight toward the tree he would roost in for the night and landed effortlessly on one of its highest branches. Sarena stared at the tree for several minutes, then picked up the hina Lanakila had brought her and walked off into the night.

It was a fine evening for a stroll. Sarena was feeling much better than she had for quite a while. The nagging pain in her stomach was almost gone. Almost, but not entirely. It was a start, though.

Sarena walked through thick chaparral, not heading in any direction in particular. Her mind was completely absorbed with all of the possibilities. Lanakila could help her find other pumas! He said he had never seen another one, but that didn't matter. He hadn't really been *looking* before. He might actually have seen one and not even have noticed.

She wondered where the ahila had come from. For all he talked, he rarely said anything about himself. Sarena knew this would change as soon as they got to be more comfortable together. After their first successful hunt as a team, things would be just fine.

When Lanakila swooped down from the eucalyptus, Sarena was already wide awake and anxious to go. She was very eager to try out their new system of hunting, and even more eager to spend more time chatting with Lanakila.

Sarena took a position on a high point along the Canyon wall. From there she had a clear view of the skies stretching over the valley where Lanakila would be patrolling. She could only see limited areas of ground from her position, since the terrain was very rugged and thick sage blocked most of her view.

Lanakila took off and began to circle high above the Canyon. Sarena smiled as she watched the great bird. She wished she could be with him, so they could soar across the Canyon together. She felt as though she were with him in spirit. Her eyes never left his majestic wings.

Sarena trembled slightly with nervous energy. She had not intentionally hunted in months. If by chance, during her travels, she had happened to come upon an unsuspecting alleen, then she had indeed made a kill. Otherwise she had gone on about her business of searching for other pumas.

Sarena expected the ahila to start a hover at any moment—her signal to move. Lanakila would begin a tight circle once he spotted an alleen, then try to maintain a position directly above it. Sarena pawed at the ground nervously, hoping her friend would hurry.

He did. It was only a few minutes before Lanakila had begun a tight circle, only to cut it off abruptly and dive toward Sarena. He landed on the branch of a holly tree near where she was keeping vigil.

"There are two," said Lanakila.

"Okay," said Sarena. "I'm ready."

"They're both bucks."

"Oh. I don't know if I can take down a buck," said Sarena. "At least not by myself. I guess it depends upon how big it is."

Lanakila hissed but said nothing. He did not appear to be angry, only perplexed.

"Maybe I can," said Sarena. "I've never really tried. Right now I feel like I have enough energy to give it a shot."

"Good," said Lanakila. "Follow me."

"Wait," said Sarena. "The last time I tried to catch alleen, thunder broke out in a cloudless sky. It killed one of them. I have never seen anything like it."

"There are no men in the Canyon today," said Lanakila.
"Men?"
"Yes. They control the cloudless thunder you speak
of. It is in a stick they carry. I'll explain later."
"But it didn't smell like men," said Sarena.
"No. They have ways of masking their scent. They do
it to fool the alleen. Now follow me, before it's too late."
Lanakila spread his wings and shot skyward. Sarena
knew the area he was headed for and began a calculated
trot in that direction. She was careful not to get too
winded, knowing she would need every ounce of strength
she had to pull down a buck. She hoped to catch the
alleen completely by surprise, minimizing the potential
for a fight.

She looked up constantly as she made her way through
the sage. Lanakila had begun his hovering less than a
hundred yards from where she now was. There was virtually no wind, giving her both advantage and disadvan-
tage. Her scent would not be carried to the buck, but
neither would her footfalls be masked by rustling leaves.

Sarena looked up again and wondered how the alleen
could miss such a huge bird directly above them. Then
she realized how Lanakila had behaved exactly the same
with her and she had never noticed either. Unlike hina
and other small rodents, larger animals just assume nothing will fall out of the sky to harm them. So far, nothing
had.

Lanakila was getting closer. It was a strange sensation
for Sarena, stalking something she knew was there but
had not yet seen or smelled. At least she hoped something was there. She would be very upset if this was one
of the ahila's practical jokes.

Suddenly Lanakila began to dive. His piercing screech
froze Sarena in her tracks. She lifted her head to peer
over the sage and saw the two alleen, who were staring
up at the diving ahila. Lanakila changed direction and
angled directly at the bucks. When they broke into a run,
Sarena jumped.

No one on the ground was prepared for what happened
next. The ahila grabbed the antlers of the smaller buck,
and yanked him toward Sarena. The bird held on tight,
flapping his wings and screaming loudly into the buck's
face. The terrified alleen was too busy trying to run and

shake the ahila off his head to notice the mountain lion racing at him from the left.

Sarena couldn't believe her eyes, but she never stopped to think about it. The buck never saw her. Sarena jolted into the air, slamming into his left shoulder and dropping him to the ground and Lanakila into the air with one quick motion. The buck screamed with terror as he landed hard on his right side. Sarena had his throat before he ever had the chance to make another move.

Lanakila swooped down and landed on the dead alleen's antlers. He looked down at the kill, then up at Sarena.

"Thought you could use the help," he said.

"You scared the fur right off of me!" complained Sarena. "Why didn't you at least tell me?"

"Didn't occur to me until it was too late," said Lanakila. "And besides, it was fun. I've never done anything like that before."

"I've never *heard* of anything like that before," said Sarena. "It looked so ridiculous, it was almost funny."

"It worked," said Lanakila, looking down at the fallen alleen.

"Yes. It worked."

Someone else had never heard of such a thing, either. Grash was completely amazed at the teamwork and efficiency the puma and ahila had demonstrated in bringing down the alleen. It looked so well coordinated he assumed they had worked together for many seasons.

It had occurred to Grash to try hunting the alleen. They seemed to be a logical solution to the imminent food shortage the tribe was faced with. He had seen them frequently in the Canyon, but he feared they were far too fast for the tribe. There was simply too much open space for the style of calculated attack the tribe was trained in. Part of Grash's plans was to adapt the tribe for large-scale Canyon maneuvers, and he believed he had just received a valuable lesson.

The tribe had still been sleeping when he had awakened and decided to stretch out and spray some bushes. The sight of the ahila piqued his curiosity, since he had never before seen such a tremendous bird. His curiosity turned to astonishment when he saw the ahila dive down and land beside the largest cat he had ever seen. From his perspective, the cat might even have been larger than he was.

Grash was certain this was the owner of the wild, exotic scent the tribe had picked up, which left them shaking. He was also certain it was the owner of the name *puma*, which struck terror into the Canyon at the mere whisper of its name alone. After witnessing its work on the alleen, he understood why.

He also understood that the puma was vulnerable.

What he didn't understand was the ahila's role in all of this. Certainly the big cat was capable of hunting for itself. Had the bird been forced to bargain for its life? Grash thought so. The puma probably had threatened to eat the bird unless it agreed to help out. This was an interesting arrangement. Grash nodded, thinking about how useful such a bird could be to the tribe.

He watched the cat and the bird feast on the fallen buck. What a combination: a cat and a bird. Grash decided the bird probably would be happier hunting with the tribe. It would take only a minimal amount of diplomacy to convince it to join up. The only problem was getting rid of the cat.

Grash looked back at the sleeping tribe and smiled. No problem.

When Sarena and Lanakila had eaten their fill, Sarena dragged the alleen carcass into a thicket of greasewood. It was more of a struggle than she was used to, since she had never before pulled the weight of a buck. She made a quick check of the terrain for identifying markers so she could find it easily again.

"I'm stuffed, Fur Ball," said Lanakila, stretching out his wings. "I never dreamed the alleen would taste so good."

"I'm full too, dearest," said Sarena. "We will not have to hunt again for weeks."

Lanakila cocked his head, giving Sarena a curious look. He did not expect their catch to last as long as Sarena apparently did. He had no way of knowing that pumas stored extra fat in their tails as a reserve against lean times.

"The morning is so young, and already I feel sleepy

as a cat," said Lanakila. "I might even nap with you if you can find us a soft place."

"It would be a pleasure," said Sarena. "A nap in the sun is always a treat after such a feast."

Lanakila hopped onto Sarena's shoulders. Even with a full stomach he was very light, which was good, since Sarena was getting tired. All of the crazy events of the hunt had worn her out.

"So, sweetness, you'll sleep on the ground again?" asked Sarena.

"I will gladly nap on the ground while the sun still rules," said Lanakila. "After dark is when I must seek the trees."

"You mentioned kribas before," said Sarena as she began to walk. "I have never seen one in the Canyon."

Lanakila's grip tightened on Sarena's fur. He felt lighter. She stopped, looked up, and noticed his wings were spread. His legs trembled slightly.

"What's wrong, love?" Sarena asked.

"There is a pack of them," said Lanakila. "Wild kribas. Killer kribas. It's been a cycle of the moon since they moved into the Canyon."

"Yes?" asked Sarena. "Kribas are not much different than krahstas, your 'howling cowards of the Canyon.' In fact from what I have observed, they are even bigger cowards than the krahstas."

"These are not," said Lanakila. "These kribas are huge and mean, and they fear nothing. They have spread their own terror through the bushes. They mostly hunt the pets of men, but they have also done damage in the Canyon."

Sarena began to walk again. She understood how a smaller creature like Lanakila could be upset by such news, but to her it meant nothing. A pack of kribas would not affect her hunting patterns one whisker.

"You're afraid they'll eat all the hina?" Sarena asked. "Don't worry. We'll catch plenty of alleen."

"I'm afraid of being eaten myself," said Lanakila. "My Fur Ball is not listening. These kribas are *huge*. Some, I believe, are as large as you. And there are eight of them."

"Have you seen them?" Sarena asked.

"Yes," said Lanakila. "They . . . I'd rather not think

about them. My warning to you is to avoid them. If you smell them, just go the other way."

Sarena began to laugh, then hissed when Lanakila jabbed at her ear.

"Listen to me, Sarena!" demanded Lanakila. "I have seen them. They are trouble. Put away your big puma ego and walk the other way if you know they are about. We will be leaving here soon, anyway. They're not worth chancing a run-in."

Sarena walked silently for several strides. Her new friend sounded very frightened. Enough so to call her by her real name for the first time since they'd met. She noticed the bird's grip was even tighter than before. Yet she couldn't imagine anything, especially a pack of kribas, being fierce enough to stand up to a puma. Still, Lanakila was right. Since there were no other pumas or ahilas in the area they would be leaving soon anyway. Why take a chance on injuring a paw while ripping a kriba's lungs out?

By the time Sarena had found them a soft spot to rest she was no longer sleepy. She was still physically tired, but she found herself in the unusual position of not being able to pass out immediately. Lanakila actually fell asleep before she did.

A deep, internal warning was starting to ring within her. It had something to do with kribas, but she couldn't exactly place what it was. It seemed hazy, as if it was coming from someone else's memories rather than her own. As she began to drift into the foggy realm between waking and sleeping, she had a brief vision of Lady Farri, who was urgently bidding her to move along.

CHAPTER 10

It was only nine o'clock in the morning, and already there were three phone messages waiting for Laura when she walked into the office. The first one was from a guy she had gone out with once several weeks ago. He had repeatedly called her, and never took the hint when she refused to return his calls. Once had been enough. The second was from Brad Berglund of Mountain Lions Forever, who obviously had something to say about her article, which had appeared in that morning's paper. The third was from Keith Gallatin.

She sat down at her desk and put her briefcase and purse on the floor. The newsroom was crowded and noisy with reporters discussing stories for the day. She quickly glanced across her assignment sheet concerning the pack of wild dogs. It was going to take lots of calls and lots of driving.

She decided to hit the cafeteria for some coffee. Her date the night before had been a doozie. The guy had seemed fine when she had met him on a story a couple of weeks ago, only to turn into a boring prima donna when they went out. Laura shook her head, wondering why the men who boasted they had the most to offer usually had the least.

When Laura got back to her desk she returned the call from Brad Berglund, but got no answer. She stared at the message from Gallatin, wondering what he might want. The phone number on the message was not one of the six she had seen the day before.

He was probably mad at her for quoting him in the article. She didn't care. He hadn't really said anything, anyway. She wondered if he was always so evasive and

57

diplomatic. She could understand why he would be, but it certainly didn't fit his rock-star image. He was supposed to be rude, crude, and lewd.

Laura dialed the number and listened to it ring. Was he at the apartment of some young star-collector? He certainly had a notorious reputation for such.

"Keith. Speak," came the voice at the other end.

"This is Laura Kay, returning your call."

"Oh, hello. Just calling to compliment you on the article," said Keith.

"Thank you," said Laura. She was somewhat surprised, but knew there had to be more.

"I like your style," said Keith.

"Thank you," said Laura.

"Of writing. I guess I should have said that."

"Oh. Now I don't know whether to be complimented or insulted," Laura replied, laughing.

"Complimented," Keith said, a little strained. "I guess I blew that. Anyway, I was kinda wondering why you mentioned me. I really didn't have anything to do with the story."

"True, but you were there," said Laura. "I mentioned you because people in this town think you're important."

Keith burst into laughter. Laura looked into the phone, very surprised at his reaction. She had not meant it to be funny, and had actually thought he might be offended.

"Yes, they do," said Keith, still chuckling. "Strange, isn't it?"

Laura bit her tongue. She decided to quit while she was behind. This guy was turning out to be far different from what she had thought he would be.

"No comment?" Keith asked. "Okay. Well, I thought you might be interested in a little tip."

"Yes?" Laura asked cautiously.

"The Fish and Game Commission is holding its meeting in Long Beach next week. You might be very interested in attending."

"Why?"

"You know when you jammed me up yesterday for not getting involved?"

"Yes."

"Well, after we hung up I was really mad at you," said

Keith. "But then I realized you were right. If I don't get involved, the mountain lions will be stuck with those freaks as their only representation."

"What are you going to do?" asked Laura.

"I can't say exactly, yet," said Keith, "because I'm not exactly sure what I can put together by then. Let's just say it should be interesting."

"Okay, I'll be there."

"Do you know where it is?"

"I'll find out," said Laura.

"Good, I hope to see you there."

"By the way," Laura said innocently. "Is this a good number to reach you at?"

"This is my office number at home," said Keith. "You can usually reach me here or leave a message."

"Okay, I'll see you next week," said Laura.

"Oh, and would you like another tip?" Keith asked.

"Sure."

"You need to give your dates more than just one chance," said Keith.

"What?"

"Gotta go. Bye." Keith hung up before Laura could respond.

Laura looked down at the phone for several minutes. She couldn't help but like him, even though he was so sober and businesslike with her. She thought about his last remark, wondering who his sources might be. It could be practically anyone. Laura's dating failures were legendary around the paper. She sometimes felt as though she had dated half of San Diego at least once.

Keith Gallatin. There were so many Keith Gallatin stories. She wondered how he could stand the gossip. Celebrities were such easy targets for dirt. His picture was constantly appearing in the celebrity rags, always at some social function with one of a select group of female stars. There were constant rumors, but he always shrugged them off and said the ladies were "just friends."

Laura wondered what Keith would be like on a date. Not her type, she knew, but at least he wouldn't be boring like most of the men she dated. Keith probably had a few stories of his own to tell. But would he tell them? He seemed awfully cautious.

The phone rang, startling Laura back to reality.

"Hi, this is Brad Berglund. I'm just calling to say I liked your story. It was really fair."

"Thank you," said Laura, rolling her eyes and waiting for the real reason for the call.

"I was wondering if you were going to cover the Commission next week in Long Beach," said Brad.

"Yes, I'll be there," said Laura. She wondered if Brad knew about Gallatin, but didn't want to ask.

"Good," said Brad. "Oh, and next time you do the story . . . ?"

"Yes."

"You might mention *how* lions were hunted back when it was legal."

"How?"

"Since the hunters would never have been able to find a mountain lion on their own," said Brad, "they used dogs."

"Dogs?"

"Yes," said Brad. "The hounds would track them down and chase them relentlessly until they were exhausted. Cats don't have the lung capacity that dogs do, so dogs can run much greater distances."

"So the dogs would chase it down?" Laura asked.

"Right. The mountain lion would finally give up and climb a tree. Then the hunters would arrive and shoot it down."

Broed was the last of the tribe to finally awaken and stretch out. Grash had waited patiently, wanting to keep everyone, especially Broed, as relaxed as possible. Any member of a group as volatile as this tribe could cause serious problems if upset, and clearly Broed was the most dangerous. Grash understood this well enough to let everyone get as much rest as they needed.

Kroth looked at Grash expectantly. It seemed as though he always knew when Grash was ready to make a statement, which usually took the form of handing out assignments. This time would be different.

The sun had already climbed high into the mid-morning sky. Even Grash had taken another nap since witnessing the cat and the bird. He pawed gently at some of the stickers his coat had snagged in the sage, trying to appear relaxed. Nothing could be farther from the truth. Grash was ecstatic.

"I have witnessed the strangest event of my life," said Grash. The other tribe members perked up their ears. "It is an event which may some day free us from ever having to raid the streets again."

Grash expected a response, any response, but got none. The others simply continued to give him their unwavering attention. Grash nodded, remembering they were skilled in discipline and obedience, not imagination. He gave each of them an individual look of affection, as they lounged on their forepaws in the shade of a thicket of brown sagebrush.

Taking a deep breath, Grash began his story. He told them all about the puma and how it had worked with an ahila to take down an alleen. He talked for several minutes, leaving out no detail of the event. He closed the tale with a description of the duo feasting on their kill.

The reaction of the tribe was frightening. Grash had expected them to be as excited as he was, but in their eyes was fear and concern. Not fear of the puma and ahila, but fear that their leader had gone mad. The tribe sat motionless in a very heavy silence.

Grash did not know what to say. He began to tense up inside. He needed to think of a quick way to reassure them of his sanity.

"He speaks the truth," said Kroth, finally breaking the silence.

All heads turned to the Doberman who masterminded their raids. He was sitting up and panting, his eyes darting around the tribe.

"I was afraid of receiving the same reaction you all gave Grash," said Kroth. "In fact I did not even believe my own eyes, so how was I to convince the tribe?"

"You saw the attack?" asked Grash. "I thought you were asleep."

"No, I didn't see the attack," said Kroth. "It was yesterday that I saw them. I was terrified, because I thought I was coming down with the crazy sickness."

"What did you see?" asked Telsh.

"I saw the puma," said Kroth. "It walked openly

through the bottom of the ravine. It walked with an ahila perched on its back."

The entire tribe gasped at once. Each kriba stood up and began to pant.

"On its back?" demanded Broed.

"You can see why I was reluctant to say anything," said Kroth. "But it's true. I saw it yesterday when you were all out hunting the ram. I thought I must have been dreaming, until I heard the tale of Grash."

"We have all smelled the puma," said Telsh. Like the others, he had begun to pace within the tight confines of brush. "I am not ashamed to say it has made me tremble. I can see it had the same effect on us all."

All of the kribas barked in agreement. The scent had driven them crazy, both with fascination and fear. Part of the reason they had always remained together as a group when in the Canyon was the unspoken dread of being alone and running into the owner of such a scent.

"Okay, let's relax," said Grash, trying to regain control. "Let's all sit back down and discuss this rationally."

Each member of the tribe sat down immediately as ordered. Grash was instantly relieved, despite their continued ragged panting. At least they would still follow orders without question. Grash waited for them to settle down even more before he spoke again.

"I believe the ahila is held against its will," said Grash, to a caucus of questioning eyes. "The puma has been forcing it to oblige, probably for many seasons. I believe the bird would welcome an escape, and would gratefully help *us* hunt the alleen in return for its liberation from the puma."

CHAPTER 11

Laura was always amazed at how close rural farmland was to America's sixth largest city. In the same county, only a few miles from traffic jams and crowded tract houses, sat miles of open-space avocado and citrus groves.

The man Laura met with first was named Carl Spring. He was a warm man in his fifties, with graying brown hair and thick glasses. His hands were large and worn, yet somehow delicate. He worked as a machinist in the city of Escondido but lived on a one-acre parcel of land in the outskirts of Vista in North County.

"This is where they attacked my lamb," Carl said, showing Laura a small pen in his backyard. "I heard a racket like you wouldn't believe. The sheep were making the noise, you see. Nothing else. Well, I thought someone was trying to steal them, so I got my flashlight and my shotgun."

"What time was this?" Laura asked, surveying the pen. There were six sheep feeding from a bail of hay Carl had just thrown in.

"Oh, nine o'clock," said Carl.

"At night?" Laura asked.

"Right. Well, I came charging out through the door, but it was too late. They had already drug the little guy through the fence. There was blood all over everywhere."

"Did you see them?" asked Laura.

"No," said Carl. "At first I thought it was coyotes. We have problems with them out here, you know. Well, I got to thinkin' about how quiet they were. Not a peep. Coyotes, you know, make enough racket to wake the dead."

63

"Yes," said Laura, nodding.

"Well, when I saw the tracks, I knew it wasn't no coyotes," said Carl. He looked down at his feet and shook his head. He pulled off his glasses, then wiped the sweat from his brow.

"How big were they?" Laura asked.

"Three, maybe four times the size of what you'd expect from a coyote," said Carl, putting his glasses back in place.

"Really? That big?"

"That big," Carl said and nodded. "There was a bunch of 'em, too. As many as five animals."

"Wow, I'm surprised they picked just one lamb," said Laura.

"Me too," said Carl. "They were awfully organized. They went straight for the easiest one. Didn't touch any of the others."

"Has anyone seen these dogs?"

"Debbie McNalty, right up the hill there," said Carl, pointing to a lime-green house at the end of the road. "They made off with her ram, right in broad daylight. All the other attacks happened at night."

"Any idea where these dogs came from?" Laura asked.

"My guess is they're from that guard dog place at the edge of town," said Carl. "You know, someone broke in and set a bunch of 'em free a while back."

"No, I didn't know," said Laura, raising her eyebrows. "What's the name of it?"

"Gordon's K-9," answered Carl.

Lanakila was gone when Sarena finally woke up. She was not surprised; in fact she was glad, considering how she felt. Most of the day was already past, with only a couple hours of sun left. Sarena stretched, then began to groom.

She normally liked to sleep even longer after a good meal. This time, however, crazy nightmares had forced her to awaken. Her slumbers were often troubled, but never like this. Loneliness was usually the dominant subject to infiltrate her dreams. It had a nasty way of creeping in, no matter how benign the topic. Not this time.

Sarena had dreamed of a chase. She had run hard and

fast until she could no longer breathe. The ludicrous part was, it was her who was being chased. She had not even known who or what was behind her, only that she had to hurry up or perish. She'd woken up gasping for air.

It was time to move on again. There were no pumas in the area, and obviously something was amiss. Even Lanakila had been anxious about a pack of wild kribas. He would probably welcome a move.

Sarena could sense a change in the dynamics of the Canyon. There was nothing concrete, since no one ever confided in pumas. At least, not until she had met the ahila. Still, she observed other animals constantly, even when she wasn't interested in hunting. While her presence alone would cause edginess in the area, she had never seen anxiety as rampant as it was now.

An awkward movement in the brush brought Sarena to her feet. She sniffed the air, quickly assessing the animal as nonhazardous. Of course, nothing in the wilds of Southern California threatened a puma. Sarena cocked her head in astonishment when she identified the scent of a skerris, the common-speech word for raccoon.

She could see the branches of buckwheat begin to move as the other animal got closer. It had to smell her by now, yet it continued its deliberate passage. When it had reached the small clearing where Sarena waited, it stood trembling as it looked up at her. When their eyes met, the smaller animal instantly dropped its gaze.

"Well, my little friend," Sarena said kindly. "These days in the Canyon get stranger still. I have never been approached by one of your line."

The skerris looked up then instantly looked back down, quickly rubbing its front paws together. Sarena glanced down at her own paws. Sometimes she wished her image weren't so intimidating. The mere scent of puma was enough to scare most animals out of their fur. This little skerris obviously had something very important to say in order to brave such a risk, yet he couldn't open his mouth to get it out.

"You are quite a handsome fellow," said Sarena, trying to relax her visitor. "I have never seen a skerris so closely before." The skerris let out a long breath, obviously relieved. If the puma had not seen one so close she had not eaten one, either. Sarena smiled and walked toward her guest. It backed up cautiously, but stopped when Sarena did.

"Just wanted a closer look," said Sarena. The skerris only sniffed.

Sarena truly had never been so close to a skerris. This was partly because she had never been hungry enough to stalk an animal with such an unappealing aroma. The skerrises she had seen picked up her scent and took off immediately. They had no intention of finding out just how hungry Sarena might be.

Sarena thought skerrises were the most unusual animals in the Canyon. Her visitor had big black circles around his eyes, making it hard to determine exactly which direction he was looking in. His coat was a unique blend of gray and brown, turning into alternate rings around his tail. He supported very long whiskers, stemming from a long snout crowned with a shiny black nose.

"I suppose we could spend all night staring at each other," said Sarena.

"I suppose not," said the skerris.

"Oh. Well, my name is Sarena. Please relax. If I was going to bite, I would have done so already."

The skerris acknowledged her words with a nod. "My name is Joris."

"Well, my little friend, what brings you here on such an errand?" Sarena asked. "I guess it must be important for you to risk such a meeting."

"There is risk, but you have eaten," said Joris flatly.

"Yes," nodded Sarena. It was never a secret. Every living animal in the Canyon gave a sigh of relief when pumas had a full belly.

Joris sat back on his honches to assess Sarena. She wondered what the skerris thought of her. He was still terrified, but beginning to relax.

"Most animals pray for you to perish," Joris said abruptly.

Sarena looked off into the sage. This was certainly no surprise, yet hearing it ripped open a lonely wound inside. Never before had she felt so isolated. She looked back at the skerris and had to fight back an urge to mangle him and run off into the night.

"Still, you are one of us," said Joris.

"One of who?" asked Sarena.

"One of the Canyon. You are from here, and belong here. While others in the Canyon may not like it, we must all accept it. You are here for a reason, just as are we all."

"So have you come to lecture me on the cycles of life?" Sarena asked, still hurting from Joris's earlier words.

"No."

"Then what can a puma do for you?"

"It is what *I* can do for *you*," said Joris. "All of us."

"Yes?"

"I watched you kill the alleen today," said Joris. "Many animals of the Canyon were witness. Your friendship with the ahila is no longer a secret, if in fact it ever was."

Sarena shrugged. She had wondered what the rest of the Canyon would think. She got the feeling she was about to find out.

"There are rumors in the Canyon," said Joris. "Rumors about a dangerous pack of kribas. It is true. I saw them today. One of them watched you take down the alleen."

Sarena rolled her eyes. It seemed like smaller animals were afraid of *everything*. Who cared about kribas?

"I followed it," said Joris. "It may have smelled me, but it didn't care. It wanted *you*."

"Yes?" Sarena asked impatiently. "Who doesn't?"

"I heard it tell the others in its pack," said Joris. "They are planning an attack."

Sarena began to laugh. She didn't mean to. She could see it offended the skerris, but it only made her laugh the more.

"Why tell me all of this?" Sarena finally asked when she'd stopped laughing. "As you said, everyone wants me dead anyway."

"Not everyone," said Joris. "Even so, most would agree to your importance here. You are of the Canyon; they are not. You belong; they do not. It's true you hunt the alleen, but it's important for us all that you do. Otherwise they would eat all the food and we would all go hungry."

Sarena looked at the skerris in wonder. She hunted for food when she was hungry, never giving it a second thought until meeting Lanakila. She had never dreamed her actions might be of some benefit to the rest of the canyon.

"Still, they are only kribas," said Sarena.

"They are *big* kribas," said Joris. "There are eight of them, and they are very organized and vicious."

"If you are really so concerned, then I shall take all precautions to avoid them," said Sarena.

"This warning is quite a favor, puma," said Joris. "You must take it more seriously. This pack is a very formidable foe."

"I will avoid them, then," said Sarena. "It sounds as though you expect a favor in return."

"Avoid the pack," said Joris. "But if you happen to catch one of them alone . . ."

Even on nice autumn days it was hot in Vista. It had to be eighty degrees when Laura stepped out of her RX-7 in front of Gordy's K-9. The storefront was part of a block that looked far more like a small town in the Midwest than Southern California.

The office was untidy and hot. Large, poorly shot pictures of Dobermans and German shepherds had been hung randomly about the fading yellow walls. Laura stood in a small waiting area while a plain middle-aged woman went to get Gordon. Laura looked down at an old wooden coffee table that held dog magazines and literature on assault weapons. This probably would not go very well.

"Good morning!" boomed a voice from behind her.

Laura turned around and involuntarily took a quick breath. A huge man, presumably Gordon, was walking into the room with his hand extended. He was easily twice Laura's size, with short black hair. He smiled a toothy grin, which was almost hidden behind a very thick beard. He grabbed Laura's hand in a large, fleshy grip.

"Gordon Jones," he said. "What can I do for you?"

"Good morning, I'm Laura Kay from the *Union*. I understand you had some problems with vandals recently."

"Yes, ma'am," agreed Gordon, his smile fading.

"What happened?"

"How did you hear about it?" asked Gordon.

"Police reports," lied Laura. She hoped he had indeed called the police, or she might be in trouble. It was always best to blame the police anyway, instead of possibly burning a source.

Gordon snorted, acknowledging a police report, but said nothing. He ran his right hand through his thick beard. Laura was glad he'd taken the bait. Now if Gordon blew her off she could check with the authorities as to what had actually happened.

"Did any of your dogs get loose?" asked Laura.

"Come on outside," said Gordon. "I'll show you."

Laura followed him out the back door toward the kennel area. She was surprised. It seemed as if Gordon was going to cooperate.

A thunder of deep barking greeted them when the dogs saw a stranger. Laura flinched, but relaxed when she saw that all of them were caged. Each of the fifteen kennels held either a German shepherd or a Doberman. All of them were on their feet, barking.

"Quiet, you old biddies!" Gordon yelled, raising his right arm.

The silence was immediate. Every dog sat on the floor and looked up at Gordon. One shepherd uttered the slightest whimper, but the others maintained their hush.

"Good babies," said Gordon to the dogs. He put his hand up to the kennel of the whiner. "You're such a pretty baby. Yes you are."

The shepherd stood up and licked his hand through the bars. Laura winced, thinking about how sweet this dog wanted to be and how vicious it was being trained to be.

"Some of 'em you gotta treat like children," said Gordon. "Some of 'em you gotta treat like old folks. I guess that means about the same thing."

"It can, yes," said Laura, still amazed at the dog licking Gordon's hand. "How did your dogs get out?"

"Someone came in through there," said Gordon, pointing at a window above a row of cages. "Whoever it was knew dogs. Knew *my* dogs. Knew them well enough to know the right signs. He cut 'em loose and took off without getting bit."

"What kind of security do you have?" Laura asked.

"I had fifteen attack dogs in here that night," said Gordon.

Laura chuckled, feeling silly, It took either a lot of guts or a lot of stupidity to break into a guard dog kennel.

"How many people work here?" Laura asked.

"Only three. It wasn't us. Coulda been anyone, really. Anyone who knows dogs."

"Eight got away?" Laura asked.

"Right. Seven just stayed put. But eight of 'em took right on off."

"How well were they trained?" Laura asked.

"All my dogs are top-notch," boasted Gordon.

"I know," said Laura. "I meant, to what level of guard duty had they been trained?"

"All the way," said Gordon. "They were ready to go. They were good. My two best dogs went with 'em."

"What did the police say?" Laura asked.

"It was sheriffs," said Gordon. "They don't care about anything unless there's someone they can bust over the head."

Laura nodded. Probably the only thing she had in common with Gordon Jones was his dislike of the local law enforcement, although probably their reasons were different.

"Do you think these dogs would stick together?" Laura asked.

"Hard to say," said Gordon. "Probably most of them."

"Would they be dangerous to neighbors?"

"I would hate to run into any of them if I didn't know the commands," said Gordon. "But hell, we hunted all all over for those dogs. We never saw a one. They're gone."

"Have you heard about the dogs who are attacking pets close to here?"

"It could be them," Gordon said. "I hope not."

Laura scribbled some notes on her pad. She hoped it wasn't Gordon's dogs either. Not just for the obvious reason of their size and destructive capabilities, but also because Gordon was a nice guy. Despite his overbearing appearance, he seemed to be just another honest businessman trying to get by.

"Anything I haven't asked that you think is important?" Laura asked.

"It's important for people to know that they're out there," said Gordon. "That's why I'm cooperating with you. People need to know to stay away if they see 'em. Climb a tree, jump on a car, anything."

"Thanks for your time," said Laura. "I hope they're not yours."

"I love my dogs," said Gordon. "But I hope they all got run down by cars. Every one. Otherwise . . . Well, let's just say they'd be one mean pack."

CHAPTER 12

Grash was already beginning to see serious flaws in the tribe's ability to hunt the Canyon. The efficient agility they evinced when raiding penned-in livestock turned to clumsy mush when pursuing wild animals with no boundaries. For all their efforts in two days of exclusively hunting the Canyon, they had managed only a few unsuspecting hina to feed the entire tribe.

Tempers were starting to flare. So much energy had been spent for so little reward. The tribe had worked relentlessly, tracking as much of the open space as their tired bodies would manage, without even a glimpse of an alleen.

Still, they hunted. Kroth had marshaled them into a loose-knit pack, and they trotted aimlessly through the chaparral. They had been roaming all morning and into the afternoon, and Grash thought they would be too tired to run down an alleen even if they did find one.

Grash stole a sideways glance at his brother, who trotted a few yards to his right. Telsh looked horrible. He looked nearly exhausted, with glazed-over eyes. His tongue flopped out to the side with labored pants. In only two days he had lost noticeable weight. They all had.

There was going to be trouble if things didn't change soon. The tribe was too high-strung to deal with such pressure. They had been easy to control when things were going well, but now they were flirting with disaster.

Grash was just about to call for them to stop when he smelled it. They all found the scent at the same instant. It was wild, familiar yet distant, and definitely not prey. It was a predator, and without even a word the tribe became alert again. They quickly tightened their formation, then stopped.

The scent got closer, with a strength and substance Grash thought he could touch. It was so ancient and wild. It painted a picture in Grash's mind he didn't understand, even though it felt so familiar. He was not afraid, but he was not encouraged either. He braved a quick glance, and saw the others were experiencing the same thing.

When a large pack of krahstas appeared from out of the surrounding bushes of scrub oak, Grash understood. He had never seen a truly wild dog before, but now the concept made perfect sense. Until now he had foolishly considered the tribe to be wild. The faces of the krahstas proved otherwise.

There were twelve of the gray animals. Their golden eyes looked cold and on fire, both at the same time. They wore long whiskers and long, bushy tails. They stood in height only one third the size of most of the tribe members, yet they stood without fear. Their heads were high and their shoulders back. They sniffed curiously at the tribe. It was several moments before anyone in either of the two groups moved or spoke.

"You are disturbing our territory," said one of the krahstas. He stepped forward and scanned a look across each member of the tribe.

"But this is the Canyon," said Grash. "No one owns the Canyon."

"We don't own the Canyon," said the krahsta. "Only the Creator can own land. But this is our territory. You do not even belong here."

Grash did not answer. The krahsta was right and he knew it.

"My name is Dropno," said the krahsta. "We have watched you since your arrival in the Canyon. We had little quarrel when you raided the man-homes, but now you are harassing our hunting grounds."

Grash could sense the tribe's reaction. They were close to starvation after only two days on these hunting grounds, yet the krahstas did not look hungry in the least. The tribe was worn out and close to exhaustion, in stark contrast to the freshness of the krahstas.

"At first we objected to your raids," said Dropno.

"We feared the men would think it was us, and vow retaliation. But then we realized how big you are. The men could not mistake our tracks or our scent."

"Go back to hunting the streets," said another of the krahstas. "You did well there. You are too awkward and noisy for the Canyon. Your footsteps alone are heavy enough to be heard all the way across the ravine."

"We are not the only large predators in the Canyon," said Grash, finally coming up with an argument. "We are aware of at least one puma. Why don't you chase it off your territory?"

The entire pack of krahstas winced at Grash's mention of the puma. Clearly he had hit a sore point. He hoped it was one he could exploit.

"The puma belongs in the Canyon," Dropno said carefully. "You do not. The puma will move on soon. They always do. It is none of your concern."

"Sounds like you hate the puma more than you hate us," said Grash.

"The Canyon has been very tense since the arrival of the puma," said Dropno. "But as I said, it will be moving on soon."

"And what if I told you that we plan to get rid of the puma completely?" asked Grash.

The leader stood before a pack of accusing eyes. They were tired, hungry, and mad. Grash knew his words would have to be perfect, or he might well be the tribe's next meal.

He hoped his handling of the krahstas had scored points with the tribe. He had taken a desperate situation and turned it around to their favor. The only obstacle now was convincing the tribe to make good on it.

"As you all know, we have a number of concerns," Grash began. He paced slowly in the shade of a eucalyptus tree. Everyone else was down on their forepaws, save for Telsh, who sat upright.

"We need to eat!" said Broed, to the growled approval of the others.

"You're absolutely right," said Grash. "We will do it soon. Today."

"Do we raid a house?" asked Kroth, hopefully. Besides the prospect of food, he was clearly interested in orchestrating another plan they could actually work with. He had not done so well in the Canyon.

"As I see it, all of these issues are bound together," said Grash. "Eating, the raids, the krahstas, the puma, and the ahila are all different parts of the same dilemma. They are all problems we will take care of."

"I was embarrassed today," said Grallus, one of the young black shepherds. "We were threatened by a bunch of krahstas less than half our size. And we did nothing! We couldn't even run them off."

Grash began to speak but was cut off.

"How will we maul a puma if we cannot even chase off krahstas?" demanded Krayde, the largest Doberman. The others echoed with various snorts and growls.

"Let the leader talk," said Telsh.

"Thank you," said Grash, when the others had stopped grumbling. "As I said, these are all part of the same problem. But the first part of it is, we all must eat. Soon."

The others woofed agreement in unison.

"It is true. We are not yet ready to hunt the Canyon," said Grash. "We must therefore go back to hunting the streets, as our dear friends the krahstas have recommended. But this we will do only for a short time."

"When do we start?" asked Kroth.

"After we have rested," said Grash. "I would wait until tonight, but I believe we will make today the exception. We will go this afternoon, as soon as we have regained our strength."

The entire tribe growled their approval. Grash could see Kroth already beginning to think up a scheme. Only Telsh looked apprehensive.

"After today we will make our raids only at night," said Grash. "We will do this only until we have again become strong."

"*Then* what?" asked Kroth, snapping out of his scheming with a look of worry.

"Then we find the puma," said Grash. "You, Kroth, will be called upon to devise your finest plan of ambush. We will eliminate the puma, and liberate the ahila. 'Eliminate and liberate' shall be our motto."

This statement received no response at all. The tribe

stared back at Grash with blank expressions. No one was quite sure how to feel about this.

"Once we have the ahila on our side," said Grash, "hunting the Canyon will be simple. The puma has done it for many seasons. If she can, so can we."

"What about the krahstas?" asked Grallus.

"Once we have proven our strength by eliminating the puma, the krahstas will be no problem," said Grash. "We will search them out to settle a score, and they will scatter like the wind and find new territory."

"Grash, so far, except for one careless afternoon, we have been cautious," said Telsh. "This caution has paid off, I think. Won't this plan of eliminating a puma be dangerous?"

"Yes, my brother, it will," said Grash. "But I believe it is a risk worth taking. The rewards are tremendous. Having an ahila in our debt will bring unlimited capabilities. Plus, imagine the respect associated with the destruction of a puma."

"But Grash," said Telsh. "What if the ahila and puma are friends?"

"Impossible," said Grash. "Pumas don't have any friends."

CHAPTER 13

Sarena was beginning to worry. The sun was well into the sky and she had not yet seen Lanakila. The ahila often left her when she napped, but he usually appeared shortly after she woke. So far he hadn't shown up all day.

This was a new sensation for Sarena. She had never worried before in her life. She had rarely felt anything other than loneliness and despair.

Lanakila. In only a few short days he had changed her whole existence. The loneliness was gone. True, there was still a small, empty space inside, but no longer was it overwhelming. Not only had it become manageable, but it was rarely thought of anymore. The space instead was being filled up by a lighter sensation of happiness, something else Sarena had experienced only brief flashes of in the past. This was all due to the unexpected arrival of a smart-aleck bird.

She needed to talk to him. It was time to move on. There were no other pumas or ahilas in the area. While this used to be the sole motivation for Sarena's travels, this time there were others. This time there were kribas.

Despite the warnings of both Lanakila and the skerris, Sarena was still laughing it off. They were, after all, only kribas. But the dreams she could not laugh off. They were becoming more frequent and specific, if not scary. One could dream of Lady Farri only so much without getting a little nervous.

The dreams were never exactly the same yet they always carried the same theme. There were kribas and chases, concluding with Lady Farri telling her to leave. The scenario of the kribas chasing her was so familiar, yet she could not place it. In waking life she had never been chased by *anything*.

There were no more excuses. She and Lanakila had finished off the last of their catch late yesterday afternoon. They would begin their journey as soon as Lanakila arrived, if it wasn't getting dark yet.

He would have to show up soon or she would be ready for another nap. This was one of the few areas in which she envied other animals. Cats were condemned to sleep most of their lives away, and there was no getting around it. But even sleep had changed for her since Lanakila's arrival. Whereas before she used to welcome it to help stave off the loneliness, now she dreaded it for the dreams. She also wanted to spend more time with Lanakila.

Raiding the streets was a great idea. The deathly look worn by the tribe only an hour earlier had been replaced by enthusiastic vigor. They loped up the side of the ravine together, waiting to part instantly at Grash's command, putting into motion an attack plan devised by Kroth.

Morale was high again. Grash could feel it. They were still physically weak, he knew, but it would pass. With the new strength would come new resolve to follow him as the unquestioned leader. This was important.

The plan they were about to use this afternoon was not new. Kroth had already worked it out the day before Grash's decision to hunt the Canyon. If successful, which the tribe held no doubt it would be, it would both feed them well and put an end to their afternoon haunts. All future raids would be under the cover of darkness.

The house in question held two adult sheep and several penned hina in the backyard. The hina were of no concern to the tribe, but the sheep were everything. The yard was wide open, with no fences. This gave the attackers the advantage of surrounding the prey from a distance, enabling them to reach full running speed by the time their targets even noticed. The sheep would be dragged down before they'd taken two steps, minimizing the potential for noise.

This time both Grash and Telsh were on the attack team. Since speed was critical in this particular adventure

Broed was tagged for security, instead of for his usual
role of project-finisher. The pit bull grumbled slightly at
this assignment, but as the slowest member of the tribe
he recognized the logic of it and went along without comment. He would be the only one of the eight not directly
involved with the attack—another unusual aspect of this
maneuver. Normally a minimum of two kribas covered
the street for safety purposes.

Grash barked the order, splitting the tribe. They began
to fan out into a large circle around the house, with
Broed heading for the street to sound first alarm if necessary. The wind was in their favor: There was none. Their
only obstacle was the brightness of the mid-afternoon
sunlight on a cloudless day.

Grash took his position behind a small tree on the
north side of the property. He stood nearly fifty yards
from the prey. Since everyone in the tribe knew the status of the sheep, all eyes would be on him. As soon as
he moved, the others would follow from their respective
positions.

The sheep had no idea any of this was going on. They
stood with faces down, chewing on some kind of green
mush. This would be a perfect operation.

Lifting his tail high, Grash focused both eyes on the
sheep and began his sprint.

As if summoned by Sarena's thoughts, the great bird
circled low and swooped down beside her. He held his
wings up for a moment, then tucked them in at his side.
He looked at her sideways, as he always did, wearing the
same impossible-to-read expression.

"Lanakila." Sarena smiled. "Aren't you ever happy to
see me?"

"I see you constantly," said Lanakila. "But you're
always asleep. I am happy to see you awake."

"Then why don't you smile for a change?" Sarena
asked.

"I am smiling," said Lanakila.

Sarena tilted her head. As far as she could tell his beak
was cast in a permanent frown. It only changed when he
spoke.

"Whatever you say," said Sarena. She figured he probably was smiling, in some strange way, but she would need time to figure it out.

"I have important news," said Lanakila.

"You saw another puma?" Sarena asked as she jumped up.

"No, no," said Lanakila. "Sorry."

Sarena looked down at her paws. She knew better than to expect so much, so quickly. It wasn't "so quickly"; she had been searching for many seasons. The emptiness expanded again.

"We'll find someone for both of us," said Lanakila. "We will. I can feel it in my wings. They are not as far off as we think."

"You're right," said Sarena hopefully. She hoped he was right, anyway. "What is your news?"

"The news I have is not so good," said Lanakila. "It concerns the kribas I have spoken of."

"Yes," said Sarena. "We need to talk about that. I've dreamed about them constantly since you first mentioned it."

"For you to say you have dreamed constantly about it is truly a scary thing." Lanakila laughed. "Since all my Fur Ball does is sleep, these dreams must be uncountable."

Sarena hissed and took a playful swipe at the bird. Lanakila returned the hiss.

"I saw the kribas today," he said. "At first the news appeared to be good. They were trying to hunt the Canyon, as they have been for three days. They have failed miserably. They were near exhaustion, and I thought some would be dead by tomorrow."

"Then what happened?" Sarena asked.

"They met up with a pack of krahstas," said the bird. "I was too far to hear what was said."

"Did they fight?" Sarena asked.

"No, but they did not seem friendly. I believe the krahstas threatened the others and warned them off their turf."

"And the kribas left?" Sarena asked, surprised.

"Yes."

"Then we have nothing to fear from them," said Sarena. "Anything run off by a scrawny pack of krahstas will be no match for us."

"I don't think they were run off," said Lanakila. "I think they simply made a deal. The kribas have gone back to raiding the streets. They are moving in on a man's home as we speak."

"What kind of deal?"

"I'm afraid to imagine," said Lanakila.

Sarena regarded the bird carefully. His beak still had not changed, but his eyes held concern.

"Sarena, there are no pumas or ahilas in this area," said Lanakila. "I believe it is time for us to move on."

Sarena nodded thoughtfully. This was only the second time the bird had called her by her real name. Both times he had been distressed.

"You are right, my little friend," said Sarena. "We . . ."

Her words were interrupted by three loud explosions.

"The man-made thunder!" cried Lanakila.

Grash was only halfway to the sheep when the disaster began. His training as a guard dog had taught him to recognize the sound of gunfire immediately. It was one of the big ones, the one that the men carried like a stick.

The entire tribe was committed and exposed. They all ran from different directions, but all toward a central goal. Grash saw the man standing at the back door of the house, pointing the gun in his general direction. He put his head down and ran harder, counting on speed for his escape. He hoped the others would do the same and not try to turn and disarm him as they had been trained.

As if in slow motion, Grash could see it all unfolding. The faces of the others, who ran in his direction toward the sheep, were wide-eyed with horror. There was nothing they could do but run for the Canyon and hope the man missed.

The sheep began to scream the instant the first shot exploded; first from the noise, then from the sight of the ambushing tribe. The sheep had no way of knowing the gunfire had just saved their lives.

The man fired a second shot, and this time Grash heard it hit. He broke his stride momentarily to look back, only to see Telsh tumble in the dirt. Without so much as a whimper his brother had died.

Grash bit down hard and bolted for the sage. There was nothing else he could do. He could not help his brother, and getting killed would only damage the tribe even more. He had to make it.

It had seemed so close only moments before. Now it seemed farther away than the alleen they had not been able to find when hunting the same canyon.

A third shot exploded from behind. Grash was not hit, and this time did not turn to see who was. He heard, though. It was Krayde, one of the Dobermans, who burst into painful yelps. The yelps turned to howls just as Grash hit the sage.

The shots stopped, but the howls did not. These lingered behind, telling everyone in the tribe that Krayde was too hurt to follow. Grash could hear the cries even as he crashed through the brush. Each one ripped through his soul like a cold, knotted whip. Grash had never heard a sadder sound.

When the surviving tribe members met at their first rendezvous point under a holly tree the howls had faded back to whimpers, but they were still loud enough to be heard throughout the Canyon. Like all of the others in the tribe Grash hoped the cries would stop soon, before they completely broke his heart. Within moments a fourth and final gunshot gave him his wish.

Grash winced at the sound. He glanced across at the wild eyes of the tribe. None of them was seeing clearly. They all panted violently, wearing expressions that were impossible to read.

There would be further catastrophe if the man followed them. The tribe was in no condition to run anymore, not without first catching its breath. Some of them were actually shaking. In this state it was hard to envision them as a fierce, well-trained group of attack dogs. They looked more like terrified poodles.

Looking at their frenzied faces, Grash knew any words now would be a serious mistake. He tried to listen for clumsy human footsteps over the gasping pants, but was relieved to hear nothing.

"Grash!" barked Kroth through heavy breaths, startling the leader and making him jump. "Grash, we are in trouble."

CHAPTER 14

Laura sat on the couch, relaxing in her living room. It was going to be another one of those nights, she could feel it already. Another first date, and probably the last. A lawyer named Terry. She had met him on a story and he'd seemed nice, but "nice" didn't guarantee personality. In fact, nice usually *excluded* personality.

She had another ten minutes before she needed to leave. She preferred to meet her dates elsewhere, which cut down on the amount of time spent cleaning up her condo. It was usually nice enough because she was rarely home, but of course the one time someone was picking her up here was the one time the cats had gone on a rampage.

She smiled, thinking about the cats. They had become so much a part of her life. She stroked Celestine, who calmly purred on her lap. The other two both were curled up at her feet.

This was part of the pre-date ritual. Laura would relax with the kitties, getting a respectable amount of cat hair on her clothing. This would tip her off immediately to the date's sensitivity to cats. Anyone who whined about cat hair wasn't worth her time. She especially despised people who claimed to be allergic to them.

Jazz stretched with a huge yawn, then plopped his chin down on her foot. He was the most recent of the three strays to show up on her door looking for a home. He was pitch-black and talked with a voice that sounded more like a saxophone than a meow. He had walked inside and taken to the others as if he had lived with them all his life. He was always the first one on Laura's lap, although tonight he had given ground to Celestine.

Fables had been the first of the three to arrive on Laura's door, nearly six months before Celestine. Laura had been sitting on the same couch, writing in longhand a short story about a knight in shining armor, when she'd heard the soft cries from outside. She opened the door and the young tabby charged in. It was love at first sight.

Celestine had arrived on the rarest of nights: a Friday the Thirteenth with a full moon. The long-haired calico howled for twenty minutes at the front door, then looked irritated when Laura finally answered. She walked inside with her head up, as if she had lived there all her life. She took to Laura instantly, and never went a night without sleeping between Laura's feet.

Laura smiled down at her children. As long as she could remember, cats had run to her when they saw her. All cats. All animals, really. She could never figure it out. Even at the zoo, sleeping zebras would wake up and walk over as close as they could when Laura came by. People always joked about it, but sometimes it made Laura nervous.

Not her cats, though. She loved her cats. She didn't love people who were allergic to them.

When the doorbell rang, Laura winced. She had gotten too comfortable on the couch for what was probably a salesman. She normally might have ignored it, but it was time to get up anyway. It was time to go meet Terry.

She tossed Celestine to the floor and stood up. Stepping over the other two felines she walked across the living room to the front door, picking up her purse on the way. She would make this sales pitch short.

She opened the door, but the man standing on the porch looked like less of a salesman than she did. He was dressed nicely in a gray suit, but appeared out of place with a collar and tie. Laura quickly assessed him as a man who would be happier in blue jeans and a baseball cap.

"Hello, I'd like to speak to Laura Kay, if she's at home," the man said.

"I'm Laura," she said, immediately umcomfortable.

"My name is Jake Cotter," he said. "I'm with the National Rifle Association. I was wondering if I could talk to you a minute about your article today."

Laura was stunned. She involuntarily took a step back,

gritting her teeth. She decided not to bother concealing her anger.

"Look, I'm off duty now," she said tersely. "I'm not interested in talking to you or anyone else about work. You had all day to call me. It's very inappropriate for you to show up on my doorstep like this."

"I tried to call you, but you were out."

"I got no messages," said Laura.

Cotter shrugged.

"Call me tomorrow," said Laura, "but don't ever come here again."

"Just give me one minute and I won't have to call," said Cotter.

"Fine. One minute. But hurry, I'm late."

"I was just upset that you could write an article like that and miss the whole point of those mountain lion people," said Cotter. "They're just anti-gun, that's all. All this bunk about saving the species is nothing more than another attempt to sabotage our constitutional right to own weapons."

"I heard the same thing from the Fish and Game Commissioner I talked to," said Laura. "It's nothing you couldn't have told me over the phone. I'll keep it in mind the next time I work on the story."

"It's true," said Cotter. "These are the same people who lobbied so hard on the disgraceful automatic weapons ban. The governor should be ashamed of himself on that one."

"Mr. Cotter, if you'll excuse me, I'm very busy," said Laura. "In the future, I'd appreciate it if you'd call me at the office instead of showing up on my doorstep."

She began to close the door, having decided to step back and stay home for a few more minutes. He reached out to her, offering a business card.

"Call me the next time you work on a hunting story," he said. She took the card and closed the door.

He was gone and she was furious. She sat back down on the couch, clenching her fists. She hadn't even bothered asking how he had found her. She had worked in the media long enough to know how easy it was to find people if you wanted to.

This was scary. The man hadn't threatened her, but still . . . Threats didn't have to be verbal to be real. What did he want from her? If this man truly represented the NRA, as he claimed, he should know better than to approach a member of the news media in this manner. She had a lot of work to do tomorrow.

Lanakila gazed westward, squinting slightly at the sinking sun. Sarena looked down and began to groom her forepaws impatiently.

"It is best to wait until first light," Lanakila said.

"I'm ready to go now," said Sarena. "You can ride on my back. You won't need to see."

"For someone who isn't supposed to be afraid of a lousy pack of kribas, you—"

"It's not that," interrupted Sarena. "I think the man-made thunder was an omen. There is a strangeness in the wind I cannot describe."

"Yes," agreed Lanakila, "the whole Canyon feels strange. But still, I won't travel at night."

Sarena stood up and began to pace with frustration.

"There is no reason why you can't go tonight," said Lanakila. "You are a big girl. I will be able to find you easily in the morning."

"Are you sure?" Sarena asked.

"No doubt you will be asleep by then," chided Lanakila. "Just find an open spot so I can see you from the air."

"Are you sure?" repeated Sarena. She knew the ahila could cover far more distance than she could, faster, and with little effort. Still, she did not want to risk losing track of her only friend.

"You don't move very fast," said Lanakila. "Just tell me which direction you're going. I'll find you without any problem."

Sarena sat down and began to groom again. Another decision. Which way would it be this time? So far, it hadn't really mattered.

"Decide quickly, Fur Ball," said Lanakila. "The sun will be gone soon."

"Then I will follow the sun," said Sarena.

"Toward the sea," said Lanakila. "You will be easy to spot."

"The what?"

*   *   *

It was an act of desperation, but then, the situation was desperate. The tribe had to eat.

They were scared; all of them. Even in the dark, Grash could see it clearly in the faces of his five companions. They could probably see it on his face. It didn't matter. They had to eat.

Five companions. The loss was devastating, especially to Grash. Telsh was gone. His brother. His friend. His sanity. It hurt in ways Grash had never dreamed possible.

The others felt it as well, but in a different way. Grash could see that in their faces, too. It could have been them. It could have been any of them. What if the man had pointed at them instead of Telsh? What if they had tripped and fallen? What if it was their turn next time? What if . . . ?

True, Grash was asking the same questions, but it was different. They weren't feeling it the same way. To Grash, it was as if a physical part of him had been cut off. It was piercing, like a deep, open wound somewhere in his belly.

Of the others, only Bruether seemed his equal in despair. He and Krayde had been very close. Brothers like Grash and Telsh, they had been inseparable since the great escape. Now, like Grash and Telsh, they would never see each other again.

What would happen next? They would eat or they would die, Grash was certain. They could not go on any longer without food. He knew the others inwardly would be blaming him for the disaster earlier in the afternoon. Outwardly they would be blaming him soon if they were not fed.

They looked down on the small yard from a hill at the edge of the Canyon. Taking no chances, even in the dark, they hid within the cover of thick, dry manzanita.

This was a double chance. Not only were they about to attempt a raid only hours after the death of their comrades, but a raid on a house they had already hit once before. All of them had feebly agreed it was a calculated risk worth taking. There really was no alternative.

Grash looked at Kroth, who had quickly devised a plan for six instead of eight assailants. Kroth looked very worried, and that was bad. Grash suspected his attack coordinator was feeling sole responsibility for the day's earlier fiasco. Kroth was probably the only one who put the blame on himself. The others, Grash was sure, put the blame on the tribe's leader.

The tribe was lost in thought. Each of them wore the glassy expression of minds someplace else. Grash wondered where they were, but decided it was best not to know.

Finally the leader gave the signal, snapping them all back to the brush on the hill. Without so much as a snort, the tribe began its silent descent upon the yard.

This was the last time Laura would ever agree to go on a date without first knowing the destination. She loved the theater, but *Romeo and Juliet* was a bit much for a first date. Especially this particular version, which seemed to be going on forever.

The evening had not gone well, which was mostly her fault. She had met Terry at The Beachcomber for a drink, where she'd snapped and grumbled about the jerk from the NRA, whom she vowed to do some serious checking on. She had felt badly about her foul mood, but wasn't able to recover very well. She'd sunk even further upon finding out that their destination was The Globe.

Why were they like this? Why did they have to be so heavy and mushy on a first date? Didn't they know they were only blowing it?

At least this was better than the last guy, who'd made the fatal mistake of taking her over to meet his parents. She never took a call from him again. Laura probably would give Terry another try, but wondered if she'd ever get a call from him again. If her mood didn't improve remarkably, Terry was going to be just one more first and last date.

It was always like this: Something wrong with him, or something wrong with her. The sad part was, there were so many of them. At least once a week there was someone asking her out. There were first dates constantly, but rarely seconds. It had been almost two years since she had gone out with someone, other than her male friends, more than twice.

She bit down hard, wondering what it was. She told

herself constantly it was time to at least commit to a boyfriend. She really wanted someone to care about, but something was in the way. She just couldn't figure out the problem.

She tried to get her mind off it, but it was difficult. She studied the actors, who seemed flat and disinterested tonight. She stole a glance at Terry, who appeared to be teetering on the brink of sleep.

Laura frowned and shook her head. In a world seriously overcrowded with people, she wondered why she had never met another person even remotely compatible. She gazed up at the colorful stage lights and softly whispered, "Is there anybody out there?"

Sarena walked while Lanakila slept. She found this concept mildly amusing, since the reverse was customarily true. Sarena slept, and Lanakila . . . flew.

The Canyon was unusually quiet for a warm, fall evening. Nothing much stirred, save for the occasional buzz of a night-flying insect. Even the krahstas were silent.

Sarena barely noticed the silence, which normally might have put her on the alert for something amiss. Tonight she was too lost in thought. She walked openly on a path, with her eyes cast down at the dirt before her rather than constantly scanning the surrounding bushes for signs of life.

The Canyon had become a strange place. At least, this part of it had. Kribas, ahilas, and skerrises all approaching a puma. Well, the kribas hadn't yet, but it sounded as though they intended to. And the dreams . . . she didn't want to think about those. She knew they had to tie in with everything else. It was enough to keep a puma up all night.

Sarena continued heading west, toward what Lanakila had called "the sea." She continually ran into areas where the Canyon ended and the hard man-ground began. She would stop to look at the places where the man lived, but she never got too close. After a few minutes she would move on again.

There were so many of them, and every day they wanted more and more of the Canyon. So many. Why couldn't there be as many pumas? Was it the man who had scared them all away?

She came upon a strange part of the Canyon. It turned from heavy chaparral into a broad field of wild grass. At the far end of the field, suspended high in the air, was the largest piece of man-ground Sarena had ever seen. It was all lit up, with thousands of man's moving machines on it. Sarena decided to walk toward it.

As she began her walk on the field she found the ground beneath her feet was damp, which was peculiar because it had not rained since before summer. The grass was not very high, leaving her virtually no cover at all. Still she decided to walk on, being drawn by something she couldn't explain.

When she reached the road, it was too high for her to see clearly. She wondered what magic the man could use to suspend his designs so high in the air. She could hear the rumbles it made, and its foul odors burned her sensitive nose. She marveled at how the man could stand it.

She sat down and looked back across the field she had just crossed. The ground was even wetter here than it was where she had come from. She looked west again, and after a short rest decided to move on. She walked underneath the great suspended road, completely unaware of the powerful set of eyes trained directly on her and following her all the way until her feet left the grass and touched sand.

The sand was hard to walk on, but Sarena managed it for several steps until she'd cleared the edge of a cliff that blocked her view to the west. When she stepped into the open she stopped instantly, staring with awe at the beauty before her. She stood motionless, absorbing its intensity with all of her senses. This obviously was what Lanakila had talked about, when Sarena had mentioned following the sun.

It was so beautiful and relaxing. Sarena stared at it for over an hour, listening to and smelling things she had never before experienced. She watched the waves repeatedly crashing onto the shore, then pulling back out. With each cycle, it seemed as if they took some of Sarena's worries with them.

She would have to come back and share this with Lanakila. It was very peaceful here; a good place to be alone and to be with someone you cared about. She wondered about how safe it would be in the daylight. She wished Lanakila could move about at night.

This would also be a nice place to visit with another puma. She decided to come back when she finally met one. If she ever met one.

Sarena looked up at the stars. She could sense Lady Farri was up there, watching her. She humbly looked down at her paws, then back up to the stars. She thought about it long and hard, then finally, when she'd gotten up the courage, asked, "Lady Farri, is there anybody out there?"

CHAPTER 15

As the sun began to nose its way above the mountains in the east, Grash opened his eyes to watch. Although very tired, he was a happy kriba this morning. The hunt had gone well the night before.

While barely moving, Grash scanned his sleeping companions. They all snored loudly, and Grash was glad. He needed the sleep as well, but he welcomed the chance to think things over free of the questioning stares of the tribe.

They were back to performing like a team again. They had taken their prey without the slightest hitch. Now, with full bellies, they slept like puppies.

But it was all a mistake. While fun at first, Grash now realized how much better off they had been in the prison. This was quite an admission, since the mere thought of how coarsely they had been treated made his stomach tighten. But at least they had been well fed.

There were other mistakes, too. He never should have told the krahstas of his ludicrous plans to kill the puma. In the current condition of the tribe, they would be lucky just to get out of the area without any more casualties.

Beginning a stretch, Grash wondered about the puma. The krahstas said pumas always moved on. Which way would this one go? And when? Grash hoped it would wait awhile, and go the opposite direction of the tribe. This would solve a major problem.

But what about the ahila? It was still intriguing, the way the two of them hunted. The tribe would be free forever if they had such a bird for a friend. Grash wondered if there were other ahilas about who might be coaxed into joining the tribe, or whether the one he had seen could be freed from the puma. If only he could get a chance to speak with it alone . . .

It didn't matter. Grash and the tribe would be moving on in the afternoon and leaving the puma, the ahila, and the krahstas behind. Still, the thought of having the ahila tugged ever so slightly at his soul, momentarily prompting a desire to stay and check into the possibility further.

The more he thought about it, the easier it seemed. There were, after all, six members of the tribe, and only one puma. One cat. He seemed to remember some kind of secret about cats that he momentarily couldn't recall. It had to do with certain weaknesses carried by all of their lines. If he could remember what they were, it might solve all the tribe's problems.

Grash started to feel the drowsiness begin to take over again. He still had numerous questions, but knew they would have to be thought out some other time. He hoped some of the answers might visit him in his dreams, as they sometimes did.

He began to curl up into a comfortable position, then looked to the east one more time for another glimpse of the climbing sun. The sight instantly brought him to his feet, as he saw, high in the eastern sky, the circling silhouette of an ahila.

Another stack of messages. Every morning they sat in Laura's mailbox, only one of two greetings she was likely to get. She picked up the pile of pink notes and walked toward her desk. The newsroom was virtually empty, except for the few in-house people who never went out on stories.

The phone was ringing when she arrived at her desk—her second greeting. She plopped her briefcase, purse, and messages onto the desk top, and picked up the phone.

"Hi Laura, this is Lieutenant Carl Langton from the Border Patrol."

"Ah, hi Lieutenant," said Laura. She had worked with Langton on an illegal alien story several months ago.

"I saw your story on the mountain lions," said Langton. "Nicely done."

"Thanks," said Laura, waiting for the pitch.

"I have something you might be interested in," said Langton. "Last night, two of our agents spotted a mountain lion walking through a field in Carlsbad."

"Really? What time?"

"About eleven o'clock," said Langton. "They were using their night scope to look for illegals. It walked under the freeway and headed for the beach."

"Did they see where it went?"

"No. It disappeared around a cliff."

"How often do you guys see mountain lions?" Laura asked.

"Never," said Langton. "That's why I called you. All the hours we spend out in the hills, this is the first time any of my men've reported seeing a big cat."

Laura thanked him and hung up. She wrote down some notes to remind herself about it for the next time she did a mountain lion story. She decided she would later ask one of the editors if they would be interested in running something on it.

After clearing off her desk, she began to look through her messages. The first one was from a man she had interviewed the day before on the attack dog story. She still needed a lot more information before she could put the piece together, so she decided to call him first.

"I'm glad you called," said Bud Kader. "There've been two more raids by the dogs. One last night, one in the afternoon."

"Two more?" asked Laura "Where?"

"A block away from where I live. The good news is, old Jim Matson killed two of 'em."

"How?" Laura asked, startled.

"Shot 'em dead, right in his yard," said Bud. "A Doberman and a shepherd."

"Do you have Mr. Matson's number?"

When Laura hung up, she slapped her palms on the desk top. Despite her elation at the new twist to her story, she was furious that she'd found out a day late. It would've been nice to have gotten pictures of the man and the dead dogs.

She picked up the phone to call Jim Matson but got his answering machine. She left a message and began to pick up her purse for another long drive to San Marcos. She hated going anywhere, especially so far, without having something set up first, but in this case she would have to wing it. She was about to walk over to the assignment desk to request a photographer when the phone rang again.

"Hi, this is Keith Gallatin."

"Oh, you. Great timing. I'm running out the door."

"Figures," said Keith. "I get the same line from all the girls."

"Goon," said Laura. "What can I do for you?"

"I don't want to keep you," said Keith. "I just have some more info about the Fish and Game meeting next week."

"Oh, good," said Laura. "By the way, a guy from the Border Patrol just called. His guys saw a mountain lion in Carlsbad last night with their night scope."

"Really?" asked Keith. Laura thought he sounded excited.

"Yeah," said Laura. "It walked through a field, then under the freeway towards the beach. They lost it when it walked around a cliff."

"All *right*," said Keith. "Probably went out to catch some waves."

"Probably," Laura agreed, with a laugh. "Either that or it went grunion hunting."

"Is that what you're going out on?" asked Keith.

"No," said Laura. "There's a pack of wild attack dogs running loose in North County. Some guy shot two of them yesterday afternoon when they attacked his sheep."

Silence. Keith's response was heavy enough to feel.

"Is something wrong?" asked Laura, a little nervous. She had not expected such a reaction.

"They're related," said Keith.

"What's related?" asked Laura.

"The mountain lion and the dogs," said Keith. "They're connected somehow."

Now it was Laura's turn to grow silent. Even if it hadn't been so unlikely that they could be connected, it was an odd thing to say.

"I can't explain it," said Keith, as if reading her thoughts.

"But how could a mountain lion in Carlsbad be connected to a pack of dogs in San Marcos? And even if they were, how would you know?"

"They just are," said Keith. "Maybe they're so far apart because they're trying to avoid each other. I don't know. But I've just got this feeling."

"Okay," said Laura. "What would you like me to do about it?"

"You can start by not patronizing me," said Keith.

"I'm not," said Laura. "I merely asked a reasonable question."

"Tone of voice," said Keith. "Anyway, are you leaving right now?"

"In a couple of minutes," said Laura.

"Can I go along?"

Laura snapped her head away from the phone. She hadn't been expecting anything like this. Obviously he was up to something.

"Hello?" asked Keith.

"Yes, I'm here," said Laura. "If you'd like to go, sure. I'm leaving in a few minutes. Where would you like me to meet you?"

"McDonald's."

"Where?"

Laura went into the ladies room to change. The prospect of walking around in a nice skirt and shoes on dirty farmland was not very appealing. She quickly changed into a pair of jeans and sneakers she kept in her car for exactly this type of situation. When dressed, she walked back into the newsroom for her purse and notebook, then went out to the parking lot.

As she crouched down into her aging RX-7, she wondered what the arrangement would be with Gallatin. She didn't want to be stuck cruising out to a news story in a limo, if indeed Gallatin showed up in one. But then, looking around the disaster area of scattered objects cluttering her own car, the idea of having a rock star for a passenger wasn't very appealing either. Gallatin's bodyguard wouldn't fit in the back, anyway. She shrugged, and decided Keith and company would just have to follow her.

As she pulled out of the parking lot she wondered why she was doing this. She never took guests along on a story. It was probably forbidden by company policy, anyway. And someone as famous and distracting as Keith Gallatin would probably get in the way.

Laura's frown was replaced by a smile she tried to deny. The idea of wandering around with a rock star was pretty intriguing, and it never hurt to have friends in influential places. She pulled into the fast-food parking lot, deciding to be very careful.

When she'd found a parking spot, she suddenly remembered she needed a photographer. She slapped her hands on the steering wheel, knowing what a hassle it would be to call the assignment desk by phone and get one now. She decided to forget about it and use her own camera, if there was anything left to shoot by the time she got to North County.

After writing down the directions to the house in San Marcos for Gallatin, she climbed out of the car and walked inside to buy a drink. She stood in line, looking up at the menu.

"So, do you come here often?" asked a man beside her.

Laura turned, expecting to see Keith, but instead saw someone she didn't recognize. His hair and beard were light brown, and he smiled at her through bright blue eyes. He seemed familiar, and Laura suspected it was someone she had interviewed in the past, but she couldn't remember. He obviously remembered her.

"Do I know you?" asked Laura, slightly embarrassed.

"Well, technically I guess we've never met, but we have talked over the phone. My name's Keith."

Laura opened her mouth and squinted at the same time. She looked closely, pictured his face through the disguise, then began to laugh.

"Oh, my!" exclaimed Laura, surprised. "I never would have recognized you!"

"Good," said Keith. "That's the point. Gets me into places I normally would never be able to go. What can I get you?"

"Iced tea," said Laura.

"I would have worn it the day you first saw me, but I

had a league meeting after the Fish and Game hearing,"
said Keith. "I had to go to that dressed as myself."

Laura nodded, looking over the disguise. It was very
well done. The wig and beard seemed very real.
The colored contacts added a nice touch. The green T-
shirt with a mountain lion was the only hint, however
slight.

When Keith had bought their drinks, they walked out
to the parking lot.

"I guess you should follow me," said Laura. "I wrote
out directions for you, in case we get separated."

"Oh," said Keith.

"Something wrong?" asked Laura.

"Well, I was expecting to ride with you. My driver
dropped me off and has left already."

"Oh," said Laura, thinking about the mess in her car.
This would not be a good first impression.

"It's okay, I don't bite . . ."

"It's not that," said Laura.

". . . very hard," finished Keith.

Laura rolled her eyes and began walking toward her
car. This was going to be an interesting ride.

Sarena bolted through the sage, working desperately
to outpace the charging kribas. She could turn and fight,
but there were so many and they were so loud, with the
scent of something strange behind them. Her internal
warning system demanded that she race on. She darted
around the brush with an advantage she knew she could
not keep.

They were closer. They would catch her at this pace,
she was sure. She was already tired and losing her breath,
but the kribas howled on with closing determination.

Sarena's heart pounded in her ears, even as she ran.
She had never run from anything before. She smashed
into a jagged branch of brush, which cut into her right
side. The pain ripped through her, but she dared not
stop or look back.

A tree. It was her only hope. She could jump up
quickly and fight off the kribas if they tried to follow.
She bounded off a huge boulder and flew toward the
lowest branches, landing perfectly and clutching with

extended claws. Gasping for air, she turned to face her pursuers.

A sudden jab at her tail jolted her around with a hiss, but there was nothing there. Confused, she turned back to the approaching kribas, only to feel the jab again.

"Fur Ball!" yelled Lanakila. He sounded muffled, and Sarena couldn't see him. Another jab at her tail, this time more severe.

Suddenly Sarena was on the ground, on her feet, looking up at the ahila, who was standing on a slab of granite. Sarena was nearly choking for lack of air, and Lanakila stared at her with concern in his eyes.

"My Fur Ball was having a nasty dream," said Lanakila.

Sarena was too winded to respond. Shaking all over, she nervously looked around the brush, but felt no signs of kribas or any other predators. She looked back up at the ahila, who remained motionless as he stared at her from above. Sarena sat down to calm herself.

"What are your dreams?" asked Lanakila.

Sarena looked up, then crouched down to her forepaws. It had been so real, she wasn't sure it was a just a dream. Her shoulders and back still were shaking slightly.

"I dreamed last night, too," said Lanakila. "Of course I dream with every sleep, but I believe last night was a dream of warning."

Sarena looked up with questioning eyes. She wasn't sure enough of her voice to attempt speaking, yet.

"There are two kinds of dreams," said Lanakila. "The common dreams, which are incidental, and the dreams of warning, which are prophecy to disaster if heed is not taken."

"How can you tell the two apart?" asked Sarena, finally able to speak.

"They can't be mistaken," said Lanakila. "The dreams of warning are as real as life. Just like the one you had. And they always put you in real situations."

"Do they always come true?" asked Sarena.

"They don't have to," said Lanakila. "That's why they're called dreams of warning. They warn you about conditions which could put you in the situation of the dream if you don't take care."

"What did you dream about?" Sarena asked.

"You must tell me first," said Lanakila, "since yours is the freshest. You will forget quickly, so tell me now."

"I dreamed I was being chased by kribas. . . ."

"Kribas!" said Lanakila. "This is bad."

"I don't think it was the ones in the Canyon," said Sarena. "They had a reason for chasing me. A purpose."

"What was it?"

"I don't know," said Sarena. "They just did. I could tell. They just had to catch me."

"It's time to move on," said Lanakila.

"What was *your* dream?" asked Sarena.

"I dreamed a man pointed his thunder stick at the sky."

With her passenger in disguise, Laura cruised north on Interstate 15. So far the entire ordeal had been humiliating. After finally clearing all of the debris into the back so Keith could have a seat in the front, Laura nearly got hit as she pulled out onto the main road. Then her car decided to act like it was suffering from a case of diarrhea.

"You need a new car," Keith said finally.

"I know," said Laura with a wince.

"Sorry," said Keith. "I didn't mean it like that."

Laura bit lightly on her lower lip. "It's okay."

They drove for two more miles without a word, which made Laura even more nervous. She couldn't understand the problem. Over the five years she'd worked as a reporter, she had met countless stars and various other celebrities. She was so used to them, she was no longer impressed by anything. She didn't think she should be too impressed with Keith Gallatin, either, but somehow it was strange playing taxi driver to a rock star.

"So, tell me about what you have going for the Fish and Game meeting next week," Laura finally requested.

"I have a signed petition from all of the basketball owners," said Keith. "They're all opposed to the hunt. And all of the teams in the league will have a representative at the meeting for support. In several cases the actual owners themselves will be there."

"Pretty impressive," said Laura. "Do you think it will help?"

"I think so," said Keith. "Most of those guys on the Board looked like they were sports fans. And I also got several people from the entertainment industry to commit to showing. They all have good followings and should carry some weight."

"Are they going to speak?"

"Most of them, yes," said Keith. "I've even convinced them to get there early so we can all speak before those Mountain Lions Forever bozos make a spectacle of themselves again."

"Does anyone else know about this?" asked Laura. "Anyone in the media, or the Mountain Lions Forever people?"

"No," said Keith. "We'll probably do a press release at the last minute, but otherwise it's a bombshell."

Laura nodded, then hit the brake to avoid getting hit by a slow car pulling into her lane and cutting her off. She changed lanes and passed the offender, and she and Keith both shook their heads when they saw that the driver was an old woman.

"What a cliché," said Keith straight-faced, shaking his head.

For some reason it hit a funny spot, and Laura burst out laughing. It was a terrific release. Out of everything that could have gone wrong everything had, and Keith still seemed to be taking it very well.

"You know the last thing an old lady sees when she pulls off the freeway?" asked Keith.

Laura shook her head, still laughing.

Keith grimaced and held up his middle finger in Laura's face.

This caught Laura by surprise, making it even funnier. She laughed so hard her eyes watered, which was not a good idea at sixty miles per hour. The car weaved to the right and Laura jerked it back to center, then checked the rearview mirror for police. She laughed even more, realizing her move had resembled an old lady driver's.

Keith, the experienced comedian working on a kill, crossed his arms and looked completely disgusted. He shook his head and leaned up against the passenger door.

"I think we'll get along fine," said Laura finally, as she wiped a tear from her eye.

Keith snorted. "I don't know."

Laura smiled and looked over at her famous passenger. He might be human, after all.

"Does the act go along with the disguise, or are you always this cute?" asked Laura.

"It's a little bit me and a little bit act," said Keith. "After all of this time I guess everything I do is a little bit of an act. It would be easier for me if you really didn't know who I was. Easier and harder."

"Seems like you've got the charming routine down," said Laura. "I'll bet the girls fall all over you, even with the disguise."

"They do fall all over me," nodded Keith. "But not when I'm in the disguise."

"You must not try, then," said Laura.

"Yes, I do. All the time. I go to parties and clubs constantly, but I rarely get any dates. I obviously have no problem without the disguise, but when they don't know who I am they don't give me the time of day."

"Really?" asked Laura. "Interesting."

Keith shrugged and turned away to look out the window. They were passing the countless rows of overnight housing developments that had ripped into the hills on the east side of the freeway.

"How do you feel about that?" asked Laura, not expecting an answer. Keith was known for his love of privacy.

"It's humbling," said Keith. He turned back toward Laura. "It's depressing, sometimes. Keith the rock-star millionaire is the great catch, not Keith the person."

"Do you really wear the disguise a lot?"

"Yes. I have several variations. Some don't include the beard at all. I can usually get by with a little hair tint and some light makeup. People expect to see Keith Gallatin in rock-star stage clothing, not jeans and a T-shirt. They might look twice, but they really don't expect to see Keith Gallatin at all so they just think I'm a good look-alike."

"Have you gone out with women who didn't know it was you?"

"Yes, many times. There have been times where I've gone out with someone several times and really gotten interested."

"Then what?"

"That happened with three different women, and each one of them dumped me."

"No!"

"Yes, three different times," said Keith, shaking his head.

"Did they ever find out?"

"Yes, all of them."

"Then what?"

"Then they were interested all of a sudden."

"I'll bet," said Laura.

"The last one, I wasn't even wearing a disguise when we met. She just didn't recognize me. She does now."

"Do you still see her?"

"No way," said Keith. "She had her chance. She dumped me."

"Wow," said Laura. "I can't believe it."

"This isn't for public knowledge," said Keith.

"Okay, okay. I'm actually surprised you're even telling me this."

"Me too."

They turned west onto Highway 78 and headed for San Marcos. Laura smiled and looked over at Keith, who had turned away again and was looking out the window.

"You're really cute, even with the disguise," said Laura. "I guess I should say, 'charming.' "

"Thank you," said Keith, still looking out the window. "You're not too bad yourself."

"You say that to all the girls," said Laura.

"So?"

"Do you have a girlfriend now?" asked Laura.

Keith glared at her, then shrugged his shoulders.

"Oh, come on. Don't clam up on me now! You don't have to tell me who she is."

"I don't have one," said Keith.

"Why not?" asked Laura. "I'm sure you could play the rock star and find plenty of women if you wanted."

"I don't want to do it that way," said Keith. "I want the other person to care about Keith the person, not Keith the rock star."

"The rock star is part of Keith the person, though,"

said Laura. "What do you tell these women you do for a living?"

"I work for the Pumas," said Keith. "I do public relations. It's true enough. Depending upon the person, sometimes I say I work for the radio station."

"Why don't you just go out with other rock stars or celebrities?" asked Laura.

"Have you ever talked to another rock star?" asked Keith. "They're all flakes. Airheads, spaced out on coke and God knows what else."

"That's right," smiled Laura, making fun of what had once been a nasty situation. "You're not into drugs."

Keith blinked and crossed his arms. He turned his face away and looked straight ahead.

"Just giving you a hard time," said Laura.

"I know," said Keith, and smiled.

The Pumas had released one of their star players as a result of a second drug-related offense. Keith had taken immense heat from the sports media after one of the reporters had pointed to a Gallatin song containing a frivolous line about smoking pot. Keith was called a hypocrite for condoning drug use on the one hand and being hard-nosed with his players on the other.

Keith had responded by saying he'd only been playing a role when he sang a song he did not write, and that he and Danielle did not do drugs of any kind.

The situation had gotten worse and worse, as the Pumas went from being contenders to bums after the loss of their guard. Keith finally silenced his critics by telling of a movie he had seen starring Ronald Reagan, in which Reagan's character belts a woman hard across the face. Keith said he didn't think the man who was then President of the United States condoned the battering of women.

"It's a tough balance," said Keith. "The rock community and my music fans expect me to have a crazy rock-and-roll image, while the sporting community expects me to be a respectable businessman. Those two images are contradictions."

"Very true." Laura laughed. It was hard to picture the man sitting beside her as the same person who danced around in rock videos on MTV.

Laura pulled up to the driveway at the address Bud

Kader had given her. She was happy to see a pickup truck near the barn.

"Your turn on the way back," said Keith, as he opened his door.

"For what?" Laura queried, grinning.

"Kiss and tell."

CHAPTER 16

The tribe was up and stretching. Grash thought they looked grim, but much better than he had expected considering the disaster of the day before. They stood up straight with their heads high; professionals, no matter what.

Grash did not feel as good as the tribe looked, and he hoped he looked better than he felt. Telsh was gone. Part of Grash was gone. This would not change no matter how successful the tribe was in the future. Grash wanted to run off howling into the Canyon and never return.

Questioning faces. The tribe was focused on its leader again. What to do now? There had never been a more pressing time for Grash to appear confident and in control. They were all relying on him for survival now. After the events of the day before, it was clear they would never be accepted back into the world of men.

"As you all know," Grash began, "it's time to move on."

All of the tribe members grunted in agreement. There had never been any question as to this, only as to where they would go.

"We'll stay in the Canyon," continued Grash. "We'll stay well hidden from now on, but close to the streets where we can execute our strikes. We'll stay in new areas for a few days, then move on."

"Why move?" asked Broed.

"It'll be safer," said Grash. "The more we move, the harder we'll be to find. Safety should now be our number-one objective. We've learned painful and costly lessons. We can't afford any more mistakes."

"Grash, where do we go?" asked Kroth.

"When we stalked the house last night," said Grash, "I watched the sunset. I felt it calling to me somehow. Then last night when we slept, I dreamed about it. I believe it is the direction we should go."

The rest of the tribe snorted in amazement. Dreams were not to be taken lightly. They almost always carried a significant message from Lord Kriba. If Grash had experienced a special dream, then there could be no questioning the direction.

"What about our krahsta friends, and the puma?" asked Kroth.

"The krahstas will be glad of our leaving," said Grash. "As for the puma . . . well, it is a disappointment. I would truly love to have the ahila for an assistant, but we must go."

Each member of the tribe exhaled a silent breath of relief at this news. None of them had been looking forward to an encounter with the owner of the scent they had experienced, although none of them would admit to such cowardice. The announcement by Grash was a terrific way out of a potentially awful situation.

"When we're stronger we might return," said Grash. "I'm still interested in pursuing the ahila somehow. And I have a strange feeling about the puma. I think it's very likely that our paths will cross sometime. If we do meet, then it will be a good day for us."

The tribe members listened without comment. They were trained to follow orders, no matter what. They would follow orders, no matter what. They just hoped the orders would lead them away from the puma.

"For now, though, it's time to move on," said Grash. "We have slept for most of the day, and the sun moves on to its place of rest. So let's follow the sun."

Lanakila rode on Sarena's shoulders as she walked along a small path in the chaparral. The autumn air had gotten cooler but still there had been no rain, and the brush was brown and crackly-dry. Small, sharp pieces of broken-off shrub stabbed at the bottoms of Sarena's paws.

"So my Fur Ball saw the sea," said Lanakila.

"Yes," said Sarena. "They were the most peaceful

moments I've ever had. I would love to just stay there, but there were too many signs of the man to be safe."

"Yes," said Lanakila. "During the days, they cover the sands along the sea."

"That's too bad," said Sarena. "I'd like to see it during the daytime."

"It is beautiful," said Lanakila. "Especially when the sun sets over the waves. Unfortunately I don't think it's safe enough for my Fur Ball to see."

Sarena lowered her head. She wished she had the wings to fly like a bird, so she could see all of the things Lanakila saw and do so safely. No one ever bothered birds. They were so out of reach—nothing could touch them unless they were on the ground, or careless. Sarena knew if she could fly she would never land.

"Is something wrong, Fur Ball?"

"No," said Sarena. "You just don't know how lucky you are."

"I do know how lucky I am," said Lanakila. "I just wish you knew how lucky you are."

"You mean we drove all the way to San Marcos and this guy might not even be home?" asked Keith.

"Right," said Laura. "But someone around here will be."

They walked up the long, dirt driveway toward the house. The yard was huge; nearly two acres, if Laura guessed correctly. She and Keith were almost to the house when a green Ford Bronco pulled into the driveway behind them.

Laura recognized the car and its driver immediately. The vehicle supported a tri-colored light bar on its roof, with Fish and Game emblems on the doors. The driver was Dennis Jack.

"Hi, Laura," said Dennis, as he pulled up and rolled down his window.

"Dennis, what brings you here?" asked Laura.

"Probably the same thing that brings you," said Dennis, as he began to pull forward toward the house. Laura looked over at Keith, who was smiling at her and flashing her a wink.

Dennis parked the car and climbed out. A man in his early thirties, he was tall and slender, with brown hair and green eyes. He supported a thick, police-style macho mustache and wore dark sunglasses. He watched Laura and Keith walk up the driveway, then turned to survey the yard.

"How's life, Laura?" asked Dennis.

"Pretty good."

"You never call, you never write," said Dennis, laughing.

"You don't either," Laura said and grinned. "By the way, Dennis, this is my friend . . ."

"Keith Galloway," he said stepping in just in time to save her. He reached over and shook hands with Dennis, who clearly had no idea whom he was meeting. Laura glanced at Keith and shook her head.

"Dennis helped me out on a poaching story I did a few months ago," said Laura.

"Really helped out," Dennis said nodding. "They stopped cold—until last week. We think they've started up again."

"Poaching what?" asked Keith.

"Deer," said Dennis. "We've found the remains of two that have been neatly butchered."

Keith looked at the ground, and Laura thought he looked like he'd been struck.

"Maybe we'll do another story," said Laura.

"Just let me know," said Dennis.

"So, Dennis, what's the deal?" asked Laura, motioning toward the house of Jim Matson.

"There's been a rash of attacks by a pack of killer dogs," said Dennis. "They prey mostly on people's sheep and goats. Last night they hit here, and from what I understand the guy blew two of them away with his shotgun."

"Have you seen the dogs yet?" asked Laura.

"No, I just got here," said Dennis. "Hopefully he hasn't buried them."

"Which reminds me," said Laura. "I need my camera."

She turned around and began to walk down the driveway to her car, cursing herself for forgetting and wondering what the two men would talk about in her absence. She turned around and saw them going up to the front door. She broke into a trot, hoping to get her camera and get back up there quickly, and thankful she had changed shoes.

Laura grabbed her camera bag, then winced at the politics that would be involved to use her pictures, if indeed there was anything left to shoot. She might even have to lie about the origin of the photos to get them in print. The paper frequently paid outsiders for pictures of events that had happened out of sight of their own regular photographers, but almost never from the staff of reporters, when one of them got a picture himself. Too many union problems.

By the time Laura made it back up the driveway Jim Matson was outside, talking to Dennis and Keith. Jim was a man in his late forties, and he wore a red-checkered, long-sleeved flannel shirt. Laura wondered how he could stand to do so on such a warm morning.

"Yep, I buried 'em," said Jim. "Just before sunset, yesterday. Come on around here and I'll show you where they attacked."

"How many?" asked Laura.

"Hard to tell," said Jim. "Half dozen or more. They run like hell, though, when I began shooting."

"I wish you could've waited until I got here before you buried them," said Dennis.

"I done called you folks yesterday after it happened," said Jim. "You aren't here until now. I can't keep dead dogs on my property forever."

They walked into the yard behind Jim's house. He showed them where the attack had taken place, where he had fired the shots from, and where the dogs had fallen. He brought them to the edge of the Canyon and showed them the escape route the dogs had taken. He had started to explain how he had followed the wounded dog into the Canyon when they heard the phone ring. Matson excused himself and went inside.

"Isn't it illegal to be shooting guns out here?" Keith asked.

"No," said Dennis. "This isn't incorporated area. There's plenty of space between houses and this isn't city limits, so technically they can shoot away out here."

"That's pretty scary," said Keith.

"With some of these characters who live out here, I

agree," said Dennis. "But hey, right to keep and bear arms, and all that stuff."

Keith rolled his eyes, then walked over to the edge of the yard where the canyon met Jim's property. He looked out over the sage with his hands on his hips. Matson came back outside, but Laura walked over to Keith. Matson and Dennis walked the other way, toward the barn.

"Is something wrong?" Laura asked, when the others were out of earshot.

"Yes. Very wrong."

"Dennis is right," said Laura. "There's nothing illegal about shooting out here. Especially to protect your property."

"That's not the problem," said Keith. "It is a problem, but not what's bothering me."

"Yes?"

"These dogs. I know I told you this over the phone, and I know it sounds strange, but somehow these dogs are involved with the mountain lion you told me about."

"You're right. It does sound strange."

"Intuition. A hunch. I don't know. I just feel it. The mountain lion is in trouble."

"A lot of mountain lions are in trouble," said Laura. "Remember?"

"True," said Keith. "I'm happy to hear that Dennis doesn't support his bosses in Sacramento. He's against the hunt."

"I know."

"This is different," said Keith. "I think our attack dog friends here have it in for the cougar."

"How?" asked Laura. "The mountain lion was in Carlsbad, near the beach. We're twenty miles from there."

"Yes, we are," said Keith, looking out across the canyon. "But the cougar isn't there anymore. And the dogs are gone."

By midday Sarena and Lanakila had traveled east, back into the thick part of the canyon, far away from the sea and all of the men. The long night hours Sarena had spent walking without a rest were beginning to wear her down. She had not slept in over twelve hours, and the weight of Lanakila had become too much for her to handle.

"I need to rest, my love," said Sarena.

"You're not going to sleep all day again," said Lanakila.

"I just need a short nap," said Sarena, not sounding very convincing. "I was walking all night and morning. A cat needs her sleep."

Lanakila hissed and shook his head. He jumped off of Sarena and onto the lower branches of a dried-out tree.

"I guess it might be best for you to nap," agreed the bird. "I can scout around for a while, and maybe figure out our best path to follow."

"I'll leave it up to you, dear," said Sarena, her eyes already drooping. She began to search for a soft place to stretch out in the sun.

Lanakila hissed again, obviously irritated. He began to bite at a brittle branch extending before him.

"I can't help it," said Sarena. "I need to sleep. You already know it's the curse of all cats."

"It'll be your bane as well," said Lanakila. "Sleep now, and if I don't awaken you then sleep through the night as well. We will need all of your strength tomorrow."

"Okay," said Sarena, then plopped down in a dying growth of long grass. She closed her eyes and fell asleep immediately.

Lanakila watched the huge cat for several moments, then hissed again and launched skyward.

The tribe loped in silence. Only the occasional bark to warn of nearby houses broke the sound of paws padding through the sage. As Grash had ordered they headed west, toward the line where the sun sank in the evenings.

Grash hated the silence, but knew it was probably the best condition under the circumstances. Anything said might be a problem. He didn't expect them to say anything critical even if they did speak, but silence was a guarantee.

Suddenly, two hina bolted from the path of the tribe, sending them all into a frenzied chase. The hina split in different directions, and the tribe responded beautifully. Three kribas chased the first victim, leaving the others to follow the second. The results were spectacular.

The hina had been caught within only a few strides. Kroth nabbed the first one, which had darted to the left, and Bruether grabbed the second. Howls of victory were raised by everyone the instant the chase was over.

Grash watched his kribas rip the hina to nothing. He stood back, not partaking in the celebration despite this new festive mood. There would be plenty of time for him to eat later, so he decided to let them enjoy. He took this as a good omen. Without any words he could tell the others did, too.

CHAPTER 17

The second stop was even worse than the first. Laura and Keith listened as a twelve-year-old girl burst into tears over her fallen pet. Through the sobs she had tried to tell about how she raised the goat from its infancy, and now it was gone. Literally. In their efficiency the attackers had left nothing behind but drag marks and blood stains in the dirt.

Laura unlocked the passenger side, letting Keith in first. She walked around to the driver side, shaking her head in disgust. She climbed in, starting the car without comment.

"Does this qualify as 'Dirty Laundry'?" asked Keith.

Laura shrugged, and looked straight ahead. She hated it when people cried as they told their stories. Even on a good story like this one.

"It's not my fault those dogs attacked that girl's goat," said Laura, defensively. "This is an important story. People need to know about this."

"Okay, no problem," said Keith. "Just jamming you up. I wanted to see how you'd react."

"We take heat all the time about stuff like this," snapped Laura. "It's hard to interview someone who's lost something dear to them. At last it wasn't a human relative. And you'll notice I didn't ask the kid how she felt about her pet getting dragged off by vicious dogs."

"I know," said Keith.

Laura bit down hard as she pulled out onto the freeway. She didn't want to sound like this with Keith. True, he had baited her, but she'd reacted badly. She gave him a quick glance, then locked her eyes on the road.

"Relax," said Keith. "I was just giving you a taste of what I have to go through every day."

Laura looked over, but said nothing. She had no idea where this guy was coming from.

"Look, why don't I buy you lunch?" inquired Keith. "We'll sit down and rest for a while; maybe exchange a little gossip."

"Okay," said Laura.

"Speaking of gossip, what's the story of you and Dennis?"

"What about me and Dennis?" asked Laura. She tried to sound casual, but knew it had come out strained.

"Well you went out with him, right?"

"He must have told you we did," said Laura.

"No, but it was pretty obvious," said Keith. "You probably went out once, and some little thing was wrong so you never gave him another shot."

"You must have an incredible source on me," said Laura, a little irritated. "I guess you've heard all about my notorious reputation."

"Haven't heard a thing," said Keith. "And even if I had, I, of all people, would know how far off reputations can be."

Laura nodded in agreement, even though she knew her reputation was probably accurate enough to base decisions on. She wondered about Keith, and all of the rumors floating around about him.

"Personally, I wouldn't have the time to be involved in half the stories floating around about me," said Keith, as if reading her mind, and not for the first time.

"Do you have ESP or something?" asked Laura.

"Something," said Keith.

With the sun reaching high into the autumn sky, the tribe stopped for a quick rest in a parched thicket of greasewood. They were winded and sore, but otherwise in high spirits. Three more hina had fallen since the first two, which served nicely as a complement to the dinner from the night before. All of them sat resting, with full bellies.

Grash really liked the taste of the food the tribe had captured. It was much different than what they had been fed by the man when they were in prison. It made Grash wonder exactly what the other stuff was, since it differed in texture so much from what they had eaten on the outside.

Aside from the sound of panting kribas, the tribe sat in silence. Grash was pleased to see quiet contentment in their faces. Their eyes were beginning to droop a little, and Grash was more than happy just to let them close and take a short nap. Things were getting better, he could just feel it.

Only moments after the first snore had been heard, the entire tribe was jolted to its feet. The smell hit them first, followed by scattered rustling in the brush. The krahstas were about.

The tribe formed a tight circle, covering every possible direction of approach. Just as before, the krahstas walked into the open as a group, drawing the tribe out of their circle and into a line, facing the new arrivals.

There seemed to be more of them this time than the last. This was bad, since the tribe's number was down by two. Grash hoped the krahstas wouldn't notice, but then realized the news had probably spread throughout the entire Canyon by now.

There were more, Grash was certain. He hadn't noticed any females in the pack the last time, but now there were several. They held the same wild, hungry gaze as the males, with an exotic smell unnerving enough to make Grash shake involuntarily. They displayed strength and cunning beyond comprehension.

The krahsta leader stepped forward, looking directly at Grash. If the gray animal held any fear at all, he was a master at diguising it. Grash decided there probably wasn't any fear to disguise.

"You have crossed into our territory again," Dropno said bluntly. His words were not accusing, but merely stated what he believed to be the fact. His eyes were seething with disgust.

"We are not hunting here," said Grash, hoping his voice would remain solid. "We are moving on."

"Yes, you are," said Dropno. "And only yesterday you so boldly spoke of taking down a puma. Now you slink away with your tails between your legs."

"We have hunted out our territory and seek a new

one," said Grash. "That is all. We are all trained killers in this tribe. We don't slink away from anything."

"What is 'trained'?" asked the krahsta, confused.

Grash began to answer, but then realized how futile it would be. Canyon animals would never understand *any* contact with men.

"We are quite efficient at it," said Grash. "A cat doesn't pose any threat to us in the least."

"Then keep to your word," said Dropno. "We let you be, on your word that you would destroy a puma. Now it seems you're running away."

"We aren't running away from anything," said Grash. He could feel how nervous the tribe was, and knew he'd better hurry up and get them out of there before one or more of them did something stupid.

"Then where are you going?" asked the krahsta.

"Look," said Grash. "We've been here for several days, and haven't once seen a puma. We've picked up a few faint scents, but nothing solid. It seems to me we have just as much chance of finding a puma where we're going, as we do hanging around here. And we can't hang around here, because we've hunted out all of the food on the streets and you won't let us hunt the Canyon."

"I don't believe you at all," said Dropno. The krahsta pack moved a half step toward the tribe. "I think you're running away. I don't think you ever intended to take on a puma."

"We d-did, and we d-do," stammered Grash.

"Good," said Dropno. "We just might have an opportunity for you to prove it."

The problem was, there were no decent restaurants in the inland section of North County. Laura drove west along Highway 78 until they'd reached the city of Oceanside, which despite its pretty name was a pit, then turned south on Interstate 5. They pulled off in Carlsbad, where they found a nice beach-side cafe.

They sat outside at a table near the sand. Their feet touched a wooden deck and a large umbrella protected them from sun rays and sea gull droppings. The air was probably twenty degrees cooler than it had been in San Marcos, and Laura was glad. She looked out over the ocean, which was framed by bright sand and a cloudless sky. She leaned back in her chair and let out a long breath of air. The ocean was always so relaxing.

"There's nothing more spiritual than water," said Keith. "I find that when I'm thinking about a certain problem, if I imagine putting it into the ocean it somehow always ends up getting solved."

"So now you're gonna get spiritual on me?" asked Laura with a smile.

"Sure, if you want me to."

"You've really surprised me," said Laura. "I was going to ask you about how you fooled your dates into thinking you were someone else. Now I know."

"How's that?" asked Keith, who now leaned forward with an amused look on his face.

"You've talked openly about a lot of things today," said Laura. "Somehow, I would've thought you'd be more secretive. But with everything you've talked about, you've never once talked about the music business, or the Pumas, or anything you're known for."

"They're my jobs," said Keith. "No one likes to talk about work when they're off duty. But if there's anything you'd like to know, feel free to ask."

Laura turned away and looked back at the water. This was an interesting situation to be in. What to ask Keith Gallatin?

"Tell me why you're getting involved in this mountain lion predicament."

"I told you already," said Keith.

"No, you sorta dodged the question when I asked you on the phone," said Laura. "And . . ."

"It's time we opened our eyes," said Keith. "Environmental concerns are a hot issue right now. Everyone's jumping on the bandwagon. But most people only think about the environment in terms of smog, pollution, and the ozone layer. Everyone forgets about the alarming rate of extinctions taking place on this planet."

"So why get involved now?" asked Laura.

"Danielle and I have been involved for years," said Keith. "We've just been low-profile about it. Now we've reached a point where low-profile just isn't going to work anymore."

Laura nodded. The Gallatins were famous for their enormous contributions to charities, despite how much the twins downplayed it. Laura couldn't recall having heard of any donations to environmental groups, but that didn't mean it had never happened.

"What I saw at the Fish and Game meeting made me sick," said Keith. "It looked like a battle between the freaks and the fascists."

Laura laughed and nodded in agreement. She was about to speak when the waitress arrived to take their order. She jotted down their requests, then scurried off without having any idea that she had a famous customer.

"When is your attack dog story coming out?" asked Keith.

"Tomorrow morning," said Laura. "I have a six o'clock deadline."

"Do we have to hurry back?" asked Keith.

"No, no," said Laura. "It's only eleven-thirty. I have the story mostly written in my head. It'll only take me about an hour to put it together."

"Where did they spot the mountain lion last night?" asked Keith.

"Not too far from here. Just a little bit south, as a matter of fact."

"You wanna go looking for it after lunch?"

"Looking for a mountain lion?" Laura asked skeptically. "Why don't we just stay here and hunt for grunion? We have about as much chance of finding them in broad daylight as we do tracking down a mountain lion."

"Very true," said Keith. "But you never know what you might find, if you only open your eyes and look. For example, if you turn back toward the water and look at the edge of the surf, you might see some dolphins."

Laura turned to her left immediately. At first she saw only the continuous, eternal crashing of waves. But suddenly, two—then four—dorsal fins appeared from behind a breaker. They sank back down, only to be followed by several others. Some reached higher and stayed up longer, as they broke water to spout and suck in new air. They rolled northward with peaceful grace.

Laura was stunned. She kept her eyes trained on the surf line, trying to count the beautiful marine mammals, but they were never all on the surface at one time. She gave a guess there were about twenty in all.

"I've never seen anything like that," said Laura. "I never knew they came in so close to shore."

"You could probably see them every day if you wanted to," said Keith. "I see them all the time. So do many other people, who know what to look for. You might have gone your whole life without seeing them if you hadn't looked. The key is, you have to look."

Laura shook her head in disbelief, while straining to see the fins as they moved farther north.

"Okay," said Laura. "We'll go look for the mountain lion."

CHAPTER 18

It was sudden and sharp; a quick, stabbing pain jolted Sarena to her feet. She was still half-asleep, and the intensity of the afternoon sun raked into her unadjusted eyes. She squinted hard and turned around frantically, but saw nothing. She might have concluded it was only a dream, but her face still hurt.

When a shadow crossed before her, she knew the answer. Lanakila landed on a stump, instantly cocking his head to the right. From the edge of his mouth dangled a long piece of hair, which Sarena instantly identified as one of her whiskers.

"What's wrong with you?" Sarena demanded. "I can't even sleep in peace with you around. I'm afraid to close my eyes in case some evil will strike me from the sky."

"I get bored watching my Fur Ball sleep," said Lanakila. "It makes my mind wander into mischief. I can't help it."

"You'd better learn to help it," said Sarena. "Or I'll learn the taste of ahila real soon."

"You'd better learn to stay awake more," Lanakila mimicked. "Or something else might learn the taste of puma."

Sarena hissed and sat down. She had been deeply asleep, and her head was banging from the sudden intrusion of sunlight. She looked up at the ahila, and couldn't decide whether she wanted to pluck off all of his feathers or thank him for caring about her. She decided to do neither.

"What's the problem now?" Sarena asked.

"The kribas are moving," said the ahila. "They are headed in this direction."

"So what? It'll take them all day to get this far. Longer. It's harder to move in the hot sun."

"They have again met up with the krahstas," said Lanakila.

Sarena looked away from her friend and stared across the great openness of the Canyon. Although she hadn't mentioned it to Lanakila before, this combination made her nervous. As far as Sarena was concerned, separate groups of kribas and krahstas posed no real threat. But the cunning wit of the Canyon-dwellers could contribute immensely to the threat posed by their larger and stronger cousins.

"We need to move again," said Lanakila.

Sarena looked up at him with a sigh. She was tired and achy already. Another march through the Canyon didn't seem to appealing.

"It's easy for you to say 'we' need to move," said Sarena. "You can move far and fast without any effort at all. It's hard for me to just get up and run from a pack of kribas I've never even seen. Especially lugging the likes of you on my back."

Lanakila fluffed up and stretched out his wings. Sarena thought he was going to fly away, but his wings came back in. He looked down at her with his never-changing expression. Sarena couldn't even read his eyes this time.

"In this case, Fur Ball, it doesn't matter if I move on or not," said Lanakila. "I'm not the one in danger. I only suggest this because I'm not interested in losing the only friend I have."

The krahsta leader motioned with his head and the pack beside him began to spread out. Not wanting to become encircled, the tribe began to back up without even waiting for Grash's command. Grash immediately decided the best way to handle this was a straight-on attack through the middle of the krahsta formation, and was about to give the order when his counterpart began to laugh.

"You still haven't learned," said Dropno. "You've lived in the Canyon all of this time, and you are as stupid as the day you walked in."

Grash froze, deciding to keep his mouth shut and try to figure out what the krahsta was talking about. The other tribe members were as uneasy as he was, and he knew they would be ready to strike immediately upon his demand.

"I'm sure you could break through our line," said Dropno. "There's no need. You're free to go. But I think you should listen to us first."

Grash had no response other than the doubtful expression he wore on his face. His opponent rolled his eyes, then looked over the tribe with a mocking smirk.

"You have promised but not delivered," said Dropno. "I'm not surprised. We should just let you go on your way, to leave our territory as cowards."

This remark struck a nerve in each of the tribe members. Grash could sense them tightening up and standing straighter.

"I think you should listen first," repeated Dropno. He looked over at another individual of his pack. "Drade?"

A krahsta to the left of Dropno stepped forward and scanned the tribe. He appeared to be older than the leader but seemed more delicate, if such a word could be applied to a krahsta. His wild, golden eyes stopped on Grash for several moments, then continued on with his evaluation of the others.

"We have discussed your plight long and hard," said Drade. "Your problems are related to ours, you see. We think we can help you out if you help us in return."

"What could you possibly have that we'd want?" asked Grash. The feelings he was getting from the krahstas were getting more and more unpleasant.

"We possess knowledge," said Drade, "which is something our kriba friends clearly lack."

Grash huffed at this, and was glad to hear snorts from the others in the tribe. He said nothing, deciding to let Drade finish with whatever caustic remarks he had to deliver. The krahsta remained silent until all of Grash's kribas had settled back into normal panting.

"Don't be so easily insulted," said Drade. "I'm only speaking the truth. When I speak of knowledge, I mean that of the Canyon. We can help you out."

"Why would you want to help us out?" asked Grash.

"Because you can help us out," said Dropno. "And I must say, you don't have much choice."

"We have mutual interests," said Drade. "None of

us are interested in a puma running around in our territory."

"So you're here to strike a deal," said Grash, finally catching on. He was so prepared for a fight he had over-looked the possibility of a truce.

"In a sense, yes," said Dropno.

"We can help you out with our canyon knowledge and hunting skills," said Drade. "We can make you totally independent from the dangers of the street. You would never have to risk attacking the animals of man again."

"That's quite an offer," said Grash. "And just what is this in exchange for?"

"Your help in the destruction of a puma," said Dropno.

Laura drove south toward the off-ramp where the mountain lion had been spotted. After deciding the big cat probably had gone inland after its night of surfing, Laura and Keith turned east and headed for the nearest and most accessible area of open space. Laura pulled over onto a small dirt road surrounded with chaparral, then stopped in the tiny curvature of a turnabout.

She looked over at Keith, who was as wide-eyed as a little kid at Disneyland. Laura shook her head, then killed the engine.

"We're gonna see a mountain lion, aren't we?" Laura asked.

"I have no idea," said Keith.

"But you seem to think so."

"I'm always open to all possibilities."

Laura gave him a wet raspberry, then opened her door.

"Is there anything you don't know?" she asked.

"I don't know anything about you," said Keith, as he climbed out of the car and closed the door. He stretched a little bit, then looked around the chaparral. There was no sign of other human life.

"I'm beginning to wonder," said Laura. "I can't tell if you have some sorta psychic powers and are reading me like a book, or if you just have terrific sources."

"What do you think?"

"Probably both," Laura said, laughing.

"You're probably right." Keith nodded.

They began to walk along the dirt road, casually looking in both directions for any movement in the brush. Laura didn't honestly expect to see anything larger than a jackrabbit, but decided to keep an open mind based on the dolphin incident.

"What do you look for in women?" Laura asked suddenly, on a whim.

Keith didn't appear to be surprised by this question, but he thought about it for a long time before answering. He looked down at his feet as they stepped in the dirt, then looked back up at the chaparral.

"I look at the eyes first," he said finally. "As the old saying goes, 'The eyes are the window to the soul.' "

"What do you see in my eyes?" asked Laura. She knew it was a loaded question, but decided to go for it anyway. Why not? After all, they were walking alone together on a dirt road out in the middle of nowhere.

"I see mirrored contact lenses," said Keith.

"Huh?"

"You've built up walls so high not even Superman could jump them. You won't voluntarily let anyone see into your soul. Your world is one big secret."

It was Laura's turn to look down at her feet. It was pretty bad when someone she'd spent only a few hours with already had encountered her walls. She didn't need a rock star to tell her about them. She'd spent most of her life carefully constructing them.

"You asked," said Keith.

"I know," said Laura. "You're right, though. How could you see the walls so quickly?"

"Maybe I've run into a couple," said Keith.

"Already?" Laura asked. She shook her head and gritted her teeth. She didn't want it to be like this.

The truth was, she didn't know what she wanted it to be like. She didn't even know this person, yet he seemed to know her much better than anything she felt comfortable with. He obviously wanted something from her, yet she couldn't figure out what. She couldn't even figure out what she wanted from him, if anything. Still here she was, walking alone with a rock star on a deserted path in the middle of a Canyon. Thirteen-year-olds everywhere would die to be part of such a scenario.

"You forgot your camera," said Keith, obviously willing to give Laura a break and change the subject if she wanted.

"Damn," said Laura, clenching her fists beside her face. She hadn't used it while they were on the attack dog story, but she'd wanted to bring it into the Canyon with her, just in case. She was certain there would be no mountain lions, but still . . .

"I guess I'm not making much of a first impression," said Laura.

Keith simply smiled and winked.

"When are we going to hunt again, Fur Ball?" asked Lanakila.

"We just finished the alleen two days ago," said Sarena. She was walking along a tiny dirt trail with the ahila on her shoulders.

"Two days ago might as well be two seasons ago!" said Lanakila. "I've gone back to eating hina again to keep me from starving."

"That's your problem," said Sarena. "I may need to sleep all the time, but at least I'm not cursed with having to eat every day."

"There's nothing wrong with eating when you're hungry," huffed the ahila.

Suddenly a loud crack sent Lanakila skyward and Sarena to the ground. She screamed in agony, as fire ripped through her left forepaw. She tried to jump up, but pain seared through her shoulder and into her back, dropping her flat onto her chin.

Something had her. She turned and kicked desperately with claws extended, but the vicious jaws did not flinch. She snarled and grabbed with her teeth, but they met with a hard, painful clink. She kicked again, making the pain even worse.

Lanakila landed and instantly began jabbing at the assailant. He struck it twice with his beak, then recoiled in pain. He hopped all around it with his wings spread, as Sarena dropped her legs and stopped kicking.

"Help me!" Sarena cried.

"It's a trap!" squawked Lanakila. "A mantrap."

"Help me!" Sarena babbled. "It hurts! Oh, Lady Farri, it hurts!"

"Oh, my Sarena!" wailed Lanakila, jumping frantically around the trap. "Be still! Be still! Oh, Sarena!"

Another jolt of pain raced through Sarena's forepaw. She howled again and kicked involuntarily, which instantly doubled the pain.

"Be still!" demanded Lanakila. "Please, my love. Please!"

Sarena couldn't respond. The rocks and bushes began to spin around her. She was panting wildly yet couldn't breathe. Her mouth was frothing as her tongue flapped out to the side.

"Oh, Sarena," repeated Lanakila. "Please, you have to help me! Please! What am I going to do?"

Sarena had no answer. She could see little more than numerous shades of gray. The ahila's voice sounded distant and hollow, with a faint echo. Then the blackness came. She ran toward it and everything disappeared.

Grash wondered what the rest of the Canyon would think of *this* arrangement. As he loped through the chaparral, he looked around at his companions. His tribe, his wild pack of highly trained kribas, was openly running in league with a pack of krahstas.

This was supposed to be the first lesson for members of the tribe. They were being taught the critical value of loping, and of doing it with the least amount of energy. They had traveled quite a distance, and so far Grash was impressed. He could tell the other students were as well.

Grash was beginning to soften in his opinion of the krahstas. They were definitely wild and unpredictable, and Grash was far from saying he would trust them, but still they weren't nearly as awful as he'd first imagined.

And they were vulnerable.

There was a lot to think about. The krahstas could learn just as much from the tribe, if Grash chose to teach them. Certainly they would learn just from being around, but the volume could be controlled. It didn't matter. Grash knew the simple combination of the two groups would make them quite the formidable foe.

Suddenly they stopped. All of them, krahsta and kriba. As one their noses went up and their tails went down.

They smelled it and they knew, and later none would admit to the slight tremors running down their spines.

It was a puma, and it was very close.

The fierce pounding in her forepaw brought Sarena back to reality. She opened her eyes to see Lanakila pushing at the space in the trap with a stick. He had wedged it into one side and was trying to manuever it with his beak, in an attempt to pry the trap open.

"We are in trouble, love," Sarena said quietly.

"We are if you don't help," said Lanakila, momentarily letting go of the stick. "We'll get you out."

"It hurts, love," Sarena whimpered.

"I know," said Lanakila. "We'll get you out."

Sarena didn't think so. The grip was like nothing she ever could have imagined. If she didn't get out very soon, she knew she would never make it.

She calmly tried to assess the damage. Fortunately the jaws held no teeth, or by now she would be a bloody mess. The bad part was the entire area was swollen, and the bone was probably broken. Even if she did get out, she might never recover well enough to hunt again.

Sarena closed her eyes and began to whimper again. She wondered how any animal could be so cruel as to set such a trap.

"Sarena, you have to help," insisted Lanakila.

"Okay," she said finally.

"This has to open, somehow," said the ahila. "It might take man-magic to open it, but I don't think so. I've been able to move it enough to give me hope."

"What can I do?" asked Sarena. She knew Lanakila was right. If she was going to get out, she needed to be strong and calm.

"Try pushing on this stick," said Lanakila. "I've had a little luck, but I don't weigh enough to make a difference."

"Okay," said Sarena, gritting her teeth.

She rolled over enough to get maximum use of her right paw. She understood what Lanakila wanted, but doubted its feasibility. Still she reached over and pushed down on the stick, which snapped within moments.

"We need a stronger stick," said Lanakila.

Sarena only grimaced with pain. She dropped back down and took deep breaths.

"It moved through," Lanakila said hopefully. "It did. I saw it, just before the stick snapped. I'll go get a bigger one."

"Hurry, love," moaned Sarena.

Lanakila launched skyward, and Sarena's eyes rolled back into her head. The pain was starting to mellow into a dull numbness, which Sarena knew was bad. She tried to focus her eyes on the trap and figure out its secret.

Surely there had to be a secret. How else could the men pull out their prey, once they had died? This was a bad thought. Sarena didn't want to think about anyone dying, other than the beast who had placed this evil device.

Lanakila dropped down with a much thicker branch in his claws. His eyes were wide and his feathers were fluffed out.

"We must hurry!" said Lanakila.

"I know," said Sarena.

"The kribas are near, and they are with a pack of krahstas!"

"Oh, Lady Farri," moaned Sarena.

The krahstas were in for a lesson on attack methods much sooner than Grash had wanted, but now there was no more time to think about it. He barked quick, barely audible orders to his tribe, and they quietly moved forward.

The plan was one of surprise. The tribe would fan out and move into positions on the other side of the puma. Once there, they would wait in ambush until the krahstas forced the cat in their direction. If possible Broed would grab the puma first, and the others would strike immediately.

Grash could still smell the puma, and was surprised by the fact that the smell hadn't seemed to change location at all. With any luck their target was sleeping and had no idea of what was going on. Surprise could only be in their favor.

The tribe was in position. They had made better time than Grash had hoped, but now they would have to wait even longer for the krahstas to chase the beast in their direction. Grash hoped pumas scared easily. They certainly didn't smell like they would.

The wait was an eternity. Grash shook from his paws to his tail and suspected the other tribe members were doing the same, perhaps with the exception of Broed. That dog didn't fear *anything*.

Suddenly Grash heard voices. He couldn't understand the words, but knew they had to do with the krahstas and their target. Obviously the puma wasn't going to run from a pack of krahstas. Grash woofed an order, and the tribe moved.

Sarena was on her feet. She stood on three legs as best she could, with Lanakila beside her. The pain was tremendous, but she barely noticed. Now her life depended on her ability to be strong.

Standing before her was a pack of krahstas. They lingered just beyond striking range, leering and snickering. They were in great shape, and they knew it. Sarena wanted desperately to reach out and rip the grin off just one of them. *One* would be enough. It would make her feel so much better.

"Does the kitty have a problem?" jeered one of the krahstas.

Sarena opened her mouth to speak but Lanakila beat her to it.

"Leave now or die," demanded the ahila.

All eyes snapped toward the bird, who stretched out his wings and hissed. Even Sarena, who had expected him to be long gone, was startled by this declaration.

"And just how do you propose to accomplish this, winged one?" asked another of the krahstas. "Seems to me your master is in a bit of a bind."

All of the krahstas laughed at this remark, but Sarena growled. She decided immediately the krahsta who had spoken would be the first to die. Even if they attacked her from all sides, she'd make sure to get that one before she fell. She'd remember him, too, even though all krahstas looked the same. She'd remember, and he'd pay.

One of the krahstas stepped forward and Lanakila immediately launched airborne with a screech, jabbing at the intruder with his claws. The krahsta yelped and stepped back. Several of the others jumped to his defense, but the ahila was already back at Sarena's side. The krahstas glared at Lanakila and growled, but none stepped close enough to risk a swipe by the puma. They were also having second thoughts about the ahila, since their comrade's nose was ripped open and bleeding.

"So the bird wants to fight," said the krahsta Sarena had pegged as the leader. "Well, I think not. My friends, let's all sit down."

The krahsta pack instantly crouched to the ground. They leaned on their forepaws, while keeping their eyes directly on their foes. Sarena and Lanakila were under siege.

Miraculously, the tribe had managed to sneak up on the unfolding event without anyone noticing, and Grash couldn't believe what he was seeing. He saw the krahstas sitting comfortably with wicked grins on their faces, waiting anxiously for the trapped puma to roll over and die. From where Grash stood it was clearly inevitable, and for a moment he pitied the great cat. A slow death from starvation and exhaustion was no way to go, especially in the obvious pain the puma was in.

Grash saw the ahila sitting next to her, and wondered why the bird hadn't flown. The tribe hadn't gotten there in time to witness the ahila's attack on the krahsta, so Grash was still unaware of the bird's loyalty to the puma. He thought about the excellent opportunity this was for them to swing the bird to their side, and silently cursed the krahstas for not thinking about it.

The puma growled, obviously in pain. This brought wide smiles to the faces of the krahstas, but not to Grash. He was a highly trained, well-disciplined killer, and he killed without the slightest concern when the tribe needed food, but this was different. Killing quickly was far different than letting another animal suffer in pain.

Grash quickly scanned through his options. With his order, the tribe could jump in quickly from behind and finish off the puma instantly. Once that task had been completed, they could begin negotiations with the ahila. The only problem was, the slightest mistake could leave one or more of them injured or dead.

He turned to his right to examine the faces of his tribe. He was getting very good at reading their expressions, and what he saw finalized his decision. They would be happy to strike.

Grash was just about to bark the order to move when he smelled it. They all did. The krahstas too were on their feet immediately, their noses to the air. The smell was unmistakable, followed by the confirmation of awkward, heavy footsteps. Men were coming.

What to do? The tribe easily could chase them off, as they had done with others before. But what if they had a gun? What if they were in the Canyon for the sole purpose of hunting the tribe? The men were still far enough away that the tribe could move on the puma now and be finished in plenty of time to escape. But then the ahila would fly off before they could talk to it. Plus, the puma seemed more alert now.

Without looking he could sense the others beside him, waiting for a command.

It seemed to take the puma several moments to understand what was happening. When the krahstas jumped up she responded with a deep growl, but dropped her voice when finally hit by the scent. She fell into a heavy pant, and Grash noticed the spasms shaking through her three good legs.

"So, the hunters have come to retrieve their prey," snickered Dropno. "At least you will be insured a quicker death. What a pity. I was beginning to enjoy this."

"Dropno, let's make sure the men find her," said Drade. "Just in case they weren't the ones who set the trap."

"Yes, my friend, you are right," said Dropno.

The entire krahsta pack broke into a chorus of howls, which raised the fur on Grash's back. This made the decision easy. He uttered a quick woof, and without a sound the tribe retreated into the Canyon.

Sarena couldn't believe what was happening. She was being set up for execution by a howling pack of cowards who didn't even have the courage to step within striking distance of her. She desperately wanted to rip their throats out, but now understood she would never get the chance. They yelped loud and long, then stopped suddenly and dashed into the brush, leaving Sarena and Lanakila to fend for themselves.

"Oh, Lanakila, what am I going to do?" whimpered Sarena. "I can't even defend myself. I've never felt like this."

Lanakila grabbed the larger stick he had brought earlier and began desperately prying at the trap. He pushed down with his beak while scratching hard at the metal with his talons. He pushed down hard with all of his strength, but the trap did not move.

"It's no use, love," said Sarena. "We don't have time."

"Shut up and help!" screamed Lanakila. "I can't let them take you."

"It's okay, love," Sarena resigned. "Even if I escape, I can't go on with a broken leg."

"Sarena!" Lanakila jabbed his beak into her tail, then turned back furiously to the stick.

"Lanakila, you must do one thing for me," Sarena said, her voice beginning to crack. "Don't let them get away! Catch them for me, and let them know why."

"I want *you* to catch them," said Lanakila, his beak still prying at the trap.

"Its up to you, love. Please, do it for me."

The footsteps were getting louder and closer. Sarena collapsed to the ground on her right side and tried to calm her panting. Her trapped leg was twisted and swollen, but she no longer noticed.

"Oh, Sarena," said Lanakila. He finally dropped the stick, after failing to move the trap any farther than it had gone before. He hopped over Sarena's shoulder and landed beside her head. He lowered his beak and began to rub his forehead against her cheek.

It was gone, finally. The lonely pain was gone. Sarena felt the ahila's feathers against her whiskers, and for the first time in her life knew what it was like truly to love someone. It was a heavy discovery, since she realized how much more it hurt to love than to be lonely.

Sarena began to groom Lanakila's face. This relaxed her enough to slow her desperate panting to almost normal breaths. She closed her eyes and pushed her face back up against Lanakila's. Then, while stuck in a deadly trap and listening to oncoming footsteps, she began to purr.

"Sarena, I can't lose you," said Lanakila. "You're the only friend I've ever had."

"And I have never had a friend other than you," said Sarena. "But be happy for me, because finally I will be in a place where many pumas walk, and the nagging pain that has followed me throughout my days will finally be past."

The footsteps stopped, and the two friends heard human voices. They were only a few paces away.

"Oh, Sarena! What can I do?"

"You must fly, my love. You were very brave against the krahstas, and I love you for it, but you cannot fight the men. You must live to find yourself a mate, so the world will have more beautiful birds like yourself."

Lanakila buried his head in Sarena's neck, then pulled away for one last look. He took a long breath, then exhaled slowly.

"I love you, Fur Ball," he said, then spread his wings and was gone.

CHAPTER 19

The howls of coyotes froze them in their tracks. Laura and Keith looked off to their right where the yapping seemed to be coming from, then looked at each other.

"Shall we?" asked Keith.

"Go chasing coyotes?" Laura asked doubtfully.

"They won't bite," said Keith.

"It sounds like there's a lot of them," said Laura, still unsure of the idea. She looked out across the chaparral, then back at Keith.

"We were looking for a cougar, for crying out loud," said Keith. "You're willing to face one of those, but not a measly pack of coyotes? Come on."

Laura hesitated, but followed when Keith marched off of the dirt path and into the sage. She placed every step carefully in the spot where his feet had been. In addition to the fear of coyotes, she suddenly had been struck by an acute fear of rattlesnakes.

Keith turned around and put his right index finger to his lips. Laura nodded, but figured the coyotes must have smelled them by now. Still, they continued to howl from the same general area.

The howling stopped and so did Keith. Laura could hear the wild dogs running off through the greasewood. Keith turned around again, looking perplexed.

"That was weird," he said.

Laura did not answer. She thought this entire adventure was weird.

"It was like they were calling us," said Keith. "But they took off as soon as we got close."

"Let's go back to the path," said Laura.

Keith stood still and turned his head, as if listening for

something. Laura listened too, but heard only a faint rustling of wind through the rye grass.

Suddenly a giant bird launched into the air only a few yards from where they stood, and exactly where the coyotes had been howling. Laura gasped and her eyes bulged wide in astonishment. She instantly cursed herself for having left her camera in the car, as she watched an American bald eagle soar into the sky.

"Look at that!" yelled Keith, pointing upward.

"Wow!" answered Laura.

They watched the great bird wing its way to a great height, then turn into a wide circle. It looked more powerful and majestic than anything Laura had ever seen. The bird seemed to be looking down at them from above, as it gracefully tilted its body to make a turn. It looked away, then began powerful strokes with its wings. Within moments it was gone over a ridge.

"I've never seen anything like that," said Keith.

"Me either," said Laura. "I can't believe it. It was beautiful. I can't believe I forgot my camera."

"Me too," said Keith. "I'd love to have a picture of him."

Keith looked over at Laura with a smile broad enough to split his face. She was smiling, too. This had turned out to be an incredible afternoon. First a school of dolphins, and now a bald eagle. She never thought she'd get close enough to either of them to actually see them in the wild.

She looked up at the sky to see if the eagle had returned, then back at Keith. He was still looking at her and smiling. For a moment she thought that if circumstances had been different, this might have been quite a romantic afternoon.

Keith turned away and looked back toward the chaparral from whence the eagle had flown. He stood motionless for several seconds, then turned back toward Laura.

"This is still weird," he said.

"I'll say," said Laura. "This whole day has been."

"What was that eagle doing with a pack of coyotes?" Keith asked, not to Laura but almost to the sky.

"It didn't say," said Laura facetiously.

"No, it didn't," said Keith, looking back at the brush.

"But the coyotes were acting like they wanted us to know it was there. I think we should go have a look around."

"We need to get going," said Laura, not sounding very convincing. "I have a deadline to make."

"We'll make your deadline," said Keith, and he began walking forward into the greasewood at the edge of the path. Laura held her ground for a moment, but then shrugged her shoulders and followed.

Keith stopped suddenly and looked down at his feet. When Laura caught up with him she saw the four gold casings at his feet, casings that had once held rifle slugs. She glanced back up at Keith, who looked pale and angry. He said nothing but only turned and walked on toward the original position of the eagle.

Between the bushes Keith found a small path. Laura took two quick steps to catch up and walk beside him on his right. The rifle shells suddenly had changed her mood and made her nervous. Keith's mood had changed as well.

Keith stopped abruptly, then looked to his right and into the chaparral on the other side of Laura. She looked over, too, but saw only large bushes of manzanita.

"Come on," said Keith, stepping past Laura toward the brush. Laura rolled her eyes, then reluctantly followed.

He pushed through the thick, dry bushes with his arms then stopped suddenly, which brought Laura's nose into his back. She stepped to the right with a giggle, then discovered the reason behind his sudden halt. There, in a small clearing just past the two large bushes they stood between, stuck in a smooth metal trap, was a full-grown mountain lion.

Sarena growled as fierce a warning as she knew how, but the two-legged beasts still arrogantly pushed their way into the clearing where she was trapped and stared down at her from a safe distance. She growled again, but this growl faded much quicker than the first. Something about the visitors seemed strange.

Lots of things seemed strange. They were obviously surprised to see her. Not just because there was a puma in the trap, but they appeared surprised to see *anything* in the trap. Sarena snarled once more, just to see their reaction. They held their ground but Sarena sensed fear, and something else she couldn't place.

These clearly were not the setters of the trap, but Sarena did not trust them. The scary part was, she wanted to. Something about their presence was relaxing, but Sarena wasn't about to let them near her. The humans were well known for their tricks and treachery. Her current situation was proof enough.

"Oh, my God," Laura finally said. "What are we gonna do?"

Keith stood motionless, biting the knuckle of his index finger. His eyes were wide with horror and disbelief, and looked just the way Laura imagined she herself looked.

"We have to do something," she persisted. "It's hurt."

Keith still said nothing. He stared at the cougar, and Laura thought he looked like a man tearing himself apart over a difficult decision.

"Why don't we call Fish and Game?" Laura asked. "They can take care of it. I can't believe someone could do this to an animal."

"She'll be dead before they get here," said Keith, shaking his head. "We have to let her out."

"Oh yeah, right," said Laura. "And just how are we supposed to go about that? She'll rip our eyes out if we even get close."

"Maybe," said Keith. "Maybe not. We have to try." He began to take a step toward the trapped animal, but it growled viciously and jerked itself around in the trap. Keith stopped immediately.

"Keith! You can't go near it! It's dangerous!"

"So are the people who set this trap," he said, still staring at the ensnared cougar. The lion was hissing and spitting, never taking its eyes off of Keith. Its eyes were wild with fury, and its ears were pinned back to its head.

"Let's go back to the car," Laura said.

"No," said Keith, finally turning to look at her. Laura could see the resolve in his eyes. He was going to try something stupid, and there was nothing she could do about it.

They were talking about her in a language she could not understand. She snarled again, showing her teeth, which was a language even the most foolish would understand.

The male had turned his attention back to Sarena, after talking briefly with the female. His stature was huge, although he didn't appear to be much larger physically than Sarena. There was something about his presence which made him seem almost larger-than-life.

The female was even stronger, if Sarena guessed correctly. She radiated strength, and Sarena felt as though she might even have been drawn to her if the situation had been different. The male took another step toward her, and she growled with everything she had left.

"Now just how in the world am I supposed to help you if you keep carrying on like that?" asked the man, in the common speech. His mouth had remained closed, yet his voice filled Sarena's ears with perfect clarity.

Sarena's growl froze in her throat. She was so surprised her mouth gaped open and her tongue dangled out to the side. She had been ready for almost anything, but a man speaking the language of the Canyon was more than she was prepared for. From everything she had ever heard, men were supposed to be deaf to the common speech. In fact it was said that they could barely communicate with each other.

She was so stunned she almost fell over, and would have if it hadn't been for the trap. The pressure on her forepaw sent a fierce wave of pain up her spine. She wondered if the man's words had been an illusion caused by the pain, since his mouth had not moved when he spoke. Yet he stood there looking at her, as if expecting a response. She growled again, which was the only response she could come up with.

"Looks like you've gotten yourself into quite a mess," came the voice, again. "And it looks like you have no choice but to let me help you. You're going to die whether I kill you or leave you for the krahstas, so you might as well take a chance and let me help you."

Sarena couldn't believe what she was hearing. Not only was the man communicating in the common speech without talking, but he was offering to help her. She thought she should hold her ground, but the way he looked at her was nonthreatening. In fact he sounded almost impatient.

"If I were going to kill you, I would have done it

already," he said, again without words. "I'm not interested in destroying such a beautiful lady as yourself. I'm going to set you free if you'll let me."

Somehow Sarena believed him. There was no threat in his voice or demeanor, only confidence and concern. Nor were there any aggressive feelings coming from the female, who remained still and silent.

"You must let me help," said the man.

Sarena opened her mouth to speak, but she was interrupted by the man's silent words.

"Save your strength, pretty girl," he said. "Speak to me with your thoughts. I can hear them as easily as you can hear mine. Please let me help you. You have nothing to lose."

"But you have everything to lose," Sarena said with her thoughts. "I could shred you into little pieces. Why do you want to help a puma?"

"Because you're such a pretty girl," said the man. "I know you can claw me up, but then what will you do? You'll never get out if you do that. You'll be stuck in there until the krahstas come back. Come on. What have you got to lose?"

Sarena's head was spinning. How could this be? This might very well be the same man who had set the trap, and now he was asking her to trust him. Was any man worth trusting? He took a step forward and she answered with a warning growl. He stopped and put his hands on his hips.

"What are you going to do if we leave and the men who set this trap come in our place?" he asked. "How long do you think you can hold *them* off?"

"You're right," Sarena said finally. "I have nothing to lose. But if you harm me . . ."

"You've already been harmed enough, my pretty girl," he said sadly. "Let me help you out of the trap."

"I have no choice," said Sarena.

Laura couldn't believe what she was witnessing. Keith was standing beside her, and somehow, mentally communicating with the trapped cougar. The strange part was, the mountain lion seemed to understand and was answering back.

Laura couldn't make it out, but she thought she could

hear bits and pieces of a conversation without words. She tried to concentrate on Keith's intense expression, but couldn't be certain if what she heard was real or imagined. Since no words actually were being spoken, it was impossible to tell.

The captured animal had stopped growling, and although it still appeared to be suspicious it had clearly relaxed as a result of whatever Keith was doing. To Laura's surprise the huge cat actually sat down, then cried out when the pressure hit her twisted leg, letting Laura and Keith know exactly how much pain she was in.

Laura immediately wanted to comfort the injured cat, but didn't know how. She wanted to walk over and pet her, but knew the cougar would probably rip her face open if she tried. Laura looked over at Keith, who had begun to walk toward the cougar.

"Keith!" she warned.

"Hey, you only die once," he said, never looking back.

The man stepped forward with deliberate determination. There was no fear on his face, yet there was no malice either. Sarena simply had to trust him.

He didn't stop until he reached the trap. He squatted down and began to examine the situation, well within Sarena's striking distance. His expression was grave as he looked at her forepaw. He picked up the stick Lanakila had used and stared at it curiously.

"Where did this come from?" he asked.

"My friend brought it," Sarena said weakly. Her head was reeling, as the new attention to her situation was answered by a severe jolt of pain through her shoulder.

"Okay, sweetheart, just relax now," he said. He looked closely at the trap from several different angles, then shook his head.

"You'll have to help," he said. "I can push the trap open, but only for a few moments. You'll have to pull yourself out. Do you think you can do that?"

"I'll try," Sarena whispered. She doubted there was enough strength left, but there was no other choice. If nothing else, she would at least do her best.

"Okay, sweetheart, here we go," he said.

Sarena's entire body seared with pain as the man

pushed the trap open. She pushed as hard as she could
with her three good legs, and fell over backward when
her bad leg cleared the evil metal jaws of the trap. She
hit the ground hard, and howled out as she was smashed
by an enormous wave of pain from her forepaw. The
metal jaws slammed shut as the man let them go.

There was only darkness and stars. The pain was too
intense for her even to open her eyes. She panted heavily
as the ground seemed to spin all around her. She snapped
at the air twice, trying to clear her head, then opened
her eyes.

She looked down at her mutilated forepaw and began
to cry. Even though she was free from the trap, its damage would result in her death. Her eyes began to water
and she felt nausea all over. She reached forward to lick
the crushed area, but the pain jabbed through her and
she was overcome by blackness.

Laura could barely breathe. There was no rational way
to explain what was happening. The cougar had simply
let Keith walk up and set it free, while Keith had somehow communicated with it. Now the poor animal was
lying unconscious.

"What . . . ?" Laura didn't know exactly what to ask.

"She'll be all right," said Keith. "I hope."

"Were you talking to it?" Laura asked.

"I didn't say a word, did I?"

"No," said Laura. "But you were communicating with
it somehow, weren't you?"

"Sure. She wouldn't have let me approach, otherwise."

"She understood?"

"You tell me," said Keith, his eyes never leaving the
fallen mountain lion.

"How . . . ?"

"Anything's possible, if you believe," said Keith. He
turned around and looked at Laura. His eyes held a question; not of her, but of himself. Laura thought he was
continuing his internal debate. He looked back down at
the unconscious cat.

"What are we gonna do now?" Laura asked. "We
can't leave her here. We've got to get her to a vet."

"It's too late," said Keith. "A vet can't help her."

Laura glanced down and bit her lip. Such a beautiful

animal, destroyed by an illegal trap. Laura's eyes began
to water.

"We have to try," she said. "We have to do something."

"See if you can open up your heart and believe in
magic," Keith said simply. "It's our only hope." He
reached down and put both of his hands on the mountain
lion's face.

It felt as though she were being led out of a dark cave,
through a vast opening and into the light. Sarena opened
her eyes and was momentarily surprised to see the man
leaning over her. She felt his hands, and they were warm.
Very warm.

Her eyes cleared as he began to lightly stroke her forehead. It seemed as though with each stroke her entire
body became lighter and more relaxed. She looked into
his eyes and recognized the expression as one of concern
and love. He clasped his hands on her two cheeks and it
felt as though a tremendous weight were being lifted
from her entire body, inside and out. She exhaled with
relief, as the heaviness of heart and body drifted away.

He looked down at her with a smile and she couldn't
help but return it. He boldly leaned forward and rubbed
his nose against hers, which surprised her and made her
giggle. She couldn't believe she was able to express
laughter at a time like this.

"You are quite a beautiful lady," he said. "I'm hon-
ored to be of assistance. My name is Keith."

Sarena opened her mouth to say his name, but knew
it was an impossible sound for her voice to make. She
simply nodded an acknowledgment.

"I am Sarena."

"Such a beautiful name," said Keith. "It's so appropriate."

Sarena smiled at the charm being exuded in her direction. This was so different from everything she had ever
heard or experienced concerning men. There was a
warmth radiating from him that washed all through her,
and if it weren't for her leg . . .

She looked down at her twisted forepaw and her heart
sank. Her spirits had been flying with brief forgetfulness,
but now the reality was back. It didn't seem to hurt as
much, but it didn't matter. She was in serious trouble.

"Oh yes, your leg," said Keith. "Well, I guess it wouldn't do to have you walking around on three for the rest of your life."

Sarena closed her eyes. She wanted to scream out, but was afraid of scaring Keith and his mate away. She opened her eyes slowly and looked up at the man, who stared down at her paw. He shook his head, then looked up at the sky. Sarena thought he looked like he was making a serious decision and asking Lady Farri for guidance.

"Okay, pretty girl, you must trust me again," said Keith. "Please trust me, and don't move a bit." He reached forward, and took Sarena's damaged leg into his hands. It hurt a little bit, as he touched the most tender part.

Keith looked up at the sky again, then back down to her leg. He began to caress it carefully with his left paw, while holding it with his right. Each stroke made the area feel lighter, which helped to relax her even more. And his hands were so *warm*.

"Okay, sweetheart, here we go," said Keith. "Close your eyes, and picture Lady Farri."

Sarena did as he said, trying to imagine what the great Queen looked like. As she did she felt movement within her damaged leg. A sudden jolt stunned her enough to cry out, as she heard something pop between Keith's paws. Her body began to shake and she opened her eyes, panting.

What she saw caused her to howl out in disbelief. Her leg was straight.

"What . . . ?"

"Careful, my love. I'm not finished," said Keith. "You have to help me concentrate."

"Okay," she said. She looked down at her forepaw. It was straight, but it was still swollen. She took a deep breath and watched, as Keith closed his eyes.

It seemed as if all of Sarena's senses suddenly were becoming more acute. Everything around her flashed with a clarity and intensity such as she had never experienced before in her life. The air felt warm and alive as it passed through her lungs and back out through her open mouth. It seemed as if a terrible pressure was somehow being lifted off of her back and neck. She was instantly more relaxed than at any time she could remember.

Every sound was exquisitely clear. Every scent whispered into her nose with delicate yet passionate finesse. Her eyes began to see with a vivid awareness she previously had never known. Everything around her seemed so . . . alive.

Keith let go and she looked back down at her forepaw. The swelling was gone, and with it all of the remaining pain. She looked up in awe at Keith, who appeared to be close to exhaustion.

"How does it feel?" he asked, the strength and confidence gone from his mental voice. There was moisture beaded up all over his forehead.

Sarena stood up slowly, cautiously. She balanced her weight on the three good legs, then carefully began to shift toward the damaged one.

There was no more pain. It felt great!

Keith leaned back and sat on his butt, and Sarena immediately jumped on him and began to rub her face against his. He wrapped his arms around her, and she began to purr loudly.

Laura had to sit down. She quickly found a large, smooth piece of rock and squatted down. She wiped her forehead and noticed she was shaking as she did so.

Either she had just witnessed a miracle or Keith had slipped some LSD into her iced tea back at the restaurant. She continued to watch the inconceivable, as a full-grown mountain lion rested her head in the crook of Keith's arm. It was more than inconceivable: It was preposterous.

The animal's seriously broken leg had simply popped back into place. Popped. Laura had heard it. Within moments the swelling was gone and the cougar was on its feet.

This was impossible.

"Her name is Sarena," said Keith.

Laura looked at the two of them wrapped together in an embrace and couldn't respond. This was too scary to think about.

"It's no big deal," said Keith, turning his head around

to see Laura. "It really isn't. In fact you even helped. You just don't realize it."

"Why doesn't she answer?" Sarena asked. She looked up curiously at the human female, who looked as though she were in shock.

"She's shy," said Keith. He began to pet Sarena between the ears. "Her name is Laura."

"She shines just like you do," said Sarena. Now that she was no longer in pain, she noticed what appeared to be a subtle white light emanating from the two companions. "I have never seen anything like it. I wouldn't even know what to call it."

Keith simply nodded, and continued stroking her face.

"I don't understand your magic, but I'm grateful for it," said Sarena. "I can feel it all around you. It's all around your mate, too, even stronger than you. It's the magic of Lady Farri. It called to me while I was stuck in the trap."

"Yes, I know"—Keith smiled—"although Laura doesn't. She has no idea. She can't even speak the common tongue. She can't communicate as we are doing."

"Really? No wonder she's so quiet."

"Yes," Keith said, nodding. "And by the way, she's not my mate."

"She's not?" Sarena asked in dismay. "But you two . . ." She didn't know how to finish. They obviously were so much alike, even for members of the same species. The fact that they could be so close together and not be mates was absurd.

"Are you siblings?" Sarena asked.

"No," said Keith. "We . . . well, it's hard to explain. Because of how different our lives are, it's impossible for us to be mates."

Sarena was horrified. She stepped out of Keith's arms and wanted to bite him for his stupidity. She looked over at Laura, then back at Keith.

"You are an idiot," she said simply, and Keith only laughed.

"My pretty girl, you don't understand," said Keith.

"I'll tell you what I understand," said Sarena. "I have been searching my entire life for a mate. No, not just a mate, *any* puma who might be out there. I've never seen one. Never!

"I have a friend," she continued, "the ahila you saw, who is in the same predicament. He's searching for a mate, too, and neither of us has ever seen another bird like him. Never. Now you have the audacity to stand there and tell me that it's impossible for you two to be mates? How dare you!"

"Sarena . . ."

"Look at her," said Sarena. "Look! Her magic calls out, even to me. How can you resist her?" She stepped over Keith's outstretched legs and began to walk toward Laura.

Laura tensed as the cougar's mood changed. Keith was trying to be casual, but the cat would have no part of it. She wondered what Keith had done to offend her. She hoped it wasn't too awful, because the grand animal was walking toward her and looked seriously pissed off.

Laura placed her hands on the rock underneath her and started to push herself to her feet.

"It's okay," said Keith. "Just sit still."

Laura glanced over at him, then quickly back to their guest. It didn't seem like a particularly good idea to stay there, but she realized if the cougar wanted to maul her she would have no chance of escape anyway.

"Sarena," as Keith had called her, approached her confidently. She walked right up to Laura and placed her nose directly against Laura's cheek. The great cat looked into her eyes, and Laura thought she saw wonder and respect. Her fear instantly vanished.

It seemed Sarena was saying something, but Laura couldn't understand. She afforded a quick look at Keith, who was looking at the ground. She looked back at Sarena, who had begun to lick her face. Laura began to laugh and brought her hands up to Sarena's shoulders.

"She likes you," said Keith.

Sarena began to nuzzle Laura's chin.

"I guess so." Laura giggled.

Sarena looked up at her and appeared to say something, then stared into her eyes, as if expecting an answer.

"Is she saying something to me?" Laura asked Keith.

"Yes," said Keith.

"What?"

"She wants to know why we're not mates," said Keith.

Laura blushed and looked down at Sarena. She grabbed the mountain lion by the ears and began to scratch affectionately. She rubbed her cheek against Sarena's.

"No, really," said Laura.

"Really," said Keith. "That's what she wants to know."

"Sounds like a pickup line to me," said Laura, although, based on the expression of Sarena, she actually believed it.

"That's what she wants to know," said Keith.

Laura looked up at Keith and then gave Sarena a hug. She held on to her for several seconds, watching Keith the entire time. He stared at the ground, never looking up.

"You're a beautiful girl," Laura said to Sarena.

Laura caught a piece of mental communication between Keith and Sarena, which Laura assumed was a translation. Sarena responded and Keith continued to stare at the ground.

"She said 'thank you,' and wants you to answer her question," said Keith, who was now looking at a bush off to the side.

Laura looked at Sarena, who stared back with questioning eyes. The mountain lion was truly a beautiful animal. She held Laura's gaze, and somehow Laura knew Keith was telling the truth. She glanced over at the rock star, who was still scanning the brush, then back at Sarena.

"He doesn't want me," Laura said to Sarena. "He's got too many other women."

"She says she thinks I have too many other mates," said Keith.

Sarena turned around and looked at Keith, who was staring at his feet.

"Do you?" asked Sarena.

"No," said Keith. "I'm very lonely."

"Then why isn't she your mate?" Sarena asked. She couldn't comprehend such a ridiculous situation.

"You don't understand, my love," said Keith. "Our world is different than yours. There are so many of us that we play silly games, and sometimes never find a mate. It's so sad. I wish I knew how to explain."

"Do you want her to be your mate?" asked Sarena.

Keith looked up at Laura, then looked back at Sarena. He shrugged his shoulders, then looked back down at his feet.

"I don't know."

"You are truly mad," said Sarena. She stepped away from Laura and walked over to Keith.

"Your foolishness is quite disturbing," she said. "But you're lucky, I guess, to have so many females to choose from. I've never even seen another puma."

She looked up at Laura, then looked up into the sky. She gritted her teeth, then closed her eyes. It was worth a try.

"Have you seen other pumas?" she asked.

"Not like you," said Keith.

"But you have seen them?" Sarena asked hopefully.

"Yes," said Keith, "but never one that was free."

"What?"

"There are places where animals are kept," said Keith. "Sometimes against their will, but not always. I have seen pumas there."

"Can you take me there?" asked Sarena.

"No," said Keith. "It's not a place for someone as majestic as you."

"Why? You said there were others. Please, I need to see other pumas."

"You can't go there," said Keith sadly. "You would hate it. You would have to give up your freedom forever."

"I would do that gladly to have a mate," pleaded Sarena.

Keith put his arms around her and began to sniffle. He held her for several moments without speaking.

"It's okay," he said finally. "I know it's tough. Believe me, I know. But you can't give up hope. There are other pumas out there. You'll find one, I know it. I can feel it. A big, handsome male who'll love to be your mate."

"Please, can't you take me to the place where you saw the pumas?" Sarena begged.

"I can't," said Keith. "But you'll find one. I promise."

Sarena leaned back and looked into his eyes. He was telling the truth. At least, if anyone would know, it would be him. After all, he had somehow managed to heal her forepaw.

"Okay," she said. "I guess I can trust you."

"I have something for you," said Keith, reaching for his neck and removing a small chain. He held it up for Sarena and she was surprised to see a small object hanging from it, which resembled the shape of a puma. "I want to put this on you, if it's okay."

"Of course," said Sarena. "What is it?"

"It's a good-luck charm," said Keith. "It also carries some of my magic." He fastened it around Sarena's neck and it seemed to fit just right.

"I mean it about the magic," said Keith. "If you're ever in trouble or you need help or guidance, think of me, and put your paw up to the chain."

"Which one?" asked Sarena.

"The one you injured today," said Keith. "Just put it up to the chain if you need help. It's also good for answering questions. If you have a problem, touch the chain and look for signs. Follow your heart. It will never let you down."

Sarena nodded. She looked over at Laura, who still sat silent. Sarena noticed Laura had no such token around her neck.

"You must go now," said Keith. "It's not safe for you to be around humans for so long. And you must never trust humans again. Never! You were lucky it was us, this time."

"Very lucky,' said Sarena. She looked back at Laura, and walked over to her again.

"I wish you spoke the common speech," said Sarena. "Hopefully he will tell you how truly beautiful you are, and will do everything he can to take you as his mate. I'm glad I met you. I hope we meet again."

Sarena began to groom the side of Laura's face, and was fascinated at how smooth skin felt when it was not covered with fur. Laura giggled, and Sarena smiled. She stepped back and looked over at Keith.

"I owe you my life," she said. "There is no way for me to pay you back, but somehow, someday, something special will happen for you. It's the way of life. Be happy."

She walked back over and gave Keith an affectionate nudge, then trotted off into the brush.

CHAPTER 20

Laura pulled out onto Interstate 5 and drove south toward San Diego. Keith had not said a word since the mountain lion had left them, and she didn't know what to say either. Keith sat motionless, holding on to his left arm and staring through his window to the west.

They had taken the trap along with them, and it was resting safely in the space behind the seats. Laura was going to call Fish and Game immediately when she got back to the office. Telling them where she'd found it would be the easy part. Telling them the circumstances would be impossible.

"I guess I have some questions," Laura finally said.

Keith didn't make any sign of acknowledgment. He continued to stare out the window.

"Of course, you could save me some time and volunteer. . . ."

"Do you really want to know?" he asked, without turning. "Think about it. Do you *really* want to know?"

This sounded like more of a warning than a question. Laura quickly went over the bizarre events in her mind and wasn't sure if she did want to know. It had all seemed like a fairy tale, or some kind of magical dream.

"I'm a reporter," said Laura. "I'm supposed to be curious."

"Why? So you can report it? It would be one hell of a story, wouldn't it? Think about it. If you wrote down what you think you saw and handed it to your editor, he'd suggest you seek employment at *The National Enquirer*."

"I never said anything about writing a story," said

Laura defensively. "What I saw out there looked similar to certain miracles I've read about in—"

"It's nothing like that," said Keith. "Look, I really don't wanna talk about it. And quite frankly, at this point, you really don't wanna know."

"Maybe I don't," said Laura. "At least, not now. But some day I will."

Keith mumbled something and looked down at his left wrist, which he continued to hold on to.

"Is something wrong?" Laura asked, glancing over at Keith's arm.

"Yes," said Keith. "We can't let them go ahead with the hunt."

As far as Grash could tell, the tribe looked relieved. The puma was as good as dead, if it wasn't deceased already. No one in the tribe would have to risk injury while trying to make good on a shaky deal. Grash just hoped the krahstas wouldn't ask for anything else instead.

It was true, the puma had fallen by mere chance, without the help of the tribe. But an argument could be made that the tribe had been there and ready to go, only their killing services hadn't been needed. It could also be argued that the puma would never have been in the vicinity of the trap had it not been for the closing presence of the tribe.

Grash studied his charges closer. They had found a nice sheltered hole in a large section of manzanita, and most of them seemed ready to curl up and take a nap. This was good. They could all use the rest.

Where were the krahstas? Grash could only wonder. He had not picked up even the slightest scent since they all had separated back where the puma was trapped. This also was good. The longer he didn't have to deal with them, the better. If he was lucky, he might never see them again. Unfortunately luck was not something he had been receiving much of recently.

Kroth was the last of them to lay his head down on his forepaws, and as Grash watched him close his eyes he wondered if they were finally ready to make it on their own in the Canyon. They had learned a lot from the krahstas, but Grash knew they had a long way to go.

The krahstas had an entire history of experience in the Canyon, the tribe had none.

What now? Should Grash lead his friends away from the krahstas, or track them down and hope the lessons would continue? And if the krahstas were amiable would there be a price attached, even though the puma was now dead?

Too many questions to think about for now. Grash was very tired, and his eyelids were beginning to stay closed more than they were staying open. He curled up on the dirt next to a small boulder and, like the others, put his chin on his forepaws. He would take a nap and decide later. For now, it seemed the krahstas couldn't possibly ask anything nearly as dangerous as they had before. After all, as far as Grash knew, there weren't any more pumas around.

He suddenly thought about the ahila. Now that the puma was gone, it would be free to join up with the tribe. With the ahila, the tribe wouldn't need any further training on Canyon survival from the krahstas. The ahila would definitely solve a lot of problems.

The only obstacle was actually finding the ahila. Once found, Grash was certain he would be able to talk it into joining the tribe. He wondered how the puma had done it. No doubt with scare tactics. Grash would handle it differently. The ahila would be happy to be a member of the tribe.

Sarena relaxed in the shade of some tall scrub oak bushes and groomed her left forepaw. She couldn't believe how good it felt. Not just the absence of pain, but an added strength and vitality which had not been present before the disaster in the trap.

And it felt warm.

It wasn't just her forepaw. It seemed as though all of the muscles in her body were refreshed and relaxed. Although not as extreme as when Keith had held her leg, her senses still remained more intense and vivid than she could ever recall.

She allowed herself a luxurious stretch, and with it she felt the strength of every individual muscle in her back. She had never noticed just how wonderful a simple flex could be.

Sarena looked skyward and wondered about Lanakila. She hoped he was safe. Knowing him, he was probably off causing trouble somewhere. She hoped he would show up soon, so she could tell him all about the man who had saved her life.

It even *sounded* strange: A man saved her life. It was pretty unbelievable. Especially the way in which the entire affair had come about. Strangely, the memory of what had actually happened was getting hazy, and it now seemed more like a dream than anything else.

Sarena decided there was no point in worrying. The great bird would probably find her when she was asleep, then swoop down on her with some nasty trick. No problem. In fact, for once, she would actually welcome his bizarre sense of humor. She couldn't wait to see him so she curled up in a patch of soft, dry grass and did what cats do best. She slept undisturbed until well after dark.

Laura stared at the computer monitor, but she couldn't concentrate well enough to finish the line. She was supposed to be writing the attack dog story, but she couldn't stop thinking about Keith and the mountain lion. The entire episode had been so phenomenal, the other story paled by comparison. It also seemed as though her interview with the man whose animals had been attacked had taken place months ago.

Keith Gallatin. What a trip. He was right about one thing: It was a story she could never write and still maintain some level of credibility. If only she had brought her camera.

"How's it going?" asked Bill Sesma, wanting to know the status of her story.

"I'll be all right," said Laura.

"Okay," said Sesma, and walked off. Sesma was one of the few editors who knew enough to leave reporters on deadline alone. Most would ask twenty questions, which only put the reporter that much further behind.

Laura shrugged and began typing. She actually worked better under pressure. She pushed the puma and Keith Gallatin out of her mind and finished the story within ten minutes. Once in the computer, it was up to the editors to do with it what they would.

The phone rang, and Laura was grateful it had waited

until she was finished. Usually the phone never stopped ringing when she was on deadline.

"Hi, this is Jake Cotter from the NRA. Remember we met the other night?"

"Oh yes, hi," said Laura. "Listen, I'm sorry for being so short with you. . . ."

"It's okay," Cotter said. "I was way outa line by just coming over like that."

"What can I do for you?" asked Laura. She still thought the guy was a jerk, but courtesy must prevail during regular business hours.

"Are you plannin' on doin' any follow-up type stories to the one you did on the mountain lions?" he asked.

"I'll probably be covering most of the Fish and Game meetings involving their proposed hunts," said Laura. She reached for her note pad, just in case this guy had anything worthwhile to say.

"I'll bet you just cover it because of those hothead protesters," said Cotter. "You know, most of them don't even have jobs. They don't have anything better to do with their time than to go and make noise."

"I'm covering it because it's an important issue," said Laura.

"It's very important," said Cotter. "There's much more at stake here than simply a hunt. Or even gun control, for that matter. Once they start chipping away at our constitutional rights like this, it'll never stop until we're a totalitarian nation. I'll bet freedom of the press is the next thing they'll attack, once they've taken the rights of gun owners away."

"You sound just like one of the Fish and Game commissioners I talked to," said Laura. "He said the exact same thing."

"Good for him," said Cotter. "At least the Commission's on the side of the Constitution."

"Okay, back to the issue at hand. What about the lack of an accurate estimate?" asked Laura. It was easy to take the opposing side with this guy. "No one knows exactly how many mountain lions there are out there."

"Not exactly, no," said Cotter. "But sightings are up all over the state. Take just the other day, for example. Right down in Mission Valley, a full-grown cougar walked right out onto a golf course in broad daylight."

"I heard about that," said Laura. "We had a reporter down there. The guy from Animal Reg said the call came in as a mountain lion, but a bobcat was far more likely."

"I talked to the golfer who saw it," said Cotter. "He told me it was as big as his cart."

"And golfers have never been known to exaggerate on a story," chided Laura.

"Well, who knows?" Cotter asked. "All I know is, there are more lions in this state than there've been in years. There's enough to hunt two hundred fifty, and then some."

"Okay," said Laura. It was getting late, and she wanted to go home. "Is there anything else I don't already know about that you can enlighten me on concerning this?"

"Yes," said Cotter. "Those freaks who scream and yell at the meetings aren't going to win this time. Take it from me. We'll beat them. They may have won a few battles, but they forget who they're dealin' with. We're the ones who know how to fight. Really fight."

Laura hung up and shook her head. Jake Cotter seemed like just the type of person to do something weird. In only two brief conversations he had revolted her enough to think he might be dangerous.

Tomorrow she would start making calls to find out just who he really was. She already had an idea of what she might find. He was probably quiet and neighborly, and his friends would swear he was the nicest guy on the planet.

Laura decided he was just the type who would someday open fire on a schoolyard with an AK-47.

She picked up the phone to call Dennis Jack, her friend at Fish and Game. It was almost six o'clock, and she was surprised to find him still in the office.

"So, who's the new boyfriend?" he chided Laura.

"Who?"

"The guy you were with today," said Dennis. "He was quite a cutie."

"Oh, cut it out," said Laura. "Keith's just a friend."

"I'll bet you say that about all your boyfriends."

"Yeah, so?"

"What can I do for you?" Dennis asked.

"First of all, I have some legal questions," Laura said.

"Shoot."

"You mentioned today the poachers may have started up again."

"Right."

"How can you tell?" Laura asked.

"People call us up and report finding butchered deer carcasses," said Dennis. "That's one way. Mostly it involves people calling us up. They've seen something strange or heard shots fired in their Canyon. Things along those lines."

"Have you seen the deer carcasses?" Laura asked, a little revolted.

"A couple, yeah," said Dennis. "Real strange. Real professional."

"Professional?"

"Yeah," said Dennis. "They're butchered clean, which is hard to do in the field. Pelts gone, the head, meat, everything. Whoever it is knows exactly what they're doing."

"You think there's more than one?" Laura asked.

"Has to be," said Dennis. "By that, I mean I think they're working together. Even though they're separate incidents, I'm positive they're related. They're just too similar not to be."

"What's the penalty for poaching?" Laura asked.

"In California, it's a misdemeanor," said Dennis. "If you shoot an animal illegally it's punishable by up to a one-thousand-dollar fine and or six months in jail."

"How about a mountain lion?" Laura asked.

"It's the same," said Dennis. "Any animal taken illegally."

"Wow," said Laura, amazed at how minor the penalty was. She thought about the mountain lion, stuck in the trap and waiting to die a terrible death. A one-thousand-dollar fine.

"What about an eagle?" Laura asked, remembering the great bird she and Keith had seen near Sarena.

"Now that's different," said Dennis. "Eagles are federally protected. I'm not sure exactly what the penalty for shooting an eagle is, but I think it's something like five years, five thousand dollars, and or both. I'm not real sure about eagles because we normally don't handle federal cases."

"Who would?" asked Laura.

"If there was a case involving an eagle, we might end up doing some of the field investigations," said Dennis. "That's only because we're set up to do so. There are some federal game wardens, but there are far more of us in the field. Chances are the FBI would be the ones who actually handled the prosecution."

"Have you ever worked on a case involving an eagle?" Laura asked.

"No, no," said Dennis. "I doubt if anyone in our office has. I doubt if there are any eagles left in the county. If there are they're way out east, hiding in the Lagunas somewhere."

"Makes sense," said Laura, not wanting to let on what she had seen earlier in the day. Not only had she seen an eagle, but it had been nowhere near the Laguna Mountains. The Canyon where the great bird had been was at least sixty miles away.

"Anything else?" Dennis asked.

"Yes, as a matter of fact," said Laura. "After I saw you today I went walking around in a Canyon in the eastern part of Carlsbad. We were looking for areas poachers might frequent. We found an animal trap."

"A trap? What kind of trap?"

"It was made of steel," said Laura. "We brought it back. I have it under my desk. I'm hoping to snag whoever's been stealing my notebooks."

"Really?"

"Well, I was just kidding about it being set, but yes, it's here at my desk."

"Can you show me where you found it?" Dennis asked.

"I probably can, tomorrow," said Laura.

"Good. That could help me out a lot."

"I don't have anything lined up for tomorrow, so just call me and let me know what time."

"Okay," said Dennis. "By the way, was the trap set when you found it?"

"Yes," Laura lied. She wasn't prepared to explain the story of Keith and Sarena, at least not to Dennis. But then, she wondered if she would ever be able to explain it to anyone.

*   *   *

Laura opened her front door to the welcome of her three cats and a ringing telephone. She decided to let the answering machine do the honors, and bent down to pet her roommates. They all seemed especially happy to see her tonight. She wondered how they might have reacted earlier, when she probably still had the smell of Sarena on her clothes.

When the outgoing message had finished on her machine, she heard Keith's voice booming through the tiny speaker. She immediately walked over and picked up the phone.

"Screening your calls, I see," said Keith.

"Yes, you never know when some weirdo might get a hold of your phone number," Laura joked.

"I know. Happens to me all the time," said Keith, turning the joke around.

"Okay, what's going on?" Laura asked.

"Well, I wanted to finish telling you about my plans for the Fish and Game meeting next week," said Keith.

"Are you calling me at home, on my own time, to discuss business?" Laura asked.

Silence.

"Because if you are," Laura continued, "I'm gonna hang up on you, just like I got rid of some creep who showed up on my doorstep last week."

"Oh no, I would never call you at home to discuss business," said Keith. "As a matter of fact, I was calling simply to tell you what beautiful eyes you have."

"Thank you," said Laura. "You can talk to me like that all night."

"Good. I thought I'd blown it there, for a second," said Keith.

"Go on," said Laura. She thought this might turn out to be very entertaining.

"Actually, I just wanted to know if you'd let me take you out to dinner," said Keith.

"Tonight?"

"Yeah."

"Oh, I'm sorry, I have plans," said Laura.

Silence. Laura wasn't sure if he didn't believe her, or if he simply wasn't used to getting turned down for anything. Or both.

"Maybe another time," Keith said finally.

"Maybe," said Laura. "Listen, I have to warn you, I'm not one of the bimbos you're probably used to."

"I guess not," said Keith.

Laura kicked herself. She hadn't meant it to sound so mean.

"I'll give you a call later in the week," said Keith. "At the office, of course. We can discuss the Fish and Game meeting."

"Keith . . ."

"It's okay. I'll talk to you later."

Laura hung up and bit her lower lip. She looked over at the cats, who were all staring at her, wondering why her mood had suddenly changed. She wished she could tell them. As Keith probably could. What a day!

She sat down on the floor and called the cats. Celestine was the first one there, and Laura scratched behind her ears.

"Never take a chance," was Laura's motto. She was quite successful at chasing away anyone who might show some interest. Or even worse, someone she might feel some stirrings for. She had just done it again.

The problem was, she still didn't know what she wanted from Keith. He was so very different from anyone she had ever met before. Keith's being a celebrity meant nothing to Laura. Even his charm was something she could easily shrug off, because charming jerks were as common as fifty-pound sewer rats in New York City.

The real attraction hadn't come until their adventure with Sarena. It was actually more curiosity than anything else. The guy somehow had communicated with a mountain lion and then healed its broken leg. Only a really special and enlightened being could pull off something so incredible. Enlightened, or insane. Judging by the way Keith acted not many people knew about this specific talent, and Laura could understand why.

In the old days, public knowledge about such things could have gotten Keith burned as a warlock. What would happen if the public found out now? Keith would still be burned, only in the tabloids instead of at the stake. Ultimately the results would be the same.

What had he done, anyway? Laura still wasn't sure, other than the obvious. He had healed the crushed paw of a ferocious animal, who had peacefully let him do it.

Laura thought this was very scary, as well as irrational. But she also thought it was terrific.

It didn't matter. She had chased him away. It was probably better, she reasoned. Keith Gallatin could have anyone he wanted, and probably did. She had heard the rumors often enough. What would he want with her, anyway? She wasn't built like some of the groupies who had no doubt followed Keith relentlessly. She had no money or prestige. He probably made more money in one week than she might make in her lifetime.

Another conquest, probably. They were easy for him, but Laura probably presented slightly more of a challenge than he might be used to. Only slightly.

After convincing herself she had done the right thing, she stood up and walked over to the refrigerator. She was starved. Instead of opening it up for food, she read the number off of a magnet stuck on the door. She dialed the number and ordered a large (because the cats would want some too) pepperoni-and-mushroom pizza.

She hung up and changed into a sweat suit. She sat on the couch, wrapped an afghan around her, and began reading the new novel her sister had recommended. Fables, Celestine, and Jazz all made themselves comfortable on the afghan, as the four of them waited for the pizza to be delivered.

CHAPTER 21

Grash watched the sunrise over the eastern mountains, with all of his thoughts focused on the great bird. As his fellow tribe members began to stir, he knew it was time for a decision. He also knew it was time to gamble.

Watching the same sunrise was Sarena. Her thoughts, too, were on Lanakila, although they often drifted to the man who had saved her and his curious non-mate.

The man had said there were other pumas. He had seen them with his own eyes. With this there was hope, even though he had said they weren't free. Sarena had thought long and hard about this but couldn't fathom the concept. How could a creature be alive and not be free? Unless they were in a trap, as Sarena had been, but somehow she didn't think that was what Keith had meant. His description of their situation had seemed authoritative.

Her thoughts trailed back to Lanakila. If there were other pumas, then probably there were other ahilas. Lanakila would be happy to hear this, although probably he would appear not to care much. Sarena wondered why he was like that. Until she saw how he'd acted when she was in the trap, she might have thought he didn't care much about anything.

The sun became stronger and Sarena blinked. It was time to be moving on again. Lanakila would find her if she walked in the sunlight. She stretched briefly, then headed north.

Another speech. A whole pack of questioning eyes. Grash was starting to get used to it. He looked them over individually, then scratched abruptly at a flea before deciding to begin.

"As you all know, the puma is dead," Grash began.

This was greeted with a number of positive snorts and pants. For the first time in quite a while, the tribe looked almost festive.

"I don't have to tell you all how much this means to us," Grash continued. "Not only is the Canyon rid of a terrible nemesis, but we are relieved of a terrible burden. At least for now."

"What other burden could be like puma?" asked Broed, who looked quite pleased for the moment. He had obviously spent many hours wondering exactly what his role would have been in the attack of the puma.

"I don't know," said Grash, honestly. "It's true the puma is gone, and we know of no others. But will the krahstas let us off the hook so easily? After all, they have spent much time teaching us the ways of the Canyon, and we did not kill the puma as we agreed to."

"But we would have," said Kroth. "We were all there. We were ready to go. I had devised plans, and everything."

Several of the others huffed agreements.

"And I agree as well," said Grash. "But if there is one thing we have learned from our wild cousins, it is how unpredictable they can be. They may well be happy with the puma's death, and may want nothing more in return."

Grash let the thought hang for a moment.

"What else could they want?" asked Kroth.

"They might want something else," said Grash. "They might want the ahila."

Now the tribe understood. There was something out there the krahstas might want. Only alive this time, not dead. The krahstas could do very well with the help of flying eyes.

"We saw bird first," said Broed.

"Yes," said Grash. "But we're not sure the krahstas want it. Like I said, they may be very happy since the puma's gone. It may not even have occurred to them to go after the bird. After all, as far as we know they've never seen it hunt with the puma like I have."

"So basically," said Kroth, "if we go back to the krahstas, they might cause problems for us."

"But they might not," said Grash.

"Do you still think we can coax the ahila into helping us?" asked Grallus.

"I have no doubt in my mind," said Grash. "All we have to do is find it."

"Do you think it'll go with us if we're hanging around with krahstas?" Kroth asked.

"I don't think anyone would want any part of us if we were hanging around with krahstas," said Grash.

"We not follow krahstas," said Broed.

"I agree, my friend," said Grash. "I think you're absolutely right."

Laura checked her message box, then walked to her desk. She hoped she looked a lot better than she felt. Although all three of the cats had slept soundly through the night, she had not. As a result she was tired and a little cranky.

She had five phone messages, none from anyone she recognized. This wasn't unusual, but this morning she wasn't in the mood to listen to people whom she didn't know pitch story ideas to her.

The only thing she had lined up for the day was a trip back to Encinitas with Dennis Jack. She wasn't sure what time he would call, so she decided to start checking up on Jake Cotter.

She checked her Rolodex and found two names listed as NRA contacts. The first was Cal Travis. Laura had spoken with him numerous times about gun-related stories. As an officer and spokesman for one of the local chapters, he was well versed in all matters related to gun control and where the NRA stood on various issues. The second name in her file was of someone she couldn't remember, so she decided to start with Travis.

Travis owned a business in El Cajon that restored antique airplanes. He was a retired navy pilot who now spent his time laboring on the same types of planes he had flown during World War II. Laura called his office number and was surprised when Cal answered the phone personally.

"Yes, I remember you," said Travis. "An old bastard like me doesn't forget a pretty young thing like you."

"Why, thank you," said Laura, blushing. "That's the nicest thing anyone's said to me in a long time."

"My pleasure," said Travis. "What can I do for you?"

"I met a man the other day whom you might know. His name is Jake Cotter."

"Don't believe I've heard of him," said Travis.

"He says he's with the NRA," said Laura.

"Well, that could be a million people in this state," said Travis. "Let me look him up."

Laura bit her lower lip as she waited for Travis to return to the phone. She liked Travis. He was always very friendly, no matter what the situation. Her request today was simple enough, but there had been times in the past when she had dealt with him in more stressful situations and he had always been polite and strictly down-to-business. His approach was very different from Jake Cotter's.

"Okay, I see his name here," said Travis, picking up the phone. "Been a member for twelve years. Never held office, never tried. Has never represented the NRA officially in any capacity. Pays his dues, and that's about it."

When Laura hung up, she stared at the card Cotter had given her for several seconds. For someone who wasn't an official representative he certainly had a slick, professional-looking card, complete with NRA logo. She hadn't told this to Cal Travis, for fear of tipping both of them off. She had some tracking to do, and the fewer people who knew what she was up to the better. After all, Cotter had told her he and his friends knew how to "really fight."

Where to start? She stared at the card again. She decided it was as good a place as any. She dialed the number and put her thumb on the handle so she could hang up immediately when she heard how the phone was answered. It took two rings.

"Jake's Gun Shop and Taxidermy."

No longer surprised at how strong her left forepaw felt, Sarena walked casually through the brush. She headed north, away from the kribas, krahstas, and trap.

She remained parallel to the sea, which in a strange way still called to her from ten miles away to the west.

She tried not to think about the pumas Keith had spoken of. At least, not specifically. She decided it was best simply to know there was hope of finding others. Keith had left her with the impression it might not be too long before she did. She wasn't sure how he could know, but he had already proven his knowledge of magic by healing her, so she had no reason to doubt he would know of other things as well.

Without thinking, Sarena looked to the sky. Since meeting Lanakila she had become used to his customary presence above, and was constantly glancing skywards to see what he might be up to. There was no visible movement in the cloudless California sky, and Sarena was reminded of the great bird's absence.

Where had he gone? She had been walking openly for most of the day. Normally it would take him only a few minutes to find her once she began to roam.

A startling, gloomy thought struck her: Lanakila believed Sarena was dead. When he had left her she was stuck in an impossible situation, with no hope of escaping alive. Upon her insistence he had reluctantly fled for his life. As far as he was concerned there was no reason for him to return.

Sarena stopped. Lanakila was gone. Her only friend. She stared up at the sky, hoping, but he wasn't there. She bit down hard, then dropped her head to her forepaws.

The warmth she had experienced since meeting Keith was quietly gone. She was alone again. No Lanakila, and no other pumas. Just as it had been for most of her life, now it was only Sarena. She growled in anger at the kribas and krahstas who had forced her in the direction of the trap. She growled in hatred at the man who had set the trap. If she ever had the chance to find him . . .

She shuddered and broke into a quick pant. She thought about Keith and Laura, and how they had saved her. Why had they done it? Why hadn't they killed her, as the man who had set the trap intended? What was it with men anyway? Animals either killed to survive or they didn't. It seemed like men couldn't make up their minds. They obviously killed, and for more reasons than simple food, but apparently not all of them did. Keith and Laura had proven that.

What was the difference? How could someone tell if a particular man was vicious or not? They all looked the same to most animals of the Canyon. Was it something in the strange pelts they wore?

Whatever it was, it made Sarena growl again with frustration. Despite the life-saving experience with Keith and Laura, men could never be trusted. The trap was testimony enough, and even Keith had told her never again to get close to men.

She looked across the open canyon of chaparral. There were man-houses around the edges in almost every direction. Each day they took more and more of the Canyon away. It was no wonder the krahstas were so territorial; there was hardly any territory left. Sadly, Sarena got the uneasy feeling there someday wouldn't be any Canyon left at all.

Completely disgusted, she stood up and began walking again. She gave one last look at the sky before finding her way to a path through the sage. Lanakila was probably better off without her. She had become too much of a liability. It was now painfully clear to her why pumas were meant to walk with other pumas, or walk alone. They were dangerous to be around no matter what the circumstances, even if one was your friend.

Sarena began to wonder about the kribas and krahstas. They too all thought she was dead. Probably they were celebrating at this very moment. Rotten dogs. They wouldn't celebrate for long. Word would get to them quickly enough. News about pumas traveled faster than hina.

Maybe not. Maybe not this time, anyway. If everyone thought she was dead, Sarena might have more room to move than usual. At least for now. She wondered whether a surprise visit to the krahstas might not prove to be entertaining. They probably wouldn't think so.

Sarena thought about the kribas. In the back of her mind she had sensed their presence somewhere, just out of sight, when she was stuck in the trap. Earlier she had thought it was simply part of the delirium she had been experiencing at the time, but now something told her they really had been there.

What would *they* have to say about a surprise visit? Even after everything Lanakila had said about them, they were, after all, only kribas. A simple pack of kribas was no match for a puma. But another voice inside told her this was not a simple pack of ordinary kribas.

She suddenly remembered the dreams. They had been awful, and continuous. They were full of visions of being chased by kribas. She involuntarily shuddered just thinking about them.

Sarena began to walk again, northward, and away from the trap and the kribas and krahstas. No surprise visits today. She would let them have their celebrations, and hopefully soon they would forget about her.

The celebrating had been brief, and it was over. The tribe moved north under the cover of overgrown sage. The sun was high in the south, but not particularly hot. Grash thought it was comfortable for a change. But it wasn't the sun from which they hid; it was unfriendly eyes.

They had learned from their wild cousins how to lope, but as they were in no hurry they walked in disciplined silence. Even their panting was barely audible over the rustle of the dried-out brush, which waved slightly in the autumn breeze.

They stopped for a short rest when they reached a small clearing. Grash directed them to sit or lie down and look skyward. He wanted all eyes searching for the ahila.

How they would get it to land he was not yet certain. The only thing he was positive of was that they had to find it first, before anything else could be done. So far they had seen not a single feather, not since the bird had ditched the dead puma while it was still stuck in the trap.

Grash wondered about the puma. He had seen the man and woman. He knew they had seen the ahila and heard the krahstas. They must have found the puma. If so they probably had killed her immediately. This was good. The puma had done enough suffering, and Grash was glad that she was out of her misery. The only problem was, none of them had heard a gunshot. They all knew guns were not the only way men killed, but in this case it certainly would have been the quickest and safest.

Grash couldn't imagine them walking up to a trapped puma with a knife.

It didn't matter. The puma was dead. If the men hadn't killed her, then obviously she was dead by now from the trauma, anyway. Grash hoped they had killed her.

His thoughts went back to the bird. They had to find it. With the help of the krahstas, they had gotten pretty good at Canyon living. But with the aerial eyes of an ahila they would become powerful beyond belief. Powerful enough to make a lonely puma seem more like a playful kitten.

Yes, they would have power and they would be feared. But first they had to find the bird.

While Grash and Sarena scanned the skies for Lanakila, another set of eyes was staring up into the vast blue as well. They were eyes of gold, cunning, wary, and wise with many seasons of running the Canyon. The eyes quickly dropped to scan the vast expanse of ravine to the south, then turned back to the sky in hopes of spotting an ahila.

Dropno had led the pack of krahstas for more seasons than he could remember. He had seen it all in the Canyon: fires, floods, the constant encroachment of man, and every species of animal imaginable. But nothing had ever been as frightening, no, *disturbing*, as what he had seen the other day.

It was unsettling enough to deal with a puma in the area. The pack had gone through it before, several times, although this was the first time they had seen one die. But even so, the big cats never stayed long anyway, and they were always alone. Always. They were never in the company of other pumas, and certainly never palling around with other animals of a different species.

And then there was the bird itself, Dropno had never seen anything like it. He didn't even know what to call it, other than a big bird. It looked fierce, and Dropno decided that he had done well by not trying to test it.

"Have you seen anything yet?" asked Ponto, the brother of Dropno's mate.

"No," said Dropno, startled at the sudden arrival of his brother. "Is it your turn to watch already?"

"Yes," said Ponto. "You need to rest with the others."

Since the experience with the puma, and the splitting with the tribe of kribas, Dropno had ordered the pack to rotate a sentry during daylight hours while the others slept. Never the type of leader to give an order for something he wouldn't do himself, Dropno took his turn just like everyone else.

"It's hard to rest," said Dropno honestly. "I can't get my mind off that bird. I've never seen anything like it."

"Nor have any of us," said Ponto. "We'll find it."

"Yes, I'm sure. I have a lot of questions for a bird who would be willing to fight and die for a puma."

"What are we going to do about the tribe?" asked Ponto.

"Good riddance," said Dropno, shaking his head.

"Good," said Ponto. "They reeked of something I couldn't describe."

"Yes," said Dropno. "Unfortunately, we may have to follow them for a while."

Ponto said nothing. He had no desire to track those filthy beasts, even though it would be easy enough. Even with all of the training the pack had given the street dogs, they were still noisy and smelly enough to wake up most of the Canyon when they moved.

"I know," said Dropno, reading his brother's eyes. "I have no desire to go near them again either. But there was something in the leader's eyes. Something. I think he knew about the bird, long before we even met up. He had a secret, but I just couldn't figure it out. Now I know."

"Why would he keep the bird a secret?"

"I don't know," said Dropno. "I just don't know. That's why we need to follow the kribas. They might know where it is, or at least how to find it."

"What are we going to do when we find it?" asked Ponto.

"Like I said, ask it some questions," said Dropno. He looked at the sky, then back down to his brother. "But first we're going to make the kriba leader squirm."

Laura stood with Dennis Jack only five feet from where Keith had freed Sarena. She decided it was best, when dealing with anyone other than Keith, to simply leave that part out.

"The trap was right there," she said simply.

"Great," said Dennis, shaking his head with disgust. "They've moved."

"Who?" asked Laura.

"Well, we have to be off the record on this," said Dennis. "I don't want them to know I'm aware of this."

"Okay," said Laura. She wasn't interested in doing another poaching story at the moment anyway. "Just let me be the first to know if you catch someone."

"Of course," said Dennis. "Anyway, they've used traps before, but this is scary because they've never been so far south. I mean, come on, we're really close to houses here. Some kid could have walked right into it."

Laura nodded, wanting to tell him exactly what *had* walked into it, but knew she couldn't.

"Do you guys regulate taxidermy shops?" Laura asked casually.

"They do come under our jurisdiction. Why?"

"Just wondering," said Laura.

"There are very few left in Southern California," said Dennis. "Most of them deal exclusively with fish, these days. There are so few places left to hunt, there just isn't anything left for them to mount."

"Mostly fish?" Laura asked.

"Yeah, sport fishing. You know, deep-sea type stuff?"

Laura nodded. She looked across the open ravine and pursed her lips.

"If you're wondering about the poachers possibly bringing their kills to a taxidermy shop, you can pretty much forget it," said Dennis. "No legitimate shop is gonna touch an out-of-season animal. In fact they'd call us immediately. They have too much to lose otherwise."

"I guess you're probably right," said Laura.

"And like I said, most of their work is fish. They might get a goose or two brought in from Imperial Valley, but even that would be rare."

"Do you hunt?" Laura asked.

"No," said Dennis.

"All of your bosses do," said Laura.

"Oh, you mean the commissioners," said Dennis. "Yeah, they all hunt."

"Does that bother you?" asked Laura.

"A little," said Dennis. "Here it's our job to protect

wildlife, and they go out and shoot it. Actually that doesn't bother me nearly as much as the whole mountain lion mess. I don't know what they're thinking about. I've been in the field for six years now and I've never seen one in my whole life. I don't know where they get the idea there's enough to shoot two hundred and fifty of them."

"You're okay, Dennis," chided Laura. "Even for someone who carries a gun."

"Hey, I carry it, but I wish it was unnecessary," said Dennis. "Hopefully, someday it will be."

CHAPTER 22

Frustrated and bored, Laura chewed on her pen. She was frustrated for several reasons, with boredom as the result. It had been a week since the incident with Sarena, and she was starting to doubt whether it had ever happened at all.

Her investigation into the life and times of Jake Cotter was going nowhere. During the week she'd spent working on him virtually nothing had materialized. He gave Laura the creeps, but there was no dirt on him anywhere. No criminal record, no problems with creditors or taxes, no difficulties with the neighbors. He did exactly what Dennis Jack had said he probably did: sold guns and made trophies out of dead fish.

The attack dog story was dead. They had not been heard from since Laura had last gone up to San Marcos, which, coincidentally, was the same day she had seen Sarena. One whole week, and not a single peep out of six dogs. They had simply vanished. Amazing.

It wasn't just her. The entire town had been dead for a week. In the past Laura had always been able to find something to stick her nose into, even in lean times. But this week was different, which made it worse. She hated tracking down stories that went nowhere.

And speaking of going nowhere, there had been no contact whatsoever with Keith Gallatin. Their last conversation had taken place, strangely enough, one week ago. Laura shook her head at another one chased off.

She glanced at her calendar. Tomorrow was the Fish and Game meeting in Long Beach, the last one before they would make their final decision about the mountain lion hunt. Laura hoped Keith would call at some point today and at least tell her about his plans. She decided she would wait until the afternoon before trying to call him.

The phone rang, and Laura smiled.

"Hi, this is Brad Berglund, from the Mountain Lions Forever organization. Remember me?"

"Oh yes, Brad," said Laura, trying to hide the disappointment in her voice. "How are you?"

"I'm great," said Brad. "Are you going to the meeting tomorrow?"

"Yes, I'll be there. It's at one o'clock, right?"

"Right," said Brad. "Anyway, I'm calling because we expect the Commission to go ahead with the hunt, so we've filed suit in Superior Court up here in San Francisco. We're going to try and beat them in court again."

"This is the third time, isn't it?" Laura asked.

"Yes," said Brad. "We've beaten them twice already. The court has overturned their proposal the past two seasons. Each year they change it a little bit and resubmit it. We should be able to beat this one, too."

"What are you going to do tomorrow?" Laura asked.

"Try to avoid the lawsuit," said Brad. "It's expensive, and you just never know. The court might change its mind one day and let them go ahead. You never know. Tomorrow we're going to plead with the Commission to stop, and avoid all the hassles."

"What do you think the chances are of that?" Laura asked.

"No way," said Brad. "But at least we'll be acting in good faith by trying."

"Have you ever considered a ballot initiative?" Laura asked.

Brad let out a long sigh.

"Yes," he said. "We can't afford one right now. It's so expensive to run a statewide campaign. And the NRA has so much money they'd blow us out of the water."

"Maybe if you worded it to their advantage . . ."

"I know," said Brad. "We still can't afford it."

"We'll talk more tomorrow," said Laura. "Thanks for calling."

"You bet."

Laura hung up and watched Bill Sesma walk toward her with an assignment sheet.

"How's your day going?" asked Bill.

"About like the rest of my life," said Laura. "Nothing's going on."

"I have something for you to check on then, if you don't mind," said Bill.

"Gladly," said Laura. "I'm going crazy trying to get something concrete to go on."

"Well, this may fizzle before you even get there," said Bill.

"Perfect," said Laura.

"It seems as though there may, and I stress *may*, be some sort of huge drug bust going on in Tijuana involving some TJ cops. We haven't been able to confirm anything at all."

"How did we hear?" asked Laura.

"Well, we know there was a bust," said Bill. "One of our sources at DEA tipped us. He had heard a rumor about it involving cops, but he couldn't be sure. He's checking for us now. If you can just start heading down there we might be able to let you know one way or the other before you cross the border."

"Aren't there any Spanish-speakers available?" Laura asked doubtfully.

"No," said Bill. "We thought of that first. Everyone's out on something else. You should be all right, though. All of the TJ cops speak English."

"Do you want me to pursue it if there are no cops involved?"

"No," said Bill. "Hopefully we'll be able to let you know, so if there aren't any cops you can just turn around before you get down there."

"Okay," said Laura.

Bill walked away and Laura shook her head. She hated not being able to speak a foreign language. She felt like an idiot every time she was sent into Mexico. She had begun to put her notebook into her purse when the phone rang.

"Hi, it's Keith Gallatin. Remember me?"

"No. Should I?" asked Laura. Her smile was broad but she tried not to sound excited.

"I guess not," said Keith. "How are you?"

"I'm fine," she said. "Haven't heard from you for a while."

"I didn't think you wanted to," said Keith. "That's why I'm calling you at the office. And strictly for business purposes."

"I hoped you would call today," said Laura. "But you know what? I have to go out on a story right now. They're sending me to TJ for some drug bust that might involve cops. I'll have to call you back. Are you going to be around? I can call you from my car phone."

"Yeah," said Keith. "I don't have anything going on today. Was it Mexican cops or American cops?"

"Mexican, I think," said Laura. "I hate going down there on stories. Especially when they send me alone. I can't speak Spanish, so I feel like a jerk. It makes it almost impossible to find anything out."

"I speak Spanish," said Keith. "You want me to go with you?"

Caught off guard, Laura sat with her mouth open, trying to respond.

"Well?" Keith asked. "It's no problem. I don't have anything to do today anyway. And besides, it would be nice to see you again."

"You speak Spanish?" Laura asked, still surprised.

"Yes," said Keith, in a long and drawn-out manner.

"Of course, how stupid of me," said Laura. "Anyone who can communicate with animals can probably speak just about any language on earth."

"Probably," said Keith. "Do you want me to go, or not?"

"Sure," said Laura. "That would be great."

After a successful morning of hunting hina, the tribe sat resting in the shade of some scrub oak and a holly tree. They were starting to look a little dirty from so long in the Canyon, but otherwise, Grash noted, they looked fine.

"When we find bird?" Broed asked, abruptly.

"I don't know," said Grash. "Soon. I think it's near."

"Me too," said Kroth. "At first, I wondered why we going this direction. I thought we should stick near the trap, and hope the bird would come back to check on the puma. But now, I'm glad we left."

Grash nodded. He was always glad when someone, especially Kroth, publicly agreed with his decisions. He had been beginning to wonder about the wisdom of their flight himself, until early yesterday, when an unidentifiable feeling got stronger and stronger the farther north they went. Whatever it was, Kroth apparently noticed it, too.

"I think we should find a road to prowl on for a while," said Roashas.

"Why?" asked Grash. "We've been doing fine in the Canyon."

"I know we're eating well, but that's not what I meant," said Roashas. "And you guys are great company. But personally, I'd like to run with some bitches for a while. Not long. Maybe one night. Maybe even less . . ."

Grallus was quick to jump to the support of Roashas.

"It's nothing personal," said Grallus. "You guys are the best friends anyone could have. But to tell you the truth, a visit to a friendly street might make us all a little happier."

All of the tribe members grunted agreement, except for Grash. He looked across all of their expectant faces, which were wide-eyed with wild thoughts. Grash knew they would follow him without question if he chose to stay in the Canyon, but also understood the potential for disaster if he led an unhappy and frustrated tribe.

Personally, Grash wanted to visit the street as well. Even with the company of the tribe, he found himself becoming lonely. But it was bad timing for distractions like bitches and visiting the street. Something inside warned against it. He wanted to wait until after they had found the ahila but knew it would be a tough argument, since no one had seen the bird since it left the puma over a week ago.

"What are your thoughts, Grash?" asked Kroth. "You look distressed."

"I would like to find the bird first, my friends," said Grash. This was greeted by an array of downtrodden faces. "But I suppose one night of romping wouldn't hurt any."

The tribe members all began to pant and smile. Although Grash still thought better of it, one night probably would be harmless enough, if they were careful about it. He would have to confer with Kroth about a plan.

"We need to find some streets, first," said Grash. "We haven't seen any for a couple of days. I think we'll continue the direction we're going for now, and as soon as we find some houses Kroth and I will plan a raid. Only this time it won't be sheep we're after."

As far as Sarena was concerned, it was time to do what cats do best. She found a soft cushion of dry grass and molded herself into it comfortably. The sky was clear and the sun was the perfect temperature for sleeping in. Sarena closed her eyes and felt it caress her face.

Spiritually, she was almost all of the way back to where she had been before Lanakila had come into her life. She was lonely, depressed, and on the move. Moving again, and probably going nowhere.

Her whiskers twitched and she sneezed. She hoped she would be asleep soon.

Where could he have gone? Sarena had kept her eyes to the sky as much as possible since he had left, but there was nothing up there. She had been careful to avoid most Canyon eyes since she had left the trap, but eyes from above would have had no trouble finding her.

Lanakila still thought she was dead. Sarena had to keep reminding herself. There was no reason for him to be looking for her, or even to be in the area. So, realistically, as far as a meeting with Lanakila was concerned, she might as well be dead.

Sleep approached. Thankfully, the dreams had stopped. At least the bad ones about the dogs. There were some strange ones, but she could never fully remember them after she had woken up. In the parts she could remember, she had always been alone.

Sleep was the only place left where the loneliness didn't hurt as much. She missed Lanakila.

Laura met Keith at the same fast-food restaurant she had before. This time she was looking for the disguise and spotted him immediately. She wondered how both times he had managed to get there so quickly, but then realized she had no idea where he lived or where he might be coming from.

Keith climbed into her RX-7, and she was glad she had cleaned it up. She had even taken it into a shop, so thankfully it was running smoother. She pulled on her seat belt and pulled out toward the freeway.

"It's good to see you," said Keith. "You look great."

"Thanks," said Laura. "But I'll bet you say that to all the girls."

"No, I mean it. Why do you say that?"

"Never mind, it's an inside joke," said Laura. "And by the way, you look pretty cute yourself. Even with the disguise."

Laura pulled onto 805 and drove south toward the border.

"So tell me about your plans for tomorrow," said Laura, trying not to smile too much. Not only was she happy to see him, but despite everything they'd been through in such a short time, it was still pretty cool to be driving around with a rock star.

"We called all the local and LA media," said Keith. "We gave them a rundown of people who'll be there. Pretty big-name celebs. Even me, ha-ha. A lot of basketball players, of course, and some other sports people. Should be interesting."

"Have you told the Mountain Lions Forever people?" Laura asked. "They're gonna be there, too."

"No, we haven't contacted them. I guess we should have. I'll have someone from my office get to them this afternoon. The last thing we want is those bozos making a scene and wrecking everything."

"Maybe you should get there early tomorrow and make sure you're the first speaker."

"Good idea," said Keith. "We'll be driving up early anyway. Say, you wanna go with me? We can ride in the limo together."

"I'll have to think about it," said Laura. "I don't want to give anyone the impression I'm biased on this story."

"Aren't you?"

"Doesn't matter if I am or not," said Laura. "I can never appear to be, either by my actions or the way I present the story."

"Spoken like a true journalist," said Keith. "But it seems to me it would be awfully hard to keep your own feelings out of every story. Especially one like this."

"Much easier than you think. Especially when you've been doing it a while. You simply say, 'There was a meeting. Person A said this, Person B countered by saying this, and the meeting ended with the Commission doing whatever.' "

"Ah, formulated journalism," said Keith.

"No. Well, maybe. Call it what you want, but at least it's fair. No one ever thinks it is, because no one thinks it's fair that you give the other guys equal time."

"By the way, what's the story we're going on again?" asked Keith, as they approached the border.

"I'll explain in a minute," said Laura. "I'd hoped the desk would have called by now."

Laura slowed the car down as they pulled up to a Mexican customs agent, who waved them through while he talked with one of his buddies. Laura's car never slowed below ten miles per hour.

She turned the car into the lane leading to "Centro," and began the large circle leading to the main drag of downtown Tijuana. Halfway into the sharpest part of the curve, her cellular phone rang.

"Laura, it's Sesma."

"Hi, what's the scoop?"

"Nothing. Come on back."

"Oh, thanks," said Laura. "Now that I've crossed the border. What happened?"

"Bad information," said Sesma. "We finally got it straight. I'm sorry. We got it as soon as we could. How long's the line coming back?"

"Long," said Laura. Actually, she hadn't even noticed.

"Sorry," said Bill. "I guess I'll see you this afternoon."

"See ya," said Laura, and hung up. "Well, we're off the hook," said Laura.

"Good," said Keith. "I didn't feel like working anyway. Do we have to go straight back?"

"No," said Laura. "We have all day. Wanna cruise TJ?"

"Sounds good to me," said Keith.

CHAPTER 23

When the sun found a cloud to hide behind, Sarena noticed the change and woke up. It was late afternoon, and she began to stretch and then claw at the trunk of a thick manzanita bush. Even with the sun behind a cloud the sky was still bright, and Sarena blinked several times before she had gotten used to being awake.

After several minutes of grooming she stood up and began walking up the side of the ravine she had been resting in. The brush was sparse over much of the top, which Sarena suspected was the result of a fire. If so it was more than two seasons past, since there was no trace of black on the ground.

At the top of the ridge she stopped and looked to the west. There below her, only a short distance away, was a road and several man-dwellings. She was startled at how close they were, since she had slept openly on the other side of the ridge. She decided caution was far more important than Lanakila's finding her when she slept, since Lanakila would never find her if someone from the man-dwellings did first.

She stared down at the houses for several minutes. The concept of living in one confined place was impossible for her to understand. She wondered what the men were afraid of, that they'd build such things to live in. Obviously they were afraid to live out in the open like other animals. What animal on earth would attack a man? None Sarena was aware of. She wondered if the men were afraid of each other.

Two children played in the street. Sarena could see them clearly as they rolled around a small spherical object. She felt secure enough, since she stood between two bushes thick enough to break her outline. The wind was light and in her face, so her scent was not a problem.

Watching the two little ones play was fascinating. They looked like any of the various cubs Sarena had seen playing in the Canyon. They were so vulnerable, yet they had no concerns in the world. Sarena wondered where there mother was, and what she might say if she found out her cubs were being watched by a puma. She probably wouldn't be too happy, even though a puma would never attack a man except in self-defense.

Sarena tensed up when an adult walked out and began talking to the two little ones. She strained her ears, hoping to hear some of the human speech. The only time she had ever heard it was when Keith spoke to Laura, and it had sounded strange and unnatural. Sarena wondered if they all spoke the same way.

They were too far away to hear clearly, and Sarena dared not go any closer. The adult picked up the two youngsters and carried them out of sight, presumably into one of the houses.

Sarena watched for quite a while, but they did not return. She thought about the little ones, and how their mother probably took them for granted. It was easy for them—there were so many of them. Sarena wondered if she would ever have cubs. She closed her eyes, then walked back into the Canyon.

When the tribe discovered the houses and the road an hour later, they were standing a mere fifty yards from where Sarena had stood watching the children play. Either they were too excited about the discovery to notice the smell of puma or, by some chance, Sarena's scent had somehow vanished on the breeze. Had it not, the tribe possibly would have been tempted to follow it, and would have stumbled upon a sleeping puma in a tuft of dry grass on the other side of the ridge.

Instead they looked down at the houses as a group, with only one thought passing between them.

"We need a plan," said Kroth.

"Agreed," said Grash. "Let's fall back into the brush and talk about it. I don't like all of us being out in the open like this."

They marched through the chaparral the way they had come and formed a small circle in the center of a small break in the sage. Dusk was still an hour away from reaching the Canyon, and everyone panted nervously. They had not charged the street for any reason in several weeks.

"We shouldn't all go at once," Grash started. "I mean we can, but if so we go separate ways. I don't want us running around as a group. If we're alone we'll go unnoticed. But together the men will recognize us and bring out their guns."

"How about a plan, like you suggested?" Kroth asked. "We'll hit the street the same way we would if it were a hunting operation. Then we'll scatter, and it's every kriba for himself."

This was greeted by grunts of approval from all of the tribe members. Although most of them had never been anywhere near a female under ideal circumstances, all of them had felt the desires. Later on tonight, hopefully, they would all experience an answer to the strange callings that tugged at their bodies.

"Ideas?" Grash asked. He knew Kroth already had it figured out.

"I'll go first," said Kroth. "Just as if it were an attack. I'll make a quick assessment while it's light, then return with the details. I'll make sure everyone knows where to go and where to meet when we're done. You can decide the time frame when I'm gone."

"Sounds good," said Grash. "We'll be here."

"I'm going to go a different route this time," said Kroth. "Just in case someone saw us on the ridge. I'm going to head a little farther up the ridge before I turn back and go down the slope. It'll be an easier climb from there, anyway."

"Good luck," said Grash.

After walking through several shops on Avenida Revolucion, the main strip in downtown Tijuana, Laura and Keith decided to turn down one of the smaller side streets. They had seen enough skulls with Nazi helmets, plaster elephants, and black suede paintings of Elvis to make Laura want to gag. She hoped Keith would want to leave soon, although she was really enjoying his company.

"So, how do you manage to have enough time to cruise Tijuana?" Laura asked.

"I don't," said Keith, as they walked past yet another liquor store. "I should be working."

"Doing what?" asked Laura. "What do you do, exactly, when you're not making records?"

"Making records takes an astronomical amount of time," said Keith.

"Okay," said Laura. "But you do more. What else?"

"There's so much," said Keith. "Danielle handles the music end and the studio, which leaves me with the TV and radio station, and the Pumas. I also do the public relations and charity coordination."

"You run all of these things yourself?" Laura asked.

"No. I hire the people to run them and let them take care of themselves. They do much better that way. Especially the basketball team. There's nothing worse than a meddling owner to screw up a good franchise."

"Then what do you do?" Laura persisted. "You still haven't answered my question."

"Each one is a full-time job," said Keith. "Just handling the PR for Gallatins is a nightmare. Everyone's a critic. Right now we're working on another album for the beginning of the year.

"Then there's the team. Dealing with the other owners is like dealing with quicksand. They're a bunch of senile old farts who don't like having to put up with a loud-mouthed rock star."

"Then if you're so busy, why are you here?" asked Laura.

"Because I'm so busy," said Keith. "I have to force myself to take a break every now and then, and I thought spending an afternoon with you in a foreign country might be fun."

A small Mexican boy approached them with a box of Chiclets, hoping for a sale. Laura began to reach into her purse, but Keith snapped at the boy in Spanish and began what looked like a lecture. The kid turned around and walked away.

"What?" Laura asked. "I usually give the kids here money. They don't have anything."

"And they won't get anything that way," said Keith. "He's being exploited, either by his parents or some shopkeeper along the strip. I told him to stop begging and go to school. It's his only chance."

Laura looked down the street at the kid, who was going after another potential sale. She looked back at Keith, who was shaking his head.

"It's not what you think," he said. "There are other ways. Better ways. Encouraging children to drop out of school and become beggars is not the answer."

The atmosphere between them thickened and Laura bit her lip. He was probably right, if there was a right answer. She decided she would slip the kid a dollar anyway when Keith wasn't looking, if she got the chance. She turned around when Keith did and they began to walk again, away from the strip.

They both stopped immediately when they saw a stuffed hawk in the window of a store they were passing. Laura looked at Keith, who was staring at the bird with obvious contempt.

"Let's go in," he said, and walked straight in the door.

Laura followed and was instantly sorry. It was a taxidermy shop.

There were stuffed animals of every description; some Laura had never seen before. Most were small, rodent-looking types. They were everywhere, lining the walls of the cramped, tiny shop. Laura looked back up at the hawk, who was perched majestically in the window, staring through plastic eyes.

"Good day," said the man in the store, who obviously was pleased to have well-dressed Americans inside his shop. "Please, look around."

Laura wanted to storm out, but Keith seemed interested. He ignored the smaller animals and kept staring back and forth between the hawk and a small coyote who was standing in the corner.

"I see you like the predators," said the shop owner, who looked to be about forty-five and had oily black hair and a thick mustache. He was very small; shorter than Laura, who was five foot six.

Keith gave only a shrug for an answer.

"If you'd like, I can show you some of my special collection," said the owner. "Please, come this way."

"I'd like that," Keith said, nodding, and followed the man into the back of the small store. Laura had no desire to follow, but her instincts were ringing an internal alarm of major magnitude.

Once in the back the store owner pushed back a curtain with a wink. Laura and Keith looked down at his special collection.

Spread out on the floor were the full pelts of six large cats. Four of them were orange with spots, and two were solid tan. Laura bit down on her lip hard, trying not to gasp.

"These are jaguars from South America," the owner said with pride. "Full size, all of them. The other two are puma."

Laura glanced up at Keith, who was staring down at the furs.

"Are the pumas from South America?" asked Keith.

"No, my friend," said the owner. "They are from north of the border."

"North?" Laura asked.

"Yes," said the owner. "I get them from a friend in America."

"How much?" asked Keith.

"For you, my friend, two hundred dollars," the owner announced, beaming.

Keith looked at the ceiling, then grabbed Laura's wrist. He turned quickly and began to lead her to the front of the store.

"Wait! One-fifty!" the owner yelled, not understanding the situation.

Keith never turned back and neither did Laura, although she did hear the owner shout, "One twenty-five!"

They walked quickly back onto Revolucion and headed straight for the Woolworth's parking lot, where Laura's car was parked.

"We could have talked him down to fifty," Keith said, shaking his head as he walked. "Fifty bucks for a puma pelt, or a jaguar pelt."

He still had a tight grip on Laura's wrist. She didn't

know what to say, although she was very interested in finding out who the owner's friend in America was who supplied him with mountain lion pelts. She looked closely at Keith, who now had large tears welling in his eyes.

CHAPTER 24

She heard the barking and started to run. It was close. Very close. The smell was all around her. She raced for higher ground, hoping to find an advantage. She took only two strides before she fell, landing hard in a patch of rye grass. She blinked twice, while panting hard.

Sarena woke up.

The bad dreams were back. There hadn't been any since meeting Keith and Laura, and this one was awful. They had never been this believable before. She began to stretch, hoping to shake off the dream, but her fur began to rise and she found herself instantly on her feet. It was real.

Her head cleared immediately. She crouched back to the ground and flexed her claws, while trying to assess the situation. Her fur stood straight up on her back, and her tail fluffed as fully as it could.

There was loud, frantic barking, and the powerful smell of kriba. It was very close, and getting closer. Sarena couldn't see anything through the brush so she remained motionless in the grass, completely prepared to attack or run.

She heard its steps, clumsy and loud. The scent was clear. There was only one. It continued toward her and Sarena coiled to strike. If there was only one, it was dead kriba meat.

It hesitated, still barking. Judging by the voice and its weight on the brush, it was quite large for a kriba. It growled with a deep, throaty snarl and Sarena heard teeth clap together.

Suddenly the brush snapped an a large black kriba burst into the small clearing where Sarena hid. It saw her

189

and erupted into a wild frenzy of barking and growling. It had huge white teeth and it showed all of them off with each snarl.

Sarena stood. It was terrified, and she knew it. She also knew the barks were not entirely intended to scare her off, since the kriba obviously knew it had no chance. It seemed to be calling for help in a language Sarena couldn't understand.

She took a step closer and the kriba crouched, still barking with insane fear. It snapped toward her, letting Sarena know his teeth could do serious damage. Sarena smiled inwardly, knowing there would be no damage done to her.

Her ears pricked up. From a distance she could hear other kribas answering faintly. They had heard their friend. Her attacker heard them as well, as he grew silent for a moment before launching into another volley of barks even wilder than those before.

Sarena held her ground but knew she had to act. The others were not very far away, and could close ground faster than Sarena felt comfortable with. She looked at the animal only a few strides from her, who was jumping from side to side and growling, with froth falling from both sides of his mouth.

She jumped. She landed quickly and stopped, feigning a move to her left. The kriba vaulted straight at her with his jaws open, but she was beside him and struck the left side of his head with her powerful right forepaw while he was still airborne. He twisted in the air and landed hard on his right shoulder. Sarena was on him instantly. She sank her teeth into the back of his neck and squeezed down, while sinking her claws into the soft of his underbelly. His howl was loud but short, as she jerked on his neck and snapped it clean.

Sarena held her grip for a moment just to make sure, but the kriba did not move. She let go and stepped back, then looked down at the fallen animal. Despite its size and strength it had gone down easily, but there were others on the way. Sarena could hear their barks getting louder. One had been easy, but several could be a serious problem. She turned and ran east into the thickest of the chaparral.

*   *   *

Grash ran as hard as he could. The others were behind him, barking and unable to keep up. Grash remained silent, listening for Kroth, who had become mute. But his scent was very loud and Grash followed it, almost step-for-step in the path Kroth had taken.

The tribe was almost there and still there was no sound from Kroth. After hearing his sudden outburst of threats and shouts for help, the tribe had broken into a charge. But his barks had been short-lived, and this made Grash nervous.

Grash stopped with a shudder the instant it hit him, as did the others when they caught up to him. It was the scent of puma, and it was coming from the same direction as the scent of Kroth.

Barking a quick order, Grash formed the tribe into a tight formation. Broed walked to the rear, with all the others watching to the sides. Grash stared straight ahead as they began slowly and quietly toward the scent. Grash was certain the puma was gone but was taking no chances.

Despite all of the training with the krahstas, it seemed as if every step crashed like thunder. Grash bit down hard, being reminded with each snapped twig of how out of place the tribe was in the Canyon. Out of place or not, the tribe, as a group, was still a formidable opponent to anyone. Even a puma.

The scent got stronger and Grash's back began to shake involuntarily. He dared not look at the others lest they notice, even though he figured they were all reacting the same way. No wonder Kroth had sounded so desperate.

Somehow Grash was not surprised when they found him. Kroth's head was twisted and bleeding. His mouth was open and his eyes stared out into nothing. There was a huge hole where his insides had been ripped open. A broken body of Kroth, but fortunately, no puma.

The tribe didn't move. They panted hard and shook a little bit but everyone held their ground, with their eyes on the corpse.

This was bad. Grash stared at his second-in-command and silently asked his dead friend for advice. He stared and stared but received no answer. Grash turned his eyes to the stars.

What now? Their chief strategist was gone, and their number now was five. How would they survive? How close was the puma, and how many more were there out there?

Grash had no answers as these questions raced through his mind. He wondered what the others were thinking but was afraid to ask. He decided they were probably asking themselves the same questions. They also probably were wondering about his ability to be a leader.

Broed stepped away from the group and walked over to the carcass of their friend. He sniffed the body for several seconds, then glanced in the direction of the scent left by the killer.

"We get puma," Broed said finally.

Sarena could go no farther without a rest. She wondered if Lady Farri's great mistake would lead to her demise. She found a large growth of red shank for cover and curled up underneath. She closed her eyes and wondered how many other cats might have fallen over the years due to lack of sleep.

She twisted slightly, trying to get comfortable, only to break into a spontaneous shudder. She opened her eyes and began panting again.

The dreams were real. They had been a warning from Lady Farri, and now the kribas were here. She had heard them, smelled them, and even killed one of them. And there were more.

There was something wrong, though. For some reason she had always gotten the impression the dreams had another meaning. She thought, anyway, the kribas were being pushed by a force beyond the Canyon. The kribas, after all, were not of the Canyon themselves. This seemed different.

Sarena rolled over and gritted her teeth. The kriba she had faced, even though she had killed it quickly, had been much larger and stronger than she would have guessed. Were the others bigger? How many of them were there? Together, a pack of them equal in size to the one she had met could do her serious damage. If confronted, she would have to run.

She thought about the dreams again. Something about them told her running would be her downfall. She thought about it and then understood. She had seen untold packs of krahstas run all night in the Canyon without stop. She would have to assume their domestic cousins could do the same. If so they could easily run her until she collapsed, since she had little endurance when it came to running any distance.

Where were they now? Why hadn't they chased her? Were there too few of them to confront a puma? Were they smaller than the one she had met? What if they came for her while she slept?

Too many questions, and Sarena had no answers. The only thing she knew for certain was she needed sleep. She tried to close her eyes again but her entire body shook. She was too nervous even to try. They were out there, somewhere.

Sarena stood up and began to pace. She was being tormented by an emotion she had never before experienced. Although she had seen it countless times in the eyes of animals she had preyed upon, she had never before known fear.

Gazing up into the star-licked sky, she looked for Lady Farri's face. She needed guidance, and she knew the Lady would be desperate to help. There were too few pumas left for the great queen to allow one to fall so needlessly.

She suddenly remembered the chain around her neck. Keith had told her to touch it with her wounded paw anytime she needed help. She instantly sat down and lifted her left forepaw to her throat. She momentarily feared it might have been lost in the battle with the kriba, but was relieved to find it beneath a lock of fur.

Everything changed. The tension and fear melted away immediately. She involuntarily let out a gasp and collapsed onto a bed of crumbled brush. She was panting again, but from relief this time, as though an immense weight had fallen from her shoulders. She looked up again and saw a star moving across the sky to the north. She took this as the sign from Lady Farri, and decided to follow it as soon as she woke up. She fell asleep at once.

CHAPTER 25

Against her better judgment, Laura climbed into the limousine of Keith Gallatin. She was followed in by Randy Schock, Keith's bodyguard, and then by Jim Simon, a Gallatin attorney. Keith was outside talking to someone else whom Laura didn't know.

"I'm glad you're going with us," said Randy. He was very tall and slender, with light skin and long blond hair. Dressed in a conservative blue pin-striped business suit, he didn't look anything like a bodyguard, but Keith had told her Randy was a black belt in Chinese *kenpo* and a local heavyweight kick-fight champion. "Keith's told me so much about you."

"Oh, he has?" Laura asked. "I'll bet."

"Only good things," Randy responded with a smile.

Laura nodded and smiled. Randy seemed very friendly, another trait not often associated with bodyguards. Keith had told her he'd hired Randy for those very reasons. Keith leaned over and climbed in, taking a seat next to Laura.

"This'll be great," said Keith. "I'm psyched."

"He rehearsed his speech all night," said Randy.

"Shhh," said Keith, putting his finger to his lips. "You weren't supposed to tell."

The limo began to move forward and Laura looked around the interior of the huge vehicle. She tried to show a poker face, as she was again reminded of how wealthy Keith really was, and of how meager her earnings were in comparison.

Before she had gotten in she had seen the personalized plates, which read KDG. Laura correctly assumed it to mean "Keith and Danielle Gallatin." Danielle's personal

194

limo had a similar inscription, only with the "D" listed first.

The inside was phenomenal. The stereo equipment alone must have cost a fortune. There was a bar, a TV set, and all of the other accommodations normally found in expensive rent-a-limos, only more elaborate. An acoustic guitar was propped up in the rear corner.

The attorney sat quietly and looked over papers while Keith and Randy continued to joke around and insult each other. Laura reached for her purse to get her note pad, but then decided against it. She would have plenty of time for note-taking later, since Long Beach, the southernmost city in Los Angeles County, was an hour and a half away. Better to sit back and enjoy the ride for a while.

It was hard to get used to seeing Keith as Keith Gallatin. There was no disguise today, although he looked unusual in a business suit and with his long brown hair combed back. Laura began to laugh at how strange everything seemed.

"What bringeth the giggles?" Keith asked.

"You," said Laura. "Ya know, I've never seen you in person, looking like you're supposed to look."

"And just how am I supposed to look?" Keith asked.

"Well, like Keith Gallatin," Laura said with a laugh. "Every time I've seen you you've either been in disguise or dressed like a conservative business man."

"Yeah, I guess so. It really is me, though."

"Sing her a song," said Randy. "Then she'll believe you."

"Yeah," said Laura. "Sing me a song."

"Let me put my earplugs in first, though," said Randy.

"We're gonna drop you off at a turkey farm if you don't shut up," said Keith to Randy.

"Come on," said Laura. "I'd love to hear you sing."

"Okay," said Keith, reaching over for the guitar. "I wanted to play one for you, anyway. I wrote it last night. It's called . . . Well, I'll tell you what it's called later."

Keith quietly began to tune the guitar, cocking his left ear closer to the strings, while looking at Laura.

"It's a good song, but I haven't decided how it's going to sound yet," said Keith, still working on the tune. "It's not a fast-paced dancer like we usually do. It's more of a ballad. Maybe we'll do a nice piano riff instead of the synthesizers we normally use. A little guitar. I really like the piano. It's a shame it's not real popular right now, 'cause it's my favorite instrument."

"Don't you normally play lead guitar?" asked Laura.

"For videos and for concerts, yes," said Keith. "But I play all sorts of things on the albums. I even play things that aren't real instruments. They just sound good. But when I write songs they're usually on the piano. I'd play one for you now, but we haven't been able to figure out how to get one into the car."

Laura smiled, and then her eyes widened with surprise as Keith began to strum at the guitar. She really hadn't expected him to sing for her. He seemed to be getting his fingers warmed up at first, but then settled into a specific rhythm. After a few chords he began to sing.

> Well, you were there,
> And you were hurting badly.
> It broke my heart to see your eyes.
> Your painful stare,
> And loss of hope around you.
> You must have heard your share of lies.
>
> Well, now I'm here,
> And still they try to hurt you.
> We'll need some strength to see this through.
> You let me near,
> And forced my eyes to open.
> I'd give it all to be with you.
>
> So hold your head up,
> And smile with me.
> We'll work together,
> And we'll be free."

Keith finished it off with a few more chords, then leaned over and put his elbows on the guitar. He looked up at Laura, who was too stunned to respond. She couldn't believe he would write something so obvious and then sing it to her in front of other people.

"We start recording tomorrow," said Keith casually. He seemed as nervous as Laura. "What do you think?"

"It's beautiful," said Laura. It was so direct and personal, she didn't know what else to say. She had never been serenaded by a rock star before. Or anyone else, for that matter.

"I talked to Danielle about it for a long time last night," said Keith. "I'm gonna be the one who sings it. Since the album won't be coming out for quite a while, we're going to release it as a single on its own."

Laura nodded then glanced at Randy, who was staring at her, but immediately looked away. The lawyer, whose name she had already forgotten, had never looked up from his notes.

She looked back at Keith, who was strumming at the guitar again and acting rather nonchalant. He was looking down at his fingers as he played nothing in particular.

"We do that, every now and then," said Keith.

"What?" asked Laura.

"Release a song without an album, if it's something close to our heart. We often go through spells where we're experiencing similar emotional ordeals. Right now is one of them. This song sorta sums up how we're feeling about certain things, so we're gonna go with it. We usually have our best luck when we're in sync like this."

"What's it called?" Laura asked.

" 'Sarena's Song,' " said Keith.

Grash was not particularly thrilled with the prospect of tracking a puma, but the tribe seemed bent on it. At least what was left of the tribe. There were only five of them now.

The puma would be easy enough to find. Its scent was strong and scarlet, and very close. The tribe would have no problem chasing it down, once they were ready. But before taking on such a task they would need to be fully rested and well fed.

Grash stopped them amidst a small thicket of greasewood. They had walked in silence all day, keeping on the outer perimeter of the puma scent. Grash believed the great cat was awfully careless, since it hadn't seemed to move in quite some time. It never occurred to him that his foe might actually be sleeping.

"Are we ready to eat?" asked Grash, who received a chorus of affirmative barks in response. None of them had eaten since the fall of Kroth.

"It's early," said Grash, "but maybe some hina will be about." They had all but given up the prospect of catching an alleen. The tribe's heavy steps just couldn't be softened, no matter how much the krahstas had barked at them.

"I've been thinking," said Grallus.

"Yes?" asked Grash. Grallus wasn't usually one to do anything but follow orders. He rarely spoke up.

"I don't think we should chase the hina today," said Grallus. "I mean, we can if we don't find anything else. But I think, since we're going to be fighting a puma soon, we ought to be getting ready."

"How do you mean?" asked Grash.

"We should go after something that can fight back," said Grallus. "We need to prepare ourselves for a nasty fight."

"I agree," said Roashas, the other black shepherd, and Grash was not surprised. Grallus and Roashas, besides looking identical, were as close as any two brothers could be.

"It makes sense," said Bruether, now the lone Doberman in the group. "We haven't actually fought anything since we've been in the Canyon. All we've done is chase goats and hina."

"We're probably out of shape," said Grallus. "A good fight will do us wonders."

Grash looked at Broed, the pit bull, who said nothing. Grash figured the bull wasn't smart enough to care one way or the other.

"Okay, you've all been in the Canyon for quite a while now," said Grash. "What do you propose that we attack that can fight back? I hope you're not thinking of going after the krahstas?"

"No," said Grallus, "although I'd dearly love to chew on a few of their hides." Grallus, of all the tribe members, had been treated with the least respect by their wild cousins. "I was thinking of maybe going after another kriba. One on the street."

This brought a heavy silence to the group. Their first major disaster had been the result of an attempt to take the animal of a man. And their most recent misfortune, the loss of Kroth, had taken place during the planning stages of another raid, albeit for reasons other than food.

"Don't you think we've had enough problems there already?" Grash asked, finally.

"Haven't you forgotten our original objective?" Grallus asked. "We were supposed to get strong enough to go back to where we're from. Don't you remember the cage-master? Don't you remember how badly we all wanted to rip him apart? We're never going to get there if we're too afraid to attack some pet kriba on the street."

Grash had forgotten all about the cage-master. The prison master, really. So much had passed since then. It seemed like an entirely different lifetime. Grash doubted they would ever come within miles of their old home again.

"And what else is there to attack?" asked Roashas. "There's nothing in the Canyon, other than the puma itself. We should be a lot more prepared before we try to take on that monster."

"Okay," said Grash. "We'll do it. It's against my better judgment, but you're definitely right about being prepared. None of us have fought anything in quite a while. Except Kroth, and we all know what happened to him."

This last statement brought the tribe to silence again. Grash had no desire to go after the puma, but it was obvious the others did. To keep them together he would have to keep them happy, even if it left them all dead, which was the guaranteed alternative should they fight amongst themselves and break apart.

"Let's go then," said Bruether. "I'm hungry."

Sarena opened her eyes. She could sense movement a fair distance away. It was nothing she could see or hear, only an internal tingling. It was the movement of an enemy, she was sure. One who had just made an important decision concerning her.

She stood up and stretched, then looked around. Nothing moved anywhere near the scrub oak where she stood.

The rest had been peaceful. No nasty dreams or disturbances of any kind. The kribas obviously had chosen to go some other direction and not chase her. Probably they had seen their friend, and decided against ending up in a similar situation.

She stretched again. It seemed as though she must

have been asleep for quite some time, because she felt
very relaxed. She looked up into the bright blue sky,
then remembered the moving star she had seen before
she slept. Without hesitation she turned north and began
walking.

Without Kroth, the tribe no longer had an attack coordinator. Grash decided they would face the street as a
group this time and see how they fared. They climbed
up a slope toward the street, which was already a disad-
vantage. They had no idea what they would be walking
into, which was very bad.

When they finally broke through the brush, there were
two houses with open yards meeting the edge of the Canyon. Once on level ground the tribe immediately could
tell there were no other kribas around. Grash barked an
order and they ran together as a group between the two
houses and toward the road.

With Grash in the lead they hit the street at a moderate stride. To the leader it was refreshing to have pave-
ment under his paws again. He could hear the clicking
of extended claws hitting the blacktop.

There were no men within view, so Grash turned to
the right and began trotting up the sidewalk. They had
passed three houses when the scent hit them. It was
unmistakable and it was in the yard behind the house
before them. It was domestic kriba.

Grash turned to his right again. He motioned for
Bruether to follow him to the left, with Grallus and
Roashas taking the right. Broed would stay in the front
yard for security. Grash ran along the side of the house,
hoping the backyard would be open from both sides.
When he turned the corner he was delighted to see it
was. He was also delighted to see the large golden kriba
lounging in the sun, chained to a tree.

CHAPTER 26

The meeting room in the State Building of Long Beach was much better lit than the one in San Diego. But it was about the same size, which was not nearly big enough.

Once inside, Laura immediately separated herself from Keith. She decided to stand again, since probably there would not be enough seats to go around. In addition to the packed audience, the room was full of news media from all over Southern California. Word had gotten out.

The crowd was amazing. Keith really had pulled some strings. There were movie stars, TV stars, rock stars, basketball stars, baseball stars, and various other celebrities Laura recognized. There were also people from Mountain Lions Forever.

It was quite a mix. The Mountain Lions Forever people still looked like they were living in the wrong decade, which contrasted how fabulously hip most of the celebrities were dressed. Even the jocks looked civilized. Keith actually looked a little square with his suit, but Laura thought it added some class.

The meeting came to order, and the mountain lion hunt was first on the agenda. The Commission listened to its staff testify to the feasibility of the hunt, and give its ultimate recommendation. This drew a chorus of hisses from the Mountain Lions Forever group.

"We're going to go to public testimony now," said Harry Klemm, chairman of the Commission. "But before we do, I'd like to ask the people in the audience to show some courtesy and respect for our meeting and not cause any commotion."

Harry Klemm sat next to Jack Dwyer, the man Laura

had interviewed at the last meeting. She decided she would try to get Klemm for a reaction this time, even though his answers would be exactly the same.

"We'll take opposition testimony first," said Klemm. "Each speaker will be allowed three minutes, but we'd appreciate it if you'd keep your speeches as short as possible. We have a lot to get through today. Now then, the first speaker is Keith Gallatin."

An immediate hush fell over the auditorium. There had been rumors that Keith Gallatin would be there, but no one had been quite sure whether to believe them or not. Not only had he shown up, but he'd brought a host of other celebrities with him.

Television cameras began rolling and still photographers began firing off their shots as soon as Keith reached the podium. No one, not even Laura, knew what to expect. Even the commissioners were leaning forward and showing interest.

For some reason Laura was tense and nervous. She stared at Keith and shuddered all the way down her spine. She was glad all eyes were on him and not on her.

"Honorable Chairman, members of the Commission," Keith began. "Thank you for letting me address you today. My name is Keith Gallatin, and I represent the San Diego Pumas basketball team. I have with me several copies of my presentation for your review, and you'll notice an endorsement from every owner of a basketball team in the Pumas' league."

Keith handed a stack of papers to the clerk, who stamped them and handed a copy to each of the commissioners.

"You gentlemen are very much aware of all the issues in this proposal," said Keith. "I'm not going to go over facts and figures, nor am I going to scream and rant and rave like others who have gone before me in past meetings. Both of those approaches would be a waste of your time.

"I'm here to speak for the animals themselves, since they have all along lacked appropriate representation in this battle. Well, not anymore."

Laura doublechecked her recorder to make sure it was rolling. She was very nervous now, even though Keith seemed very cool.

"It's your job to protect the wildlife of California," Keith continued. "I simply don't understand how you can sit there and flirt with environmental destruction like you're doing. We're not just talking about California here. The eyes of the entire planet are on us today. How can we condemn Brazil and other Third World countries for destroying rain forests and natural habitat when we ourselves are guilty of similar destruction? Hypocrisy isn't going to get us anywhere.

"You all know how few great predators there are left in the world," Keith continued. "There are even fewer of the great cats. In fact, most large felines on this planet either live in zoos or are dead. You all know this, and yet you're pushing for the elimination of two hundred and fifty great cats. Two hundred and fifty California mountain lions, and we don't even know how many of them are left. What if there are only two hundred and fifty-one?

"I know it's wrong. You know it's wrong. Ninety percent of all Californians know it's wrong. This is the last meeting. You're voting on it today. Please, do the right thing. Let's not take any more chances. Extinct is too late. Thank you."

Keith turned and headed back to his seat. After a moment of hushed silence the Mountain Lions Forever group burst into applause. Keith cast them a nasty look, and they stopped abruptly.

Laura glanced at the commissioners, who were all leaning back in their chairs with their arms crossed. No sympathetic ears on the panel, yet.

"The next speaker," said Harry Klemm, "is Danielle Gallatin."

This was a complete surprise to Laura, and she immediately stood up straight. She hadn't known Keith's sister would be there. She wasn't sure why it made a difference, but she did know she was suddenly terribly nervous.

Danielle Gallatin walked up to the podium with her head held high. She looked like royalty, brimming with self-confidence and charm. She also looked exactly like Keith, only very pretty instead of handsome.

When she reached for the microphone all of the commissioners leaned forward for a better look. Danielle was, indeed, gorgeous. Her long, dark, wavy hair was model-perfect, as was her figure and posture. She wore a red business suit, which was nowhere near as conservative as Keith's. It didn't matter anyway, since everyone in the room had seen her in wild attire on MTV.

"Good morning, my name is Danielle Gallatin," she said, looking over the commissioners. Her voice was strong and direct. "I represent Gallatin Entertainment, and I'm here to speak on behalf of California mountain lions."

She stopped for a moment, giving the room an example of a dramatic pause. It worked.

"First, I'd like to tell you a little bit about the namesake of my alma mater," Danielle continued. "I attended San Diego State University, and we called ourselves the 'Aztecs.' For those of you who aren't familiar with the real Aztecs, they were a highly civilized city of Indians who lived in the area that's now called Mexico City."

Laura had rolled her recorder for Danielle's speech, but now was wondering if it had been worth the bother. This was a strange topic for a Fish and Game meeting.

"The Aztecs were the fiercest and most bloodthirsty civilization the world has ever known," Danielle said. "They began every morning with a human sacrifice and continued with several others throughout the day, depending upon how many slaves they had been able to capture from neighboring tribes.

"Their sacrifices were carried out in several different ways. One of my personal favorites was when they would chain the leg of the victim to a tree and then let five of their strongest warriors go after him with their sharp, obsidian swords. To show their sportsmanship, the Aztecs would allow the victim to have a sword as well—only his was made out of feathers."

This was greeted with muted laughter.

"You can imagine how the man must have felt," said Danielle. "Probably not too different from a mountain lion who, after being chased relentlessly by a pack of dogs, is finally overcome by exhaustion and forced up a tree. Then, in the same sportsmanlike fashion as the Aztecs, a mighty warrior arrives and shoots him out of the tree. The only difference is . . . the mountain lions aren't offered a feather sword to defend themselves."

Danielle paused, very effectively yet again.

"The Aztecs died out several hundred years ago," she said. "Most people would agree that the world is a better place as a result. Let's not be like the Aztecs. Trophies aren't worth extinction. Stop the hunt. Thank you."

The auditorium was dead silent as Danielle walked back to her seat. Laura clicked off her recorder and was glad she had let it run. She looked over at Danielle, who was sitting down and glaring at the commissioners defiantly.

Laura looked back over at Harry Klemm, who simply touched his microphone and said, "The next speaker is Janet Donovan."

What followed was a celebrity parade. Twenty-three people, all well known in entertainment or sports, approached the podium when their names were called, and simply said, "Stop the hunt."

It took less than five minutes. Laura wondered how much effect this would have on the commissioners. They all sat motionless, with stone faces, but it had to affect them somehow. This wasn't just some group of nobodies going to the podium. Each one had a tremendous following, not only in California but nationwide. They represented an impressive amount of political clout.

Since the commissioners weren't elected, they probably wouldn't care. But their boss was elected, and no governor in America is going to support a proposal that ninety percent of the people are against. Still, none of the commissioners appeared even to flinch.

The last of the celebrity speakers said his line and walked back to his chair. There was some rustling in the crowd, but no more applause. Keith's glare had been effective.

"The next speaker is Brad Berglund," Klemm said, rolling his eyes.

"I'm here representing Mountain Lions Forever," said Brad. "You all know that. We've been through this a million times before. All I have to say is, we support Keith Gallatin and the other courageous people who stood up here before me today. And I'd like to add, you'll all be pleased to know that we won't be causing any commotion today. Thank you."

"Thank you, Mr. Berglund," said Klemm, who smiled,

along with all the other commissioners. "Thank you for your courtesy."

There were several other names on the list to speak in opposition, but all of them declined the opportunity.

"Well, this must be a new record," said Klemm. "On any issue, but especially this one. Okay, since it was so short, we'll go right to testimony in favor of the proposal. The first speaker will be Sherman Elliot."

A slender man in his late fifties approached the microphone. Laura thought he resembled a minister more than a hunting advocate. She flipped over a page in her notebook and wrote down his name.

After handing a copy of his statement to the clerk, Elliot glanced down at his own script and then up at the commissioners.

"For almost a quarter of a century now," Elliot began, "the United States of America has been plagued with a group of men in black, commonly referred to as Superior and Supreme Court judges. As I understand it the courts are to interpret the law, not to make it. Since the Earl Warren era we have had nothing but misinterpretations of constitutional law by these men in black."

Elliot paused, which everyone appreciated, as far as Laura could tell. She had no idea what he was talking about, and figured the man must have been somewhere on the moon during the first part of the meeting.

"I have a great deal of love and respect for our nation, our government, and for our courts," Elliot continued. "However, with a decision such as Roe versus Wade, which permits murder, we should not be surprised that the same group of men would say it is permissible to burn and trample upon the flag of the United States. Taking away our right to bear arms is their obvious next step. Now they also tell us there is nothing wrong with Dial-a-Porn."

An inquisitive mumble began in the crowd, but Laura figured it out. The Mountain Lions Forever group apparently had filed suit again to stop the hunt, in anticipation of losing before the Commission today. Elliot was addressing the previous decisions sent down by the California Supreme Court.

"Have we gone completely insane that we have allowed the leftist Communists to dictate American policy in place of principles? Have our men died to defend the flag in vain? Have the men who died to raise the flag in Hiroshima given their lives in vain? I say one thousand times, no!"

Laura decided to move before the Mountain Lions Forever people changed their minds and broke into an uproar. She picked out Janet Donovan, an afternoon soap star who was sitting near the aisle, and handed her a card. Laura pointed to the back of the room and Janet nodded. The two women walked toward the outer hallway as Sherman Elliot rambled on.

"The ACLU applauds this decision, while decent people everywhere are weeping. Perhaps it's time once again for the patriotic American to come out of his closet, display his flag, and stand up for his constitutional rights. . . ."

The door closed behind Laura and Janet, shutting out the wisdom of Sherman Elliot.

"Thank you for coming out," said Laura. "I wanted to get you before that guy started a riot."

"What a bozo," said Janet. "Raise the *flag* over Hiroshima? It seems to me we raised a hell of a lot more than a flag."

"Really," agreed Laura with a laugh. "Okay, now for the serious part. What brings you out here today?"

"Keith Gallatin called me up and asked me to be here," said Janet. "When he explained to me what was going on, I made sure to get here early. Hunting mountain lions is dead wrong."

"You wouldn't have come on your own?" Laura asked.

"I wouldn't have known about it," said Janet. "That's the point of my being here, and everyone else you saw in there. Not enough people know about what they're trying to do to those poor lions. Now everyone will know. As a group we'll attract enough attention to let the whole country know."

Laura nodded. There were indeed two crews from the national networks covering the meeting.

"Will your effort work?" asked Laura.

"Maybe not today," said Janet. "But it will. I'll personally yell and scream until everyone in America hears about this."

"So you don't expect to win today?" Laura asked.

"Personally, no," said Janet. "I think Keith does. He's a little naive. I've really checked into this thing since he called me a few weeks ago. We're dealing with a low corrigibility factor as far as those old clowns are concerned."

"I think you're right," said Laura. "So what's next, then?"

"I'm not sure what all of the options are," said Janet. "But now that I'm in on this I'm really going to find out as much as possible. It doesn't matter how they vote in there today. As far as I'm concerned this issue is far from over."

"Thank you," said Laura, and followed Janet back inside.

Keith had really done his homework. He had not only gotten visible celebrities, but intelligent, articulate ones who liked to talk to the media as well. Getting the word out was the single most important part of any campaign.

Laura walked back inside. Sherman Elliot was finished and another hunting advocate was at the podium. Laura looked around and was surprised to see Dennis Jack standing against the far wall. He was in full uniform, and there obviously for security purposes. Laura caught his eye and pointed to the back hall. He nodded and walked out.

"Dennis, it's so nice to see you here," said Laura. "What brings you all the way out to Long Beach?"

"They were just worried," said Dennis. "You know, with all the celebrities and media attention, they wanted as much security as possible."

"I have a question for you," said Laura. There were a few other people standing out in the hall, so Laura lowered her voice. "I was in Tijuana the other day. My friend and I went into this shop off the main strip, and this guy had jaguar and mountain lion pelts for sale. He wanted two hundred dollars each. He told us he gets his mountain lion pelts from north of the border."

Dennis's mouth opened for only an instant, then he straightened his face as if nothing were wrong.

"What?" asked Laura.

"Nothing."

"What? Tell me."

"I can't tell you here," said Dennis. "But I will. I'll call you later today. Are you going back to San Diego after the meeting?"

"Yes. You'd better tell me."

"I will, I promise. I have to go back inside now."

Laura went back inside and brought two more of the celebrities out with her. Both gave her statements similar to the one Janet Donovan had given. She thanked them and followed them back inside, where she found a local NRA activist. She gave him her card and he followed her out, while other testimony was being given.

The man was named Don Goff and Laura had seen him before, but she couldn't remember where. He was a man in his early forties, with jet-black hair and a mustache.

"I was wondering what your reaction was to all of the celebrity attention this issue is getting all of a sudden," said Laura.

"In a way I'm surprised, and in a way I'm not," said Goff. "I'm surprised because it is all of a sudden. This is the last meeting, and we haven't heard a word from these people until today. It's kinda late for them to be jumping in like this."

"Why aren't you surprised?" Laura asked.

"People in the movies and music industry have always been to the political left," said Goff. "They tend to be anti-everything. This is no exception. Most of the people in there are anti-gun and anti-hunting. They'll even tell you they are, but they say this is an isolated thing. They say they're here strictly because of the mountain lions, which is a bunch of bunk."

"Some of those people are pretty well known," said Laura. "Don't you think they can sway some public opinion against the hunt?"

"I'm sure they can," said Goff. "But it's too late. The Commission votes today, and I don't think they changed any votes. Maybe if they'd been here from the beginning like the rest of us."

"Who was the first speaker in favor of the hunt?" Laura asked. "Do you know him?"

"That guy? What a loony. I guess everyone's got a right to speak. He does more harm than good, I think.

But he's still a hell of a lot better than those Mountain Lions Forever people."

"Thank you," said Laura, and followed Goff back inside.

The public testimony had ended. Laura found a place to stand and listened as the commissioners discussed the pros and cons of the hunt for the final time before they would vote. Judging by their conversation, Laura could tell Don Goff had been right. Keith and his group of friends had failed to sway even one of the commissioners.

Their discussion was brief. They quickly took a unanimous vote, then unceremoniously went on to the next item on the agenda.

CHAPTER 27

The scent hit her and she dropped to her forepaws. It was to her left, and it was close.

Alleen.

With all of the heavy thinking, Sarena had thoroughly forgotten just how hungry she was. Her mouth began to water and she licked her lips, closing her mouth to stop the panting. Silence was imperative.

As hungry as her body was, she wasn't really in the mood to eat, let alone hunt. But she knew it could be several days before she found another opportunity, so she decided it had to be now. She quickly tightened the muscles in her back, and instinctively flexed her claws.

A slight breeze carried the alleen scent, which was to Sarena's advantage. It not only blew her identifying smell in the other direction, but it rustled the chaparral enough to cover the sound of her steps.

Sarena raised her head slightly, trying to see over the dense manzanita. Nothing yet, but the scent was getting stronger. She crouched back down and began to weave her way along a tiny path, careful not to step on anything that could snap or rustle.

She found a large boulder of granite, and risked hopping up for a better view. She raised her head as high as she dared, but could see only thick brush in every direction. The alleen was virtually invisible under such a cover.

Crouching again, Sarena decided to remain on top of the rock. She could tell by the strength of the scent the alleen was getting closer. From the rock she would maintain a slightly better view, and hold the advantage of being able to initiate attack from a higher spot.

Sarena quickly glanced at the sky, then uttered a silent hiss. Where was Lanakila now? His aerial eyes would have made all the difference. She looked back down at the brush and inwardly laughed at herself. She had hunted with the great bird only once, and already she felt dependent upon him.

She heard the brush move abruptly and she tensed up again. She quietly reminded herself that she was a big girl now, and fully capable of hunting on her own. She sniffed quickly, and identified the alleen as being alone.

Daring another peek, she pushed herself as high as she could, scanning the top of the brush in the direction of the scent. She remained upright for several moments, unable to see anything save the thick, brown sage. Frustrated, she scanned the chaparral in the other direction, seeing nothing, and then turned back toward the area where she believed the prey to be.

She barely caught it, but there was no mistake. Antlers. They were casually lowered into the high brush, and Sarena felt her heart begin to pound. She had seen the rack only for an instant, but judging by its size it sat upon quite a buck. It took a step, faintly rustling the brush, and Sarena dropped back to her crouch. The buck was headed straight for her, and obviously had no idea she was there.

Without seeing it, Sarena knew it was even larger than the one she had taken with Lanakila. It was more than she needed, and possibly more than she could handle, but she felt much stronger than she ever had before, and her confidence was running high. With the element of surprise, a good jump, and a little luck, she felt as though she could handle anything.

She heard it again. It was getting very close. She glanced around for the path the alleen most likely would use. There was only one and it was very narrow, which would make it impossible to run along without smashing into thick, dried-out clumps of brush. She was going to take a beating in this chase.

It was time. The buck was too close for Sarena to wait any longer, for fear of his picking up her scent. With any fortune at all, she would have two full strides before he knew she was there. She took in a deep breath, crouched back, and launched herself airborne.

The piercing screech struck her ears before she'd even touched the ground. Her landing was solid and her momentum carried her another bound, but she stopped awkwardly, fearing another an attack by men on the alleen.

Suddenly the brush parted and the huge buck thundered toward her. Its eyes were wide, but it never saw her. Sarena barely had a chance to react before the alleen smashed into her, flipped over her head, and landed hard on its back. Stunned by the impact, Sarena shook her head, ignored the pain from the collision with the buck's shoulder, and quickly scanned for signs of danger. She needed to decide instantly whether to attack the alleen or put her head down and run. Within a second she had concluded there was no danger, and turned on the alleen.

It had no chance. Still struggling to regain its feet, it never even saw Sarena as she pounced from only a few yards away. Within moments she had taken her second large buck, without even testing her ability to actually run one down.

Where had the screech come from? With the buck at her feet, Sarena scrutinized the area as best she could from where she was, but could see nothing. She decided it must have been another animal, possibly the buck's mate, attempting to warn him of Sarena. If so, the warning had failed.

Sarena looked down at the fallen alleen and licked her lips. The buck was huge. It had been easy, but she had paid for it. The right side of her face, where the alleen's shoulder had struck her, was pounding. But looking at her catch, she smiled at how trivial the price had been for such a reward.

A sudden shadow crossed her face and she dropped to a crouch. Her claws instinctively extended. She glanced to her right but sensed nothing threatening. She looked to her left, then quickly back to the fallen alleen. There, perched indifferently on one of its antlers, was Lanakila.

"It's you!" said Sarena, delighted to see her friend.

"Who else?" asked Lanakila. "I thought you were going to blow it there, for a second."

"What?" asked Sarena, completely confused.

"The alleen," said Lanakila. "I chased him right to you. I was afraid you'd miss him."

Sarena had no response. She simply walked over and rubbed her face against Lanakila, who lowered his head and nestled it against her ear. The two friends stood together without moving or speaking for several moments. Sarena closed her eyes and smiled, as his soft feathers tickled her whiskers.

He was back. She couldn't believe it. After an entire life of loneliness, it had seemed only appropriate to lose the only person she had grown close to. But her luck had changed. He was back, and now she knew exactly what it was like to love. It had hurt, badly, when she had lost him, but now he was back.

"I thought you were gone, Fur Ball," Lanakila said finally. Sarena noticed his voice had cracked somewhat.

"I did too, love," she said. "I did too. It's a very long story, and one I'm not sure even I believe."

"Your leg," he said simply.

"It is healed," she said. "Somehow, I don't know. We live in strange days."

"I'm glad I returned," said Lanakila. "When I thought you were lost, I didn't want to live anymore. It hurt so badly. All over. I've never felt like that. I wanted to die. I flew west, over the sea. It goes forever, you know, so I wanted to go as far out as I could before I collapsed. I hoped I would know peace then."

"Oh, Lanakila," she said.

"I flew. I flew farther than I ever have before. When I passed the distance I knew I wouldn't be able to return from, I suddenly felt better. It was over. All of the pain and loneliness was finally over. The loss of my Fur Ball still hurt, but I felt as though you were close by and I'd be seeing you soon. For this I was glad, because you were the only friend I'd ever known."

"Lanakila . . ." She didn't know what else to say, so she quickly groomed him across his face. He closed his eyes and pressed against her.

"I don't understand," said Sarena. "If you passed the

distance from where you could return, how did you make it back?"

"I can't really explain what happened," said Lanakila. "It's as if a huge claw reached out and grabbed me and yanked me around. Then I heard this voice from somewhere and it sounded like a man's voice, only it spoke the common tongue. It told me to return immediately."

"Really?" asked Sarena, startled.

"Yes. It was the strangest thing I'd ever experienced. I was literally jerked around, and facing in the direction from which I had started. Then everything changed. I no longer felt like I was alone out there. It was as if someone was flying with me, and far away I could hear your voice."

"My voice?" she asked.

"Your voice. And I felt lighter all of a sudden. It was easier to fly."

"How could *you* become lighter?" Sarena asked, almost to herself. She had carried him several times on her shoulders and had barely noticed any weight at all.

"I did become weary, though, after a while," said Lanakila. "Like I said, I was way past the point where I could safely return. And it was getting dark."

"What happened?" Sarena asked.

"There was something floating in the water," said Lanakila. "It was very hard. I think it was something made by a man. Anyway it was floating there, right out in the middle of nowhere, and it had a perfect perch on it. I landed easily, and spent the night floating on the sea."

"Wow," said Sarena.

"I couldn't believe I was being saved by something made by a man," he said. "It seemed ironic, since at that point I thought you had been killed by something made by a man."

"I did, too," she said.

"Anyway, I slept better than I had for many nights. And the next morning it felt as though I had slept for weeks. I was rested and full of energy. I flew to the shore without any trouble at all."

"What was it like out there?" Sarena asked.

"It was magnificent and peaceful. On the way in I saw a huge pack of sea animals. They were beautiful. They

were as big as you are, Fur Ball, and so full of life. They
kept jumping out of the water as if they were playing. I
think they must have been. I've always thought that of
all the Creator's works, only birds were truly free. But
now I'm proved very wrong. Those animals I saw in the
water were flying and free in their own strange way. I
was envious."

"I would love to see them, some day," said Sarena.

"I hope you can," said Lanakila. "They seemed very
friendly."

"Tell me more," said Sarena, "about your trip back."

"I kept my eyes to the water, hoping to see more of
the sea animals, when I saw something else," said Lanakila. "I don't know how, but somehow I knew it was food.
There were several of them, small creatures close to the
surface. I dove down, just as if I were hunting the hina,
and grabbed one out of the water. I had never done
anything like that before, but it felt as though I had done
it for a lifetime."

"What was it?" asked Sarena.

"It was cold and slippery," said Lanakila. "And it
tasted like nothing I have ever eaten. It was terrific."

"Then what happened?" asked Sarena.

"I reached the land, and I quickly flew here. Actually
I flew to the area where we last departed. It was painful to fly over the area, for despite the strange callings
I still thought you were gone. I circled for quite a while
but saw nothing. Even the krahstas and kribas were
gone.

"I decided to head north and it took some time, but
then I spotted you," he continued. "At first I thought I
had discovered another puma. I thought this was the cru-
elest, saddest irony I'd ever seen. All your life you had
searched for another like yourself, and now one shows
up after you're gone."

Sarena looked at her paws. She was very happy to see
Lanakila, but she still didn't like being reminded of how
lonely she was in the puma world.

"Then I noticed that arrogant strut of yours," Lanakila
chided. "I thought, 'Great. Do all pumas walk like
they're the Creator's gift to the world?' But when I circled closer, I knew there could be no doubt. It was my
Fur Ball."

Sarena didn't know whether to groom him or bite him. She pushed her face against him and nuzzled his breast feathers.

"Come on, Fur Ball, let's eat," he said. "I'm starving!"

CHAPTER 28

The mountain lion portion of the meeting was long over, but Keith was still talking with the media. He, along with several of his friends, had grouped together outside the building in what turned out to be an impromptu news conference which lasted nearly half an hour. Laura did not see Danielle in the crowd.

This was fine as far as Laura was concerned. She had wanted to talk with Danielle, but really only needed reaction from one of the twins. She could get a quote from Keith on the way back to San Diego. Most of her story was finished except for a quote from one of the commissioners, which could take a while since they were still working on the rest of their agenda. They would probably take a break in a few minutes.

Laura found a pay phone and called the newsroom. When she got Bill Sesma, she told him about the story.

"Good," said Sesma. "We'll go with a picture of the Gallatins testifying alongside your story. We'll lead B-1 with it."

"Okay," said Laura. "I'll be back sometime this afternoon." She didn't want Sesma to know anything about how she had gotten here.

"By the way," said Sesma, "I think your attack dogs have resurfaced."

"Really? Where?" asked Laura.

"Up in Carlsbad, not far from where they were last seen," said Sesma. "Apparently they attacked a golden retriever in someone's backyard early this morning."

"They attacked a *dog*?" Laura asked.

"Yep. He was chained to a tree. They ripped his collar off him and dragged him into a Canyon."

218

"Oh, my God," said Laura.

"The owner, a lady, watched from inside her house. She was too afraid to go outside. Can't say I blame her. She said there was five dogs in all."

"Five?" Laura asked.

"Five," said Sesma. "Maybe the other one stayed home."

"Okay, I'll check on it when I get back," said Laura.

Not only had Grash felt awkward about hunting another kriba, but the taste had not been rewarding, either. Grash noticed the others in the tribe were reacting the same way.

"Next time we leave kriba," said Broed, to the laughter of the others.

"It tastes awful," said Grallus. "His owner must have been feeding him something unspeakable."

"I don't think kribas were meant to be eaten," said Grash.

"If this one is any indication, I'll agree," said Grallus.

"It's our eyes," said Grash. "The Creator of all things gave kribas predator-eyes. We're supposed to eat, not be eaten."

"What do you mean, predator-eyes?" asked Bruether.

"They're directed forward," said Grash. "They're designed for pursuit. You'll notice the hina and other prey have eyes on the sides of their heads, so they can look all directions for predators."

"I never thought of that," said Grallus. "It makes sense. Cats have them, too. And the krahstas."

"And men," said Broed.

"Yes," said Grash. "They are the most ruthless predators on earth."

"Are we going to attack kribas again?" asked Bruether. "If we are, I think we should do what Broed suggested and pass up other kribas."

"I agree," said Grallus.

"If we attack kribas again," said Grash, "we should do it a lot different than this one."

"Why?" asked Grallus. "No one got hurt, and it's a pretty big kriba."

"But it didn't have a chance," said Grash. "It was tied to a tree. The reason we were supposed to do this was to get battle experience. This thing went down without a fight. Can't say I blame him."

"Okay, let's go now," said Grallus.

"Now?" asked Grash.

"Now would be the best time," said Grallus. "We're not hungry or tired. No one saw us attack this last one. Why not?"

Grash looked around the group. They all seemed non-committal except for Grallus, who apparently was politicking for more influence now that Kroth was gone.

"Well . . ."

Grash was about to agree but his words died in his throat. A sudden movement caught his eye and his gaze went skyward. All of the others followed his stare and were startled to the dog. Very high, but still very visible, was the great wingspan of the ahila.

Other eyes followed the bird's motion as well. Farther to the east, across a large ravine, the pack of krahstas sat motionless with their eyes on the sky.

"Well, well, our friend has returned," said Dropno.

"Do you think he is in league with those dreadful kribas?" asked Grahna, his mate. Grahna despised their domestic cousins, and had refused to participate when the two groups had run together.

"It's hard to say, from here," said Dropno. "I think we should watch it for a while and see where it lands. Who knows what interesting things it might lead us to."

"You don't think we can convince it to join with us, do you?" asked Ponto.

"Not a chance," said Dropno. "The kribas thought it was being held prisoner by the puma, but I disagree. It was ready to tear our eyes out if we got anywhere near the puma. Just ask Krade. That doesn't sound much like a prisoner to me."

"What if the kribas do have the bird?" asked Grahna.

"Then we'll simply take it from them," said Dropno. "Or kill it."

"Maybe we should kill them while we're at it," said Grahna.

"Maybe," said Dropno. "Maybe."

*   *   *

Grash didn't know what to do. As the bird circled high above where the tribe was sitting in a patch of manzanita, Grash had no plan. He wanted desperately to meet with the bird and talk with it, but for now it was way out of reach.

"Ideas, anyone?" asked Grash.

"I'm sure it can see us at this distance," said Grallus. "I'm sure it could hear us, too. Why don't we run out into the open and call it?"

"Call it?" asked Grash, not liking the idea. "What if we only scare it off?"

"What else can we do?" asked Grallus. "We may never see it again."

"Good point," said Grash. "We might as well try."

"It is in league with them!" said Dropno. "Hear them calling it?"

"They're across the ravine," said Ponto.

The entire pack was panting and on its feet. All fourteen of them were walking anxiously in circles, switching glances between the bird and the ground where the barks were coming from.

"Okay, everyone," said Dropno. "Let's go."

Sarena jumped to her feet the instant she heard the barking. She had been napping off her enormous meal in a bed of rye grass when it began from the cliff up above her. She immediately jumped onto a path and began running in the opposite direction.

It was the same kribas, she was certain. Their voices were the same, only the nature of their call seemed different. They didn't appear to be getting closer, but she wasn't taking any chances.

Sarena stopped for a moment to get her bearings. She could stay along the bottom of the ravine, which ran north and south, or she could head east, up a large canyon wall and the opposite direction of the barking.

She looked for Lanakila. He was up there, very high and circling. She wondered what he saw and why he didn't come down to tell her. The barking was still stationary, but she decided to move anyway. She looked up the side of the slope and began running east.

* * *

It was clear the ahila hadn't noticed them until they had started barking. The bird immediately swerved and tilted to look in their direction, but maintained its altitude. All Grash and the others could do was keep barking.

Grash wondered if the bird understood. The common speech could be tricky enough, but barked at full volume it turned into a garbled mush. Grash hoped that if the ahila could understand anything, it would be urgency.

Suddenly the bird made a wide turn and circled high across the Canyon. It stopped somewhere over the center of the ravine, fluttered momentarily, and then began a dive. Within moments it was lost from sight.

"Come on!" said Grash. "Maybe we can get over there and find it before it takes off again."

The tribe immediately broke into a run toward the bottom of the ravine. It was slow going since the terrain was so rugged, and Grash had to keep looking up to see if the ahila had gone skyward again. It was going to be a slow and rough trip.

Sarena had barely begun her ascent of the slope when something grabbed at her back. She growled fiercely and jumped around, with claws fully extended, but grabbed only air. She hissed and quickly looked in both directions, but saw nothing.

It was Lanakila. He flapped his wings above her, then lowered himself to a branch of scrub oak beside her.

"Kribas," was all Sarena could say, she was so out of breath.

"Yes, Fur Ball, I have eyes," said Lanakila. "Not only kribas but krahstas, too. You're running right to them."

"Krahstas?" Sarena gasped.

"You must run back down the hill and into the gully," said Lanakila. "Run to the right. You must hurry, because the kribas come as well."

"I don't hear them anymore," said Sarena.

"I'll explain later," said Lanakila. "You have some time, but you must go now. I'll lead them in the other direction."

"You?" asked Sarena. "You can't. It's too dangerous. I'll fight them off."

"Fur Ball, when are you going to get some sense?" asked Lanakila with exasperation. "They can't catch me. I can fly, remember? They can't. Neither can you, so you'd better go before they get here."

"Lanakila . . ."

"Go!" screeched the bird, jabbing at Sarena's tail with a quick dive. He was high in the air a moment later.

"There it is!" shouted Grallus.

Grash saw it, too, hovering low over the bottom of the ravine. It didn't seem to be in a hurry, although it was drifting to the south.

"Okay, let's keep quiet until we get there," ordered Grash. He was panting miserably, more from nerves than fatigue. So much was at stake with the ahila.

Rather than going to the bottom of the gully they stayed on the Canyon wall. At one point they were almost at an even height with the bird, who maintained a low, tight, calculated circle.

When the tribe lost their cover of brush, Grash ordered them down the slope. It was a gradual descent over rocky dirt and rye grass. They took their time, since the bird obviously would see them anyway. About halfway down, Grash ordered them to stop.

"Well, he knows we're here," said Grash. "He knows we want to talk to him. Let's see what he does."

"Should we bark some more?" asked Grallus. "He's closer. Maybe he'll hear us better."

"No," said Grash. "We'll just sit here and wait."

The krahstas sat down to wait as well. From their position across the ravine they still had the benefit of thick brush. Their domestic cousins could not see them at all, but the krahstas could see them just fine. Dropno and his pack watched eagerly through a thicket of manzanita.

As far as Dropno could tell, the bird didn't know they were there either. This was good, since secrecy was everything in spying, and spying was exactly what Dropno had in mind.

There was someone else around, though, who might know they were there. A puma was close by. The pack had picked up the scent halfway down the Canyon wall. Dropno remembered the last time they had seen a puma was the last time they had seen an ahila. He wondered if there was a connection, although the puma scent was fading and the cat apparently had been heading north, away from where the ahila currently hovered.

Suddenly the bird tucked its wings and began a slow dive. It aimed directly for the kribas and then curved off at the last moment and launched itself high again. It made a small circle and then dropped back down again. After hovering for several moments, it finally lighted on top of a large holly tree.

"Let's go!" said Grash.

It was only a short distance, and the tribe bounded over within moments. They came to a stop short of the tree, and Grash ordered them to sit down a respectable distance away. Panting hard, they all sat down and stared up at the great bird.

"Greetings!" said Grash, not knowing how else to address such a creature. He had never spoken to a bird of any kind before, much less one of such majestic stature.

The bird did not answer, but merely cocked its head and scanned the panting tribe members. It ruffled up its feathers and Grash feared it would fly, but it settled back down and continued to stare at the kribas.

The bird's expression was impossible to read. From where Grash sat the bird looked angry, but it wasn't acting aggressive or threatening. It simply sat there, as if it were waiting for something.

"We've seen you before," said Grash. "It's been several days. We thought you were gone. We're glad you came back."

"Why would you be happy to see the likes of me?" the bird asked. "I am, after all, your competition. I take hina that otherwise might feed you."

"It's okay. There's plenty of food to go around in the Canyon. That's why we're here. By the way my name is Grash, and these are my friends. We have never seen a bird such as you."

The bird seemed to wince at Grash's words, but again it was impossible to really tell what the bird's expressions meant.

"My name is Lanakila. There are no other birds like

me in these parts. I am alone. Again I must ask, though, why would you be happy to see me?"

"When we saw you before," said Grash, "you were being held against your will by the evil puma. We saw you hunt with it, and help it catch the alleen. We know the puma is dead now, but there are still plenty of alleen in the Canyon. We were wondering if you would be interested in making friends with us, and helping *us* catch the alleen."

The bird leaned back on its perch and ruffled its feathers again.

"We'll treat you much better than the puma did," said Grash. "We know it must have been very cruel to you. We're not like that. We want to be your friend."

"What about the krahstas?" Lanakila asked. "Are they also your friends?"

"No!" barked all of the tribe members at once.

"Those filthy dogs make us sick," said Grash.

"I have seen you run with them," said Lanakila.

"Not anymore," insisted Grash. "We ran with them to learn. They have nothing to teach us that we can't get from a friendship with you."

"I can't fly with you," said Lanakila.

"Why not?" asked Grash, dejectedly. He had just done the best sweet-talking of his life.

"I am held prisoner by another puma," said the bird.

"What?" asked Grash. The other tribe members barked concern.

"It's true," said the bird. "We hunted this morning. If you walk back up the hill that way, you will find the carcass of an alleen in the bushes. It was caught with my assistance."

Grash tried to think of a quick response, but was beaten by Grallus.

"Lead us to the puma," said Grallus. "We'll kill it. Then you'll be free at last."

"I'll have to think about it," said Lanakila.

"Why?" asked Grash. "It should be an easy choice."

"I'll find you when I'm ready," said the bird, and launched himself into the sky.

CHAPTER 29

The ride home was the complete opposite of the morning trip. Keith sat in virtual silence most of the way, as the stereo played rock music by a group Laura had never heard of.

Jim Simon, the attorney, was still buried in paperwork he'd taken from his briefcase. Randy sat next to Laura, with his feet on the seat and his knees bent up to his chin. Keith was on the other side, staring out the window.

There was nothing for Laura to do but work on her story. She wrote furiously on her note pad, occasionally holding her tiny recorder to her ear so she could listen to quotes taken earlier. It was hard to hear over the music, but she figured it was best to leave matters alone for now.

"How can you write with all the noise?" Randy asked her.

"Oh, this is easy," said Laura. "You should try writing in our newsroom around deadline. You can't even hear yourself think."

"Yeah, I guess you'd be used to stressful deadlines," said Randy.

Laura nodded, then reached over to the stereo and turned down the volume. She looked over at Keith, who still had his back turned to her and was continuing to stare out the window.

"I'm about finished with my story," said Laura. "The only thing left that I need is your response to the vote."

"I'm bummed," said Keith, finally turning around. "Really bummed. I can't believe they'd be so stupid."

"Is that what you want me to print?" asked Laura. "Or would you prefer to be a little more civilized?"

"Print whatever you want," said Keith, turning back around to resume staring out the window.

Sarena traveled quite a distance before sitting down to rest. She hoped Lanakila had diverted the kribas, but she didn't know how it would be possible. As far as Sarena knew, most animals never looked to the sky for anything.

After catching her breath, Sarena began to groom. She suddenly realized how lax she had been in her cleaning during the days when Lanakila was away. Most of the time she had spent merely existing, instead of living. Now she was back to feeling alive again.

Her coat needed work. The tawny fur was thick with stickers and dried dirt, but within minutes it was looking better. She had almost finished when Lanakila landed on the high rock beside her.

"Where've you been?" Sarena asked. "I've been worried about you."

"You're always worried about me, Fur Ball," said Lanakila. "You can relax. I'm a big bird now."

"Did you see the kribas?" Sarena asked.

"Yes. They're far away now, so you can rest easy," said Lanakila. "I even spoke with them."

"*What?*"

"They had a lot to say. They still think you're dead, and they thought you were holding me prisoner."

"They *what?*" asked Sarena.

"They saw us hunt," said Lanakila. "They didn't know we were friends. *Are* friends. They thought the only way I would help out a puma was if I was forced into it. I told them they were right."

"Why?" asked Sarena, startled. "It was your idea, not mine."

"I know," said the bird. "But they don't. It's better to keep them guessing. I told them I'm being forced to help another puma."

"Why?" asked Sarena. "You're so confusing. Why would you want them to know I'm around?"

"Because they already know there's a puma around," said Lanakila. "And they want me to help *them* hunt."

"Oh, my," said Sarena. "What did you say?"

"I told them I'd let them know later."

"Dear Lady Farri," said Sarena. "How do we ever get into these things?"

"I don't know, Fur Ball," said Lanakila. "But from now on, we're going to have to be very clever. Very clever."

By the time Laura sat down at her desk, the story was completely written in her note pad. In less than ten minutes it was typed neatly into her computer. She stretched out, then looked through her purse for her phone book and found a number for Dennis Jack.

"I was wondering if you were gonna call," said Dennis. "I was about to give up on you."

"Sorry," said Laura. "I didn't drive up there this morning, so I had to wait for my ride. Anyway, what's going on?"

"This is off the record, okay?" asked Dennis. "At least for now."

"Okay," said Laura. "Shoot."

"Basically, I may be asking you to help me for a change," said Dennis.

"Yeah? How?"

"I'm not sure," said Dennis. "I don't know what-all you know."

"About what?" Laura asked.

"When you first asked me about taxidermy shops, I didn't think anything of it," said Dennis. "But today, when you mentioned the shop in TJ with the cougar pelts . . . well, I guess I'd have to say it was more than a coincidence."

"What are you talking about?" asked Laura.

"You don't know? Really?"

"Not unless you make it a little clearer," said Laura.

"Okay. We've been working on a case for some time involving poachers."

"I knew that," said Laura.

"We'd heard some of the pelts and antler racks were being smuggled into Mexico and sold through taxidermy shops in TJ and Tecate."

"When I asked you about taxidermy shops, I didn't know anything about this," said Laura. "I was just trying to dig us some dirt on a guy who owns one on this side of the border."

"Jake Cotter," said Dennis.

"Yes," said Laura. "How did you know?"

"We've been trying to nail him for a long time," said Dennis. "We think the pelts are going through an American taxidermist, because the quality of the skins is too good for south of the border."

"Why do you think it's Cotter?" asked Laura.

"Rumors," said Dennis.

"Rumors? Come on."

"I gotta protect my sources, too," Dennis said, laughing.

"Okay."

"Anyway, I can't crack this case because it's out of my league," said Dennis. "We're not designed to handle international smuggling cases, or any case of this magnitude for that matter. Our function is mostly to handle people who're fishing without a license or catching over the limit."

"Who's jurisdiction is it?" asked Laura.

"Ours, to an extent," said Dennis. "But we can't do it. Actually the FBI should be handling it because it involves international smuggling, but they won't touch it."

"Why not?" asked Laura.

"Unless it's drugs or guns, they don't want anything to do with it," said Dennis. "They're just as swamped as we are."

"Who'd you talk to down there?" asked Laura.

"I can't tell you," said Dennis. "it would be too obvious."

"Okay," said Laura. "I'll go through proper channels."

"For what?"

"You want them to help, don't you?"

"Yes."

"Let me give them a call," said Laura. "Nothing can get the ball rolling faster than nosy newspaper reporters."

"Just don't mention my name," said Dennis.

"I'd never burn a source," said Laura.

"Good," said Dennis. "I have to go now. Those attack dogs have been spotted in Carlsbad."

"Oh yeah, I was supposed to ask you about that," said Laura.

"I'm gonna go set traps in the Canyon near the lady's house where they attacked."

"You're gonna set traps?" Laura asked, horrified. She thought about Sarena and her crushed forepaw.

"Not the kind you found," said Dennis. "These are big boxes that we bait with food. They're very humane. The animals won't get hurt at all. Chances are we'll catch a bunch of coyotes anyway."

"Okay, well, let me know if you catch anything," said Laura.

"You got it," said Dennis.

Laura had barely hung up when the phone rang. It was Brad Berglund.

"Quite a show, wasn't it?" Brad asked.

"Yes," said Laura. "What did you think?"

"I thought it was great. Especially the part about the Aztecs. I thought old Klemm was gonna keel over right there."

"Well, he didn't," said Laura.

"No, but it doesn't matter," said Brad. "The whole meeting was a moot point, and the commissioners knew it. That's the reason I'm calling. You've been following this pretty close, so I just wanted to let you know that we filed a lawsuit in a San Francisco Superior Court this morning. If the court rules anything like it has the past three years, and I have no doubt it will, there will be no hunt this year. The judge has issued a temporary restraining order, which will prohibit any further proceeding by the Commission until there's a ruling."

"Already?" Laura asked.

"We weren't wasting any time," said Brad. "We've been working on this for a long time. We knew what the Commission vote would be. It's just a coincidence that the ruling came down today. If Keith Gallatin had reached me earlier I would have been able to tell him not to waste his time being so dramatic, although it was a nice gesture. Don't tell him I said that."

"So what does this mean?" Laura asked.

"Hopefully, no hunt until next year," said Brad. "Third year in a row this has happened. You'd think they'd learn."

"Are you going to have to go through this every year?" Laura asked.

"I don't know," said Brad. "We're still looking at a ballot initiative. We just can't afford it."

"I wouldn't discount Keith Gallatin's help yet," said Laura.

"I'm not, and I didn't mean to sound like they were wasting their time," said Brad. "Every little bit helps, and they'll get the word out. Their publicity will especially help if we ever do get an initiative."

"The court could still rule against you though, right?" asked Laura.

"Yes," said Brad. "So far it hasn't happened, but you never know. As long as the judge follows California law, we'll be fine."

"Which is?"

"By law the Department of Fish and Game must have a reasonable estimate of any fish, bird, or mammal before it establishes a limit. As you know, there has never been *any* estimate of how many mountain lions there are."

"Where are you now?" Laura asked.

"I'm at the airport in LA" said Brad. "I'm taking off for San Francisco in a few minutes."

"Call me if anything else develops," said Laura.

She hung up and shook her head. This meant she would have to make more calls to confirm what Brad had told her, and then pull her story from the computer and rewrite parts of it. She let out a sigh, then reached for her Rolodex. She had barely begun to flip through it when the phone rang again.

"Hello, this is Danielle Gallatin."

"Hi, I'm sorry I missed you at the meeting," said Laura. "I wanted to talk to you."

"I had to run," said Danielle, "and Keith is better at talking to the media anyway."

"I was quite impressed with your speech," said Laura.

"Thank you, although it obviously didn't do much good. Listen, the reason I'm calling is that I heard Keith was a turd on the way home."

"Yes, as a matter of fact he was," said Laura.

"I hope he didn't say anything nasty," said Danielle.

Laura rolled her eyes. It was too late to be worrying about how Keith would be portrayed in the papers.

"Don't worry," said Laura. "I'm not quoting him on anything. I'm just saying he was disappointed by the outcome."

"Well, thank you, but that's not what I meant," said Danielle. "You have to understand something about Keith, he's used to things always going his way. Lately he's been under a lot of pressure, and a lot of things have gone wrong."

"So you're calling me to apologize for your brother acting like a baby?" asked Laura, a little miffed. "Don't you think he should grow up and do it himself?"

"Yes," said Danielle. "And he might. He doesn't know I'm calling. I just wanted you to know . . . Well, just don't give up on him yet."

"Give up on what?" asked Laura. "I didn't know there was anything concerning Keith to give up on."

"You know that we own a TV station, right?"

"Yes."

"Their news department had a crew at the meeting," said Danielle.

"Yes, I saw them."

"They didn't get a ride in Keith's limo," said Danielle. "Or mine either. They took their own company car."

"So?" asked Laura.

"I heard he sang to you," said Danielle. "I would have liked to have seen it, because I've never seen him sing to anyone like that before."

"Big deal," said Laura. "We were on our way to a meeting about mountain lions, and he sang me a song about mountain lions."

" 'Sarena's Song,' " said Danielle. "A real double-edged sword, if you ask me."

"How?" asked Laura.

"Listen," said Danielle. "I've gabbed enough already. Why don't you come down to the studio tomorrow? We're going to start working on the song."

"I have to work tomorrow," said Laura.

"One o'clock," said Danielle. "Figure out a way. It'll be worth it."

"We'll see," said Laura. "I'd like to get together

with you sometime and talk about Keith, if you don't mind."

"We'll see," said Danielle.

The tribe had remained as visible as possible since the ahila had left them. Grash was taking no chances. He wanted to make sure the bird could find them if it decided to work with them. So far they hadn't seen it again.

Both Grallus and Roashas were rolling around in the tall rye grass. Broed was sitting with his head down, and Bruether was stretching out in some shade. No one had talked much since Lanakila had left them. No one knew what to say.

"Weren't we supposed to go after another kriba?" asked Grallus, shaking dust and grass off his back.

Grash looked over, but then ignored him by looking back up at the sky. He had hoped that, with the arrival of the ahila, everyone would have forgotten the idea of hunting more kribas.

"It seems even more practical now," insisted Grallus. "After all, the bird said he was being held prisoner by another puma. It's probably the same one who killed Kroth. If so we have a double obligation now, and I still don't think we're ready."

Grash looked over at Grallus. Roashas was right beside him as always, and the two looked almost identical. Grallus's words had gotten Broed to his feet, and he was intently looking back and forth between Grallus and the leader. Bruether also had stood up and begun walking over.

Grash could see the challenge in the eyes of Grallus. It wasn't strong enough to suggest a fight, but it was there, and kindling. It was obvious the others could see it as well, and were wondering how Grash inevitably would handle it. As far as Grash was concerned, this was exactly what the tribe didn't need.

"Don't you think the timing is wrong?" asked Grash. "What if the bird comes back and we're gone?"

"The bird has eyes from above," said Grallus. "He'll see us no matter where we are. You know that as well as I do."

"But he'll be looking for us here," said Grash, knowing his argument would not hold up.

"He won't expect us to be stuck in one place," said Roashas. "I say we raid the street. We could have done it by now and been back."

"Exactly," agreed Grallus.

Grash looked at Broed and Bruether and both of their expressions were noncommittal, which was exactly what Grash didn't want to see. He looked back at the two brothers and then up to the sky, hoping the ahila would be there. The bird was not, and Grash reluctantly agreed to go along with the wish of Grallus and Roashas.

"Okay, let's go," said Grash. "We'll walk as openly as possible until we reach the top of the cliff. Hopefully the ahila will see us before then. If not we'll take cover in the brush, and then ambush the street like before. But this time let's go after something that can fight back."

Grallus and Roashas took off without an answer. The others followed, with Grash in the rear, a position he didn't like at all. He continued looking to the sky until the last possible moment, with no luck. Then, with the others, he ducked into the cover of the sage.

They reached the edge of the brush on the side of the houses and froze immediately. There, holding something in his hands and walking toward them, was a man in a uniform. A man with a gun on his belt.

"Back up," ordered Grash quietly.

They all obeyed without question. In moments they were well within the shelter of chaparral, but they could still see the man clearly. Obviously he had not seen them. He appeared to be more interested in the object he was carrying than in chasing wild kribas.

Grash, like all of the others, instinctively wanted to run to the man. All of their training had conditioned them to do so. A man in uniform with a gun was their friend, and someone to protect at all costs. *All* costs. And there, walking toward them, was such a man.

He looked like a friend. He projected an aura of one who cared about animals. He didn't appear to be at all threatening. He simply fumbled around with his box, or whatever it was.

The men in uniforms had never harmed them. To the contrary, only the utmost respect was shown by the men in uniforms. It was the people who lived at the cage who were the demons. This was not one of the demons but a man in uniform, who might very well have treats in his pockets, as most of the others often did.

Grash could see it in the eyes of the tribe: They wanted to go to the man. This made the decision easier, but still Grash wanted to be cautious.

"Okay, but keep a safe distance until we're sure he's okay," said Grash. "If he lifts his gun, scatter."

They broke from the brush at a full run. Grallus barked first, and soon they were all following suit. The man looked up, obviously startled, and dropped his box. He immediately reached for his gun.

"Stop!" barked Grash, unnecessarily. Everyone had done so the second the man dropped his box.

The man held his gun, but did not aim and did not shoot. He stared at the tribe in obvious fear and disbelief. He kept his position, without advancing or retreating. He didn't even appear to be breathing.

Grash was. Like the others, Grash was panting hard. And like the man, they were all standing motionless. It was a standoff, with neither side knowing what the other wanted or what to do as a result.

"Wag your tails," ordered Grash. "Let's tell him we're friendly."

The tribe broke into a chorus of gregarious barks, but the man held his position . . . and his gun. He didn't take his eyes off them for a second.

"Come on!" Grash pleaded with the man. "We're not going to hurt you! We're your friends!"

"Take us with you!" shouted Grallus. "We'll protect you!"

The man remained motionless.

"We're too intimidating," said Grash. "Let's spread out a little."

The tribe began to separate slightly, which made the man even more rigid. He began to sway his gun back and forth across the widening group.

"We would have chewed you up by now if we had wanted to," said Grash to the man. "Give us a chance."

"I know," said Grallus. "Let's lie on our backs with our paws up. Maybe if we roll around a little, he'll understand."

"Good idea," said Grash, who gave the order.

They all fell to the ground immediately. Grash went over on his back, indicating complete submission. He remained motionless for several seconds, then began to roll around a bit as the others were doing. They stayed on their backs for quite some time, without any response from the man. Grash began to lose hope.

"Forget it," Grash said dejectedly. "He's not interested. Let's go."

Slowly and sadly the tribe members got to their feet, turned, and loped back into the cover of the Canyon. Not one of them looked back.

CHAPTER 30

As usual, there were already messages in her mailbox when Laura walked into the office at nine o'clock. She grabbed four of the pink slips and walked over to her desk.

It had been a long night. She had tried to get to sleep early, but had tossed and turned for several hours before finally nodding off. She'd been wrapped up in thought about Keith and Danielle, and what a long conversation with the latter might turn up. She had meant to ask Danielle about Keith's ability to speak with animals.

She might still get the chance. Laura had decided to take Danielle up on her invitation to sit in on the recording session. If nothing else it would be a learning experience, since Laura had never witnessed the actual process of producing of a record.

Laura had a lot of work to do early if she was going to go play in the afternoon. She decided to start off by returning the four phone calls she had received, the first three of whom she didn't know and the last from Dennis Jack. She put the other three down and began dialing Dennis's number, figuring he would be the least hostile of the four.

"I'm glad you called," said Dennis. "I have two things to tell you."

"Shoot," said Laura.

"First of all," said Dennis, "thanks for getting the FBI people off their butts. I got a call from two of them yesterday afternoon, and I'm meeting with them this morning."

"No problem," said Laura. "It took one phone call to their PR flack. The last thing they want is headlines talking about their refusal to get after an international smuggling ring, no matter what it is that's being smuggled."

"Again, thanks," said Dennis. "They may not help much, but we can use whatever we can get."

"If you have any problems let me know," said Laura.

Dennis knew it was a two-way street. If and when anything broke on this he would call Laura immediately, before anyone else in the media could find out, with the complete story.

"The other thing," Dennis said, "is, I saw five of the attack dogs yesterday."

"You did? Where?"

"Carlsbad. A few miles north of where you found that trap. I was up there, ironically setting a trap of my own, and there they were. They ran out of the brush and got pretty close. It was real scary."

"What did you do?" asked Laura.

"I drew my gun," said Dennis. "That's what froze them in their tracks. Otherwise I'm sure they would have come all the way over. They obviously recognized the uniform and they seemed happy to see me, even after I pulled the gun. It was like they were trying to tell me they were friendly. They were yelping and wagging their tales like crazy, but I wasn't taking any chances."

"I can understand why," said Laura. "But you only saw five?"

"Yeah. We know eight escaped from the kennel. Two of them were killed by the guy in San Marcos who caught them trying to rip off his goat. It's possible another one dropped out for some reason, or just didn't show up yesterday."

"So you didn't catch any of them," stated Laura.

"No. I was by myself, without the proper gear. Plus there were too many of them to try and catch one by myself. They finally just ran off into the brush."

"What now?" asked Laura.

"Now that we know where they are, specifically, we're gonna have a massive hunt for them this afternoon. There'll be several officers from our office and from the Humane Society. We'll pound the brush if we have to."

"What time?"

"One o'clock," said Dennis.

Laura closed her eyes and put her left hand to her

forehead. One o'clock. Exactly when she was supposed
to visit the Gallatins as they recorded a hit song.

"Where are you going to meet?" asked Laura, resigned.

Sarena afforded herself a luxurious stretch, then carefully began to groom. She had been sleeping since well
before daylight, and now the sun was high in the clear
southern sky. She worked on her tawny coat while pon-
dering the whereabouts of Lanakila.

She finished her grooming and began to walk away
from the sun. She wondered why Lanakila had let her
sleep so late. Normally her friend would be jabbing at
her tail, or up to some other mischief. Sarena was still a
little sour over his demand that she leave her most recent
kill behind for the kribas from whom she was fleeing.

Sarena thought about the kribas and where they might
be. Perhaps Lanakila was leading them in the opposite
direction. This made her nervous, because she knew how
large the kribas were and how light Lanakila was in
comparison.

Stopping amidst a large cluster of manzanita, Sarena
looked to the sky. A hawk was gliding gracefully over
the Canyon, but no Lanakila. Sarena lowered her gaze
to the huge expanse of brush but saw virtually no movement of any kind. It was midday, and the Canyon was
napping.

A thought suddenly struck her. With all the time *she*
spent napping, the same must be true for other pumas
as well. No wonder they could never find each other—
they were too busy sleeping to find anything. It was a
wonder they even found enough food to eat.

Sarena shook her head. She was assuming, again, that
there were others like her. It had been a while since she
had thought about other pumas. A lot had happened
over the past several weeks, enough to distract her from
her primary objective.

Walking forward again, she began to growl silently to
herself. It didn't matter how much she slept, she had
never crossed anything resembling the scent of another
puma. She had managed to cross everything else. Lanakila had not seen one either, and nothing passed through
the Canyon undetected by his eyes. No, they simply were
not out there.

She wished the great bird would show up. She desperately needed someone to talk to.

It was not much better for Grash and the tribe. They had not seen the ahila either, and they were in cheerless need of good news. The disappointment with the man in uniform had dropped morale to a disheartening gloom.

It had been so sudden, Grash still could not figure it out. They had been out of touch with men for so long, no one in the tribe had seemed interested in ever pursuing a relationship with men again. To the contrary, men were considered more of an enemy than anything else they had come to face in the Canyon.

This truly had been a surprise, and now it was raising unasked questions throughout the group. It must have been the uniform. As nasty as everyone else had been to them, the men in uniform were always special.

Grash wondered what would happen if they saw another one. This one had not been friendly at all, but he had not harmed them either. He easily could have. He'd pointed his gun right at them. Still, he didn't shoot.

As the tribe hid in the cover of thick scrub oak, Grash watched them gnaw internally at themselves. They faced difficult questions with even more difficult answers.

"What think?" Broed asked Grash suddenly.

"I think, for now anyway, we should stay away from the streets until we figure out what it is we're really looking for," said Grash. "Obviously the man has had a major effect on us all. Let's be glad he didn't use his gun. Maybe the next time another one will."

"He wouldn't have," said Bruether. "I could tell. He loves all animals. He wanted to help us somehow, but was too afraid to try. I don't know how I know, I just do."

"I'll agree with you," said Grash. "Something about him was really decent, but I just couldn't put a paw on it. I think he did want to help us."

"What now?" asked Broed.

Grash glanced across the remaining tribe members. They were all panting hard, even though they had been still and resting for quite some time. It had not gone unnoticed by Grash that Grallus had not said a word since their encounter with the man.

"We've had one objective all along," said Grash. "We want to have the ahila on our side. Apparently this means we're going to have to free it from yet another puma, but I think this can be done simply enough. With any luck we can figure out the problem, then take the bird and run."

"The problem?" asked Bruether.

"The puma must be doing *something* to hold the bird hostage," said Grash. "If we can figure out what it is, we might be able to fix the problem and free the bird. Then we'll never have to face the puma."

There was no response to this remark, and Grash was perplexed. He had thought long and hard about the problem, and considered himself a genius for possibly having figured out an easier way. The tribe didn't seem so impressed. Or judging by their lack of expressions, didn't care.

Apparently the kribas had forgotten everything their cousins had spent two weeks teaching them. The krahsta pack had tailed the kribas relentlessly since the appearance and disappearance of the ahila, without ever having been discovered. As far as Dropno could tell, the kribas seemed too wrapped up in themselves to notice anything.

The run-in with the man had been scary, but worth it. The man hadn't seen the pack at all, since the kribas were barking at him like idiots, asking him to take them home.

Dropno didn't know where all of this was leading and really didn't care. To the pack it was simply entertainment. They could eat well no matter where they roamed in the Canyon, so following the kribas around was no big deal.

It was, though. To Dropno and several others in the pack, it was a very big deal. Never before had he developed such a loathing for any animal. Not even puma. The kribas were a disgrace, and he would be very happy to do them in somehow. It might also include doing in a puma at the same time, if he was clever enough. It all hinged on the actions of a very mysterious bird.

CHAPTER 31

It was late afternoon when Laura returned to the office. The hunt for the killer attack dogs had been a bust. As promised, several officers from Animal Reg, the Humane Society, and Fish and Game were out pounding the chaparral, without even one sighting.

This made it even more of a story, as far as Bill Sesma was concerned. Laura agreed, and began typing away at the computer. She had two hours until deadline, which was a long time to write an easy story with all of the elements already lined up, but she knew the phone would be ringing, as always, and answering it would take time as well.

Miraculously, she finished writing in forty-five minutes, without one interruption. There were no messages from when she had been out, either, and she wondered if she was losing her popularity with the wackos who usually called her.

There was no message from the Gallatins either.

She tried not to think about it, but it didn't matter anyway. Playing around with rock stars was all fun and good times, but the reality was she had her job to worry about. She had her *life* to worry about.

Keith Gallatin was a pro. He had probably charmed his way to success with more women than Laura could even count. She had to admit he'd succeeded in charming her as well. The only difference was, she wasn't having any part of it. Her job would still be there tomorrow. Keith Gallatin probably wouldn't.

Laura gritted her teeth in frustration. Despite all her attempts to replace emotion with logic, it still would have been nice if he had called, which was strange, since

she couldn't recall ever having concerned herself with
whether a man would call her or not. She had never
cared one way or the other, until meeting Keith.

"I have a rather strange question to ask you." Someone's voice had interrupted her thoughts. It was Bill
Sesma. Laura looked up and realized she was biting her
left index finger, which she promptly pulled from her
mouth.

"About the story?" Laura asked.

"No. About yesterday," said Sesma. "Did you ride up
to Long Beach with Keith Gallatin in his limo?"

"Yes," said Laura, without blinking. She had been
prepared for this one. "I asked him if I'd be able to
interview him ahead of time and he agreed, then invited
me to ride up there with him. I went along for two reasons: first, so I could get as much info on him as possible
to update our file, and second, so I wouldn't have to
drive back. I was able to write my story in the car."

"Okay, just asking," said Sesma. "I was hoping there
wouldn't be any conflict of interest."

"No such luck," laughed Laura. "I was just trying to
establish a good rapport for any future stories I may have
dealing with the Gallatin empire."

"What did he say about you writing your story on the
way back?" asked Sesma.

"Nothing," said Laura. "He was too busy moping
about the decision to go along with the hunt."

"He didn't know about the court ruling?"

Laura shook her head.

The phone rang and Laura was relieved. She had
known better than to ride up to Long Beach with Keith.
She wondered who had told Bill Sesma, and who all was
talking about it. The last thing she needed was a rumor
like that.

"Hi, this is Keith."

Laura answered with silence; not only because of the
coincidence, but also because she didn't know what to
say.

"I hope you're not mad at me about the other day,"
said Keith. "I'm sorry for being such a baby."

"It's okay," said Laura. "You had plenty of reason to
be upset."

"But not with you," said Keith. "And really not at all.

It was bad, yes, but in the grand scheme of life it was no big deal."

"Does this mean . . ."

"Why are you always interviewing me?" asked Keith, irritated. "Why can't you just . . . Never mind."

"Why can't I what?" asked Laura.

"We started recording 'Sarena's Song' today," said Keith, ignoring her question. "We actually got a couple of the tracks down on tape. A few more days and she might be ready."

"Terrific," said Laura.

"Danielle told me she invited you," said Keith.

"I couldn't make it," said Laura. "News happens."

"It's actually better, since we did mostly prep stuff today. Tomorrow would be a better day for listening in. If you get a chance you should come on down. We'd love to have you."

"I will if I can," said Laura. "I won't know what my day looks like until tomorrow morning. If nothing much is happening I should be able to swing it."

"Take the day off!" said Keith.

"Can't," said Laura. "I have three cats to feed."

Laura hung up and shook her head. She began to visualize sitting in on a rock session but was immediately snapped back to reality when the phone rang. It was Dennis Jack.

"Sorry about this afternoon," he said.

"It's still a good story," said Laura.

"I got some news from the folks at the FBI," said Dennis.

"Already? You just met with them this morning."

"I know," said Dennis. "Seems they have a problem with communications within their own department. Imagine that. Apparently they've had an agent working on this very case for several months, and none of the people I'd contacted even knew about it."

"I guess it's their job to be secretive," joked Laura.

"I guess, but it sure could have saved a lot of time on everyone's part if they'd talked to each other. Even the guys I met with this morning didn't know about it."

"Amazing," said Laura. "Government bureaucracy, even in the FBI. So, what did you find out?"

"Seems they almost have enough to make some

busts," said Dennis. "Real soon. And guess which shop they're gonna hit?"

"Jake's Gun Shop and Taxidermy."

"You got it."

"Let me know when it goes down," said Laura.

"You got it."

CHAPTER 32

Sarena decided not to move again until she heard from Lanakila. It was now the midpoint of the second day since she had seen him last, and she was beginning to worry. She hoped he wasn't off flying way out to sea again.

She found an open spot in the brush, which would leave her visible only from the sky. Large growths of drying red shank kept her well hidden from any other Canyon eyes.

The air was getting cooler in the late autumn afternoons. The air was dry, with a wind out of the east, which carried a little nip with it. It didn't bother Sarena at all. She was more than happy to be cool as long as she was dry. She remembered other winters that had been warmer, but sopping wet.

Without warning, Lanakila was beside her. Sarena jumped only a little, since she was getting used to his sudden appearances.

He looked different. Something about him had changed dramatically. His piercing eyes were brighter than they'd ever been. His head was held high, and he moved his shoulders from side to side. And for the first time ever, it looked to Sarena as if Lanakila was smiling.

"Where've you been?" asked Sarena.

"I've got news," said Lanakila. "Lots of it."

"Such as?"

"Big news. But first of all, I'll tell you about the kribas. The men walked all over the Canyon yesterday looking for them. They were too late, though, because the kribas had turned this way and had already left the area where the men searched."

Lanakila's words were almost too fast for Sarena to understand. He seemed very jittery, but not upset.

"What else?" asked Sarena. "Something's going on. I've never seen you like this before."

"Just happy, that's all," said Lanakila, defensively. "Anyway, the men set traps for the kribas. I saw how they work. It gave me an idea of how to get rid of the kribas."

"I'm not going near any traps," said Sarena, alarmed.

"You won't have to, Fur Ball. I haven't figured out exactly how we'll do it yet, but it should be pretty safe for both of us."

"Is that what you're so excited about?" asked Sarena, doubtfully. Lanakila talked about catching the kribas, but still didn't seem to be very interested in the project. Something else was going on.

"You'll see very shortly," said Lanakila.

It took less than a minute. A huge shadow fell between them, and suddenly another bird swooped down and lit beside Lanakila. Sarena let out an involuntary gasp, and it was several moments before any of them could speak. Words, however, were not necessary. Lanakila had found a mate.

CHAPTER 33

Everything looked good. It was a slow news day, and Laura was freed up from doing dailies so she could work on beats and future projects. Laura decided to add the Gallatins to her list of beats.

She sat at her desk in the quiet newsroom. Several of the other reporters were also in-house, but most talked quietly at their phones. There was very little movement or noise for the number of people in the office.

Most people thought her job was glamorous, running around chasing cops and robbers. But the truth was she spent most of her time on the phone, making sure people remembered her when something important happened. She began paging through her phone list, to see if there was anyone whom she really should call. She was on the third page when her phone rang.

"Hi, it's Dennis. You wanted me to call. . . ."

"Yeah, I think you just call because you like my voice," said Laura.

"I like a lot more than just your voice," said Dennis.

"You say that to all the girls," said Laura.

"But you never let me near enough . . ."

"Shut up, goon!" said Laura with a raspberry. "What do you want?"

"More info on Jake's Taxidermy," said Dennis. "The feds are making the hit late this afternoon. People from our department will be there as uniformed support."

"What? So soon?" gasped Laura.

"Turns out the reason the FBI didn't know anything about this was, they weren't working on it. The guys at ATF are handling it. Their guys have been on the case for months. Seems our friend Mr. Cotter has been smug-

248

gling a lot more than pelts into Mexico. The Mexican government has warrants out for the guy, too, so you know it must be bad."

Laura immediately turned her phone book to Alcohol, Tobacco, and Firearms. She had no current numbers listed.

"What else has he been moving?" asked Laura.

"Guns," said Dennis, simply. "He's got access to warehouses full of them, and certain people on the other side of the border pay dearly for them. Mexico is not the USA. They have no right to keep and bear arms down there."

"Damn," said Laura.

"What?"

"Oh, nothing," said Laura. "Just bad timing, again. What time is this thing going down?"

"Around four," said Dennis. "Several undercover guys'll be making the hit. We're staying back so we don't tip them off. It's unlikely we'll be needed anyway. Usually when these guys make a bust like this it's quick and painless."

"Okay," said Laura. "Four o'clock. You're sure?"

"Positive," said Dennis, a little hurt.

"Sorry," said Laura. "All right. Four o'clock. I'll see you then."

The tribe had once again picked up the scent of the puma. This seemed to lift their spirits, as far as Grash could tell. He personally had no desire to meet an animal capable of shredding Kroth to ribbons, but the tribe seemed bent on it. Grash reminded himself of the ahila, and how their only hope was tied to the puma's demise.

The scent was not strong so the puma was still quite a distance off, but the scent was strong enough to hold without any problems. Grash knew they could make up ground quickly on the big cat if they chose to, and he felt they probably would.

To Grash the tribe looked even worse than before. Even Grallus, whose eyes had been on fire only days before, was loping along without emotion. Bruether, too, whom Grash depended upon for input and support, panted along with a glazed-over expression. It was as if they were on a mission none of them wanted to survive.

Grash barked an order to halt, which was obeyed immediately without question. They all sat down, with tongues hanging out in a moderate pant.

"Is this what it's going to come down to?" asked Grash. "A tribe of fierce, highly disciplined, killer attack dogs done in by one stupid man in a uniform?"

All four of the others lowered their heads. None dared make eye contact with Grash, although he wasn't being threatening at all. He was merely trying to boost morale.

"Come on, we've worked too hard for this," Grash continued.

"It's too late, Grash," said Grallus. "We blew it. You know it, we all know it. We should never have left the cage when that man let us out."

Grash wanted to argue, but he knew it was true. After all this time, they were still no match for the Canyon and all its surprises. And worse, they were lonely for a companionship foreign to the Canyon.

Grash growled to himself. If only they hadn't seen the man in the uniform. It didn't matter. Their resistance had been weakening anyway. It was only a matter of time. Now they were out of time, and out of friends.

"It's okay, Grash," said Grallus. "You've been a good leader. We're just not cut out for this."

"Maybe not," said Grash, "but we're here, and there's nothing we can do about it. We're stuck, so we might as well make the most of it."

"We will," said Grallus. "We'll get you your ahila. If all of us have to die trying, we'll get you your ahila."

"Another ahila!" cried Sarena, the thrill beginning to hurt.

"Yes," said Lanakila. "We met yesterday. Oddly enough, near the sea."

Sarena looked at the female ahila, who was obviously nervous and shaking to prove it. She nuzzled closer to Lanakila, who beamed beside her.

"Falanika, this is my Fur Ball," said Lanakila to his mate. "This is the only friend I've ever had, until we met."

"Now I have two friends," said Sarena, still eyeing the new bird. She was slightly smaller than Lanakila, but otherwise looked exactly the same. Sarena knew she would have trouble telling them apart for a while, if they weren't together.

"I've heard so much about you," were Falanika's first words to Sarena, who no longer worried about telling them apart. Falanika's voice was higher and sweeter than the throaty song of her old friend. "Everything Lanakila has talked about has somehow involved you and your safety. You must be very special."

"Our friendship is special," said Sarena, who was starting to ache inside. "I hope our friendship will stay strong, and you two will continue to visit me often."

"Oh, Fur Ball, of course we will," said Lanakila. "Now we'll have twice as much fun. Just think of how good we'll be at hunting."

Sarena's eyes lit up momentarily. It was true: another pair of eyes in the sky, now looking almost exclusively for another puma. The situation could be a lot worse.

Still, Sarena couldn't understand the pain. What it came down to was, she had never realistically expected either of them to find another mate. Now Lanakila had, which not only reminded her of how nice it *would* be to have a mate, but at the same time it threatened to take away the only friend Sarena had ever known.

"Is that really your name? Fur Ball?" asked Falanika.

Lanakila burst into laughter, only to be hissed at by Sarena.

"And I called you a friend," said Sarena to Lanakila.

"You'll see," said Lanakila to his mate. "She sleeps all day long. From the sky she looks just like a big ball of fur wrapped up in the grass."

"My name is Sarena."

Falanika looked at Lanakila in horror.

"See what I mean? She's got an impossible name to pronounce," said Lanakila. "Just call her Fur Ball, it's a lot easier on everyone."

Sarena hissed at him again, but Lanakila only laughed.

CHAPTER 34

Laura checked her makeup in the rearview mirror one last time, then shook her head and closed her purse. She had been sitting in the parking lot of Gallisongs, the recording studios owned by Keith and Danielle. She had made it this far but was still too nervous to get out of the car. Then a security guard tapped on her window.

She immediately opened the door and jumped out, heading straight for the front door of the building.

"Laura Kay of the *San Diego Union*. I have an appointment inside." She said all of this in one breath, walking full speed, without even looking at the guard. The man shrugged his shoulders and turned away, having learned years before not to mess with a woman like that one.

Laura figured she had two hours. The bust was scheduled to go down at four, so she wanted to be nosing around the neighborhood no later than two. Depending upon how things went here she might even get there earlier, and eat lunch in her car across the street from the business in question.

Once inside, Laura was surprised to find the receptionist had been expecting her. She rang for someone to escort Laura to the studio where Keith was. It was Randy Shock who opened a side door and led her down a short hallway.

There were two rooms with thick glass windows between them, and both were fairly dark. The walls were lined with what looked like green foam-rubber eggshell cartons. Laura correctly assumed this was soundproofing for acoustical purposes.

Danielle stood with her eyes closed in the smaller one,

wearing a headset and playing an electric guitar. Keith was sitting on the floor beside her, watching her intently and also listening through a headset.

The other room contained a large production facility. A huge audio mixing board and several large tape machines were being tended by two women, while a third woman leaned up against the back wall with her eyes closed. As with Keith and Danielle, all three of them were fitted with headsets.

Laura and Randy watched from the hallway through another set of windows. Although Danielle continued to play, Laura couldn't hear a thing. She stood with Randy, completely unnoticed, until Danielle had finished.

"Even though we've been away, Fur Ball, we haven't been idle," said Lanakila.

Falanika giggled and Sarena rolled her eyes.

"As I said earlier, we saw the men setting traps," continued Lanakila, ignoring the others. "There is a way, somehow, of trapping the kribas. I know there is."

"I don't want them to be trapped as I was," said Sarena. "I wish that on no animal. Not even the evil krahstas who watched me while I suffered, although I'd still love to deal with them in my own special way sometime."

"You may get your chance," said Lanakila. "If all goes well and we're clever, we may be able to pull it off."

"How?" asked Sarena.

"The men want the kribas out of the Canyon, too," said Lanakila. "But they don't want the kribas hurt. The traps they set this time don't bite. I know, because one of them captured a lynx."

"How do you know?" asked Sarena.

"We saw it happen," said Lanakila. "We dropped down to investigate and found the animal was not hurt, as you had been. She was simply held inside a box. Having seen it work, it was easy to figure out the concept. We set the lynx free and she went on her way."

"You figured out a human trap?" Sarena asked in amazement.

"It took us both, but we managed," said Lanakila proudly. He nuzzled his mate's cheek.

"You've learned how to set animals free," said Sarena. "How will this help us trap the kribas?"

"We've learned the concept," said Lanakila, "not the technique. We'll have to devise our own method, since I have little hope of coaxing the kribas into those boxes."

"Then how do we do it?" asked Falanika.

"We think big, my love. We think big."

"I'm glad you made it," said Keith, when Randy opened the door and led Laura inside. He pulled off his headset with a smile.

"I can only stay a little while," said Laura.

"We're due for a break, anyway," said Danielle, slightly irritated. Apparently she had been playing the guitar for quite some time before Laura arrived.

"What's going on?" asked the woman who had been leaning against the wall in the other room.

"Break time," said Danielle. "By the way, Kathy, this is Laura Kay, a friend of Keith's."

"Hi," said Kathy, looking right past Laura. "Ten minutes, then I want a few more takes on Danielle's riff." She turned and walked back out.

"Producers," Keith said to Laura with a wink.

"How's it going?" Laura asked.

"Not bad," said Keith. "We're almost halfway through with laying down the sound. It'll be a couple more days, then we'll begin mixing and post-production."

"When will it finally be out?" asked Laura.

"About two months," said Danielle. "We're already working on promotion."

"We've been busy," said Keith, as they finally began to walk out of the tiny, padded room. They walked down a hall and turned into a small lounge.

"All the proceeds from 'Sarena's Song' will go to the campaign to put together and pass a mountain lion initiative," said Danielle.

"Really?" asked Laura. "Is there one?"

"There is now," said Keith. "The Gallatins have finally tossed their hat into the political arena."

They all sat down and Randy walked in with several cans of soft drinks. Laura took diet, while staring at Keith.

"We're gonna get it going," said Keith. "Not yet, though. And by the way this is all confidential, until we're about to release the song."

"Rats," said Laura.

"She only loves me for my news value," Keith said to Danielle.

"I can tell," said Danielle. "Smart girl. There isn't much else to love about you."

"So what's your goal?" asked Laura. "Are you looking at actually putting together the initiative yourselves? Or are you concerned with getting it on the ballot and getting it passed?"

Danielle looked at Keith and laughed. Keith rolled his eyes.

"What?" asked Laura. "Or are you just concerned with raising the funds?"

"Yes," said Keith. "All of the above."

"My, girl, you ask a lot of questions," said Danielle.

"I can't help it," said Laura defensively. "I'm a reporter."

"Back off, Danielle," said Keith. "You're even nosier than she is."

"Being inquisitive isn't being nosy," said Danielle.

"No, it makes you a gossip," said Keith.

"Another question," said Laura. "What's this initiative going to say?"

"We're not sure on the exact wording yet," said Keith. "We're novices at this. We'll actually be hiring professionals to handle the actual wording."

"Basically we want it to put mountain lions on the protected species list indefinitely," said Danielle. "Whatever wording it takes to keep them from being hunted."

Laura nodded and wished she had her note pad, but knew she was better off without it. She watched as Keith and Danielle continued to play off of each other, constantly filling in the blanks for each other with a series of good-natured insults. It was almost as if one soul was occupying two different bodies at the same time.

There was more to it. Laura could sense constant communication between the two, even when they weren't talking or even looking at each other. It was a bond almost strong enough to touch. Laura found it slightly unnerving, since they seemed to be secretly carrying on some kind of conversation without her hearing or seeing a thing.

"Let's go!" Kathy belted into the lounge. When she

turned away, the twins immediately stuck their tongues out at her in unison.

"Even we have bosses," said Danielle.

"I should go," said Laura. "I don't want to get in the way."

"No, stay. It's no problem," said Keith.

"I have a story I have to go on," said Laura, as they walked down the hall. "It's one you'll be interested in. Remember the shop we went into in Tijuana?"

"Yes," said Keith with a grimace.

"The feds are gonna bust one of his suppliers on this side of the border."

"Really? Great!"

"Apparently he's a gunrunner, too."

"I hope they hang him out to dry," said Keith.

"I have to talk to Kathy for a minute," said Danielle to Keith, with a very direct stare. "I'll be ready shortly."

"Okay," said Keith. "I'll walk Laura to the front door."

"Come back again," said Danielle. "The fun part will be the day after tomorrow when Keith tries to sing. You won't want to miss it."

"Thanks," said Laura. "Tell Kathy it was nice meeting her."

Danielle laughed and walked into the production control room.

"It was nice to see you," said Keith, as they walked toward the front of the building.

"It was nice seeing you, too," said Laura.

"Maybe you'll let me take you out to dinner sometime," said Keith.

"That sounds like fun."

"How about tonight?" asked Keith.

"Well, I don't know how long this bust is going to take," said Laura. "I could be . . ."

Keith let out a long sigh and shook his head.

". . . a little late," said Laura. "But if you don't mind having a late dinner, sure, I'd love to."

"Great," said Keith, smiling. "You're certainly worth waiting for."

"Thank you," said Laura. "That's sweet. I'll call you when I'm done."

She walked out to her car with a smile, while shaking

her head. She felt good about having changed her mind and let Keith take her out. She had even amazed herself by allowing him to compliment her without turning it into a mess.

As she opened her car door, she looked at her watch. The bad part was, she had allowed herself two hours with the Gallatins but had run herself out in less than twenty minutes. She sat down and closed the door. At least she was making progress.

It had been quite a while since Sarena had carried a bird on her back, and now she carried two. Falanika had gotten on reluctantly, and only after a lot of encouragement from Lanakila. Sarena hardly noticed any difference in weight with the addition of the second ahila.

Falanika rode in front. She was still very nervous about Sarena, and needed some getting used to the entire concept. With urging from Lanakila she began to tell Sarena the story of how she had come to find him, as they walked along a tiny dirt path through the sage.

"I grew up in the mountains where the sun rises," she began, looking out to the east. "I can't remember my parents, or anyone else ever looking like me. I thought I was the only ahila in the world."

Sarena nodded as she walked. Falanika's story was beginning to sound familiar already. She stopped speaking momentarily, as Sarena jumped over a small boulder blocking the path.

"I never realized how lonely I was," said Falanika. "It was bitter, never having anyone to talk to, but I didn't know how bad until I met Lanakila. I don't even think I could tell you how it felt to be so alone."

"You don't have to try, dearest," said Sarena. "Lanakila and I both know exactly how you felt."

"Yes, I suppose you do," said Falanika. "Anyway, I lived okay, eating well and flying high. I always kept my eyes open for anyone else, but never saw anything.

"Then one day I heard this strange voice," she continued. "It wasn't a bird or any animal I could recognize, but the words were clear. It was calling me. It called me to the sea."

"A voice?" asked Sarena, remembering Lanakila's tale about his flight over the sea.

"Very clear and reassuring," said Falanika. "It was beautiful. I had to follow it. I knew it was right. It led me to Lanakila."

"We talked about it, Fur Ball," said Lanakila. "I believe she heard the same voice I did. Someone called out to both of us, at the same time. We heard it the same day."

Sarena walked on but said nothing. She thought about the exact time Lanakila would have heard the voice. She thought about where she had been and what she had been doing at the time, then smiled. Keith had told her the truth about the chain he had put around her neck. It truly was magic.

Sarena started to speak, but stopped. When alone again she decided to give the chain another try. The last time she had touched it she had desperately been hoping for Lanakila to return, and it had worked. Not only had it called Lanakila but it had found him a mate as well. This time Sarena would wish for something else.

"I have a plan, Fur Ball," said Lanakila.

"For what?" she asked.

"For getting rid of the kribas," said Lanakila. "I think I've finally figured it out. It was something I saw a young man do once, and I think it'll work for us."

"A man?" asked Sarena, doubtfully.

"It will be dangerous, but I think we can pull it off," said Lanakila.

"How dangerous?" asked Sarena.

"That depends upon how high you can jump," said Lanakila. "For now, Falanika and I must fly. There is so much we need to rehearse."

CHAPTER 35

The scent was getting stronger and the tribe was getting edgy. From where they stood they could run the puma down in a few short minutes. The wind was to their advantage, so it could take even less time if they were careful.

Looking at the others, Grash could see a dramatic change. The prospect of an extreme challenge had snapped them out of their despondent lope. Their heads were high and they panted with excited anticipation. They were ready for war.

"Okay, let's do it," Grash said in a hushed voice. The others nodded in agreement. "Remember, this is the monster who killed Kroth, so I don't have to remind you to be careful. We're avenging our brother. As a team we should have no problem at all, so let's spread out and tear every limb off its body."

The others began bouncing around in circles, and Grash had to remind them to keep silent. Any noise at all could ruin their chances. Surprise was imperative.

Grash was just about to give the order to move when a piercing screech ripped out from directly above them. It was the ahila, diving at them with beak open and talons extended. There was no time to move, only to crouch. Every kriba in the tribe dropped to his forepaws as the fiery voice blasted through their ears.

The bird was almost at brush level before it broke its descent. It circled around above them, then hovered for a moment. Grash was about to order them to take cover when the bird turned and flew to the low branches of a eucalyptus tree several strides away.

Grash looked at the others, who were all still frozen

on the ground. Their eyes were on the tree, where the great ahila sat sqawking and flapping his wings.

"I guess he wants to talk to us," Grash said finally.

No one answered, and no one looked thrilled at the prospect of walking over to face a bird who had just scared the fur off them.

"It's not so bad," said Grash. "He's on our side, remember?"

"Doesn't look like it to me," said Grallus.

"No," agreed Broed.

"He didn't hurt us," said Grash. "He wanted our attention. Let's go see what he wants."

"What about the puma?" asked Grallus.

"The bird knows how close we are," said Grash. "He can advise us."

The bird was still making a tremendous racket in the tree. Reluctantly, the four others followed Grash through sparse chaparral to where the bird was perched.

"Bad timing, bad timing," said Lanakila when the tribe arrived. "The puma knows you are here. She sits in ambush, right as we speak."

"But as a group we can take her," said Grash, with a wince. The thought of Kroth being destroyed so thoroughly by a *female* was even harder to take.

"Not if two of you are killed before the others can help," said the bird.

"Then how will we know when to attack?" asked Grash, not liking the odds of going up against a puma with only two others alongside to assist.

"Tonight," said the bird. "Just before the sun reaches the sea, I will lead you to where she sleeps. You should have no trouble at all."

"What does she keep over you?" Grash asked. "How can she make you help her, when you can simply fly away?"

"She has more powers than you know," whispered the bird. "They are best not spoken of, because she gets most of them from a powerful man. How else would she know of your present location?"

Grash had no response. The prospect of facing a puma was bad enough, but one with strange powers generated from a man was turning the cause into a nightmare.

"She is weakest when the sun begins to leave," said Lanakila. "I will come for you when she sleeps."

"What is the sea?" asked Grash.

"No concern," said Lanakila. "I'll find you before the sky turns dark."

It was too hot to keep the window rolled up, but too cold to leave it open. Laura hated days like these, and she hated stakeouts even worse. She sat in the front seat of her aging RX-7 and waited for the feds to move in on Jake's Taxidermy.

Laura was parked directly across the street from the target, and she had already seen several undercover officers walk past the front of the store. She knew they were cops, because each one of them turned his head to look inside for the slightest fraction of a second, then walked on without looking back.

The employees of Jake's Taxidermy obviously had no idea of what was about to happen. Laura could see them going on about their business. The street was crowded and busy with late afternoon traffic, so the parade of men walking past their window had gone unnoticed.

Finally, it began. Laura jumped out of her car as fifty undercover officers marched toward the store from both directions. They were all clad in dark blue windbreakers marked with yellow lettering on the backs that said POLICE. Three marked San Diego Sheriff cars pulled up to the front as the feds began walking inside.

Laura ran across the street and stood by the store window as the last of the officers walked inside. She could see them fanning out through the aisles, as the employees stood motionless with stunned faces. Laura was willing to bet most of them had no idea what had been going on at their place of employment. She wondered if Jake Cotter was inside.

Laura had already been waiting two hours up to this point, and knew she would be standing outside the shop for several more. It would take the officers quite a while to go through the entire store and all of its paperwork.

"We'll need you to clear away from the area," said a man with a police blazer.

Laura held up her press ID without even giving the guy a second glance. She continued to stare through the window at the officers going through the aisles, expecting the guy beside her to hassle her some more, but he merely turned away.

"Excuse me," she said to him. "Is there a spokesman, or anyone who can tell me how long this might take?"

"I'll try to find out," the man said, and walked inside.

Laura looked at her watch. It was four-thirty. If she could get out of here in an hour she might be able to get the story written and filed by seven-thirty. Any later and Keith probably wouldn't wait for her. She stood on her tiptoes for another look inside, then bit down hard on her pen.

Walking up the edge of the Canyon, Sarena was finding that she didn't like this idea one bit. She hoped Lanakila knew what he was doing. The slightest mistake could lead to disaster.

Well, maybe not the *slightest* mistake. There was *some* room for error, but Sarena still was not thrilled with the potential consequences. Yet it didn't matter. She was on her way, and turning back would accomplish nothing.

She reached the top of the cliff and stopped. She stayed at the edge of the brush as long as possible, using its ragged pattern to break her outline. She carefully scouted her destination, scanning in all directions for signs of men. There were none.

It was time to move. Sarena took a long, deep breath, then began a calculated trot to the fence. As Lanakila had instructed, she was running directly into the dwellings of men. She stopped at the gate, risked another quick glance in all directions, then bounded inside.

The smell of man was everywhere. Their tracks were numerous in the soft dirt surrounding the harder ground in the enclosure. Most of the tracks, Sarena noticed, were small. Thankfully, the owners of all of the tracks were gone.

Sarena went to work. She began to rub against the metal barrier which separated the Canyon from the men. She rubbed against the gate and even rolled on the ground near the entrance, guaranteeing her scent would not be missed.

When she'd finished with the entrance, she repeated the exercise throughout the small enclosure. She rubbed against walls and objects she couldn't name. She left her scent *everywhere*.

Once done, she quickly examined the area for possible escape routes. There were none. Lanakila had been correct. Other than the gate, there was no access to the Canyon. Her timing would have to be perfect, or else it was going to be a long night.

She saw Lanakila circle low over the Canyon, which was her cue to move. There was only one place to hide in the enclosure; a place Sarena never would have thought of before meeting Lanakila.

The sun was failing in the western sky when Dropno saw the ahila. Others in the pack saw it the same instant, and they watched it circle high and then dive. It came closer than they had expected, but apparently it didn't see them.

It was above the kribas. The pack found the downwind scent, then saw the bird take a branch high beside them. It began to speak, but the words were too distant to be understood.

"If the kribas follow the bird," said Dropno, "we'll follow the kribas. I'd love to find out what mischief is going on in this Canyon."

"It is time," said the bird. "Time to track the evil puma."

The tribe was wiggling with excitement. Grash was pleased, since morale had not been this high since their escape. They were being led directly into the puma's lair, but there was nothing to worry about. The puma was asleep.

Grash couldn't help but think of the possibilities. This was an excellent example of how Lanakila could work for them. He could seek out their enemies, and the tribe could destroy them while they slept.

"As I said before," said Lanakila, "she sleeps with the men. You must be very careful, because her power is renewed each night, and she may be at her strongest when you meet her."

"She'll be asleep," said Grash.

"If you're careful," said the bird. "You must utter no sound, or risk serious consequences."

"What is the plan?" asked Grallus.

"She is inside the fence of a man," said Lanakila. "It has an opening, where she goes in each night. She sneaks out from the same opening before the sun rises with all its strength."

"How many of us should go in?" asked Grash, wondering about security.

"All or none," said the bird. "It will take all of you to face her. I hope it will be easy, but I fear for you all if any should remain outside."

"We need someone to watch out for men," said Grash.

"It will be me," said the bird. "I will alert you to any trouble."

Grash could tell the others liked this idea, but something seemed odd. It was one thing to face the puma on open ground, but to do so on man's territory was something else. Especially if a man was responsible for her powers.

Yet debate would be a mistake. He could see it in their eyes; they were ready to go. Grash argued it in his mind, but then had to give in. If they were going to trust this bird at all, they might as well trust it completely. If the bird was going to lead them to evil, it was best to find out now.

"Where is this place?" asked Grash finally.

"At the edge of the Canyon," said Lanakila. "You'll follow me. I'll land on the fence, directly above the opening. It's the type of fence you can see through, so your approach must be extra careful. Be silent, and be invisible."

CHAPTER 36

"Keith. Speak."

"Hi, it's Laura. I called you as soon as I could. I hope it's not too late. The raid took forever."

"Are you all finished?" asked Keith.

"Yeah. I just got through typing up my story. I can leave anytime."

"Are you hungry?" asked Keith.

"Famished."

"Good. I'll meet you at McDonald's."

The huge bird was a dark silhouette against the sunset as it glided across the western edge of the Canyon. Dropno and the pack watched it from the bottom of the eastern side of the ravine as it made its way up toward the man-homes.

When the kribas moved, Dropno silently barked the order. They filed close together and found a well-covered path along a gully. The kribas had their eyes on the bird, and had no idea the pack was behind them. The kribas were clearly on a clandestine mission, since they loped in complete silence.

The sun was now behind the far Canyon wall, making the sky look almost white. It was the perfect time for krahstas to be about, since the eyes of prey had a difficult time with such conditions and the gray krahsta coat turned them almost invisible. The multicolored kribas did not enjoy such an advantage.

After a small circle, the ahila made a sharp left turn, and dove straight for the man-homes. It flapped its wings in a short hover then landed on a high, twisted metal fence. It sat perched there with its wings extended, and the kribas ran straight for it. Dropno lowered his ears and did the same, with the pack directly behind him.

Expecting to be greeted with a disguise, Laura pulled into their favorite meeting place and found a place to park. She rubbed her eyes and made a quick check of her makeup, then opened the door. She began walking across the parking lot, having decided to go in for a caffeine fix.

Only halfway there, she stopped when Keith's limo pulled into the lot. It drove right up beside her and stopped. The driver immediately jumped out and opened a door for her. Inside was Keith—dressed as Keith—and no one else.

"You look terrific," he said.

Laura simply smiled, knowing she probably looked closer to death than terrific. She'd been on a stakeout all day, and felt as if she had been dragged through a box of cat litter.

"How did it go?" asked Keith. "Did they catch the guy?"

"No, he wasn't there," said Laura. "They did raid the store, though. They found all sorts of illegal furs, including a mountain lion pelt."

"Oh."

"Sorry. At least the guy's out of business. They also found guns. I mean obviously it was a sporting goods store, and that's what they sold, but he had enough to supply a small army."

"Really?" asked Keith.

"Yeah. I guess he's been smuggling them across the border."

"Why didn't they catch him?"

"His employees say he's out of town," said Laura. "They don't know where he is. He apparently takes off for weeks at a time. He might be in Mexico. He might not even know his store's been raided."

"He'll sure be in for a surprise when he comes back," Keith said with a laugh.

"*If* he comes back," said Laura.

"Okay, enough shop talk," said Keith.

Laura nodded and leaned back in the soft leather seat. She was still amazed at the incredible toys inside the car. Keith's guitar was still in the corner. Laura smiled, remembering her first experience of "Sarena's Song."

"Can I ask a personal question?"

"Aren't all of your questions personal?" asked Keith.

"Maybe. I don't know. Anyway, I was just wondering about songwriting. How can you write so many songs? It would seem to me that once you've written one it would be hard to come up with other tunes."

Keith shrugged with a strange smile. He looked out the window, then down at his feet.

"The music is the easy part," he said. "It never stops. Never. There's always a new tune playing in my head. Always. Twenty-four hours a day, seven days a week, unless I'm thinking of a specific song of course."

"You hear music now?" asked Laura.

"Yep. Really, it never stops. Sometimes I wish it would, just for a little while, anyway. Danielle is the same way. That's how we write so many songs. We just make up the words, and put them to whatever melody happens to be playing in our heads at the time."

"You both hear the same thing?" asked Laura.

Keith shrugged. Laura thought she should be surprised, but Keith was turning out to be so full of surprises nothing seemed impossible anymore.

"Is Italian food okay?" asked Keith.

"Sure," said Laura.

"I hope you don't mind being seen with me in public like this," said Keith. "It could wind you up on the front page of a trashy tabloid."

"I guess I don't mind, as long as you don't mind," said Laura, slightly nervous.

"Not at all," said Keith. "Not at all."

CHAPTER 37

The tribe came to an involuntary halt when first struck by the scent. It was puma, there could be no mistake. It was strong, clear, and very fresh. It arched like a wide, scarlet beam toward the gate where Lanakila sat.

They were panting harder than they should have been for such a short run. They looked as if they were ready to start howling at any moment, so Grash quietly barked them a warning, even though he felt about ready to do the same.

It was there, and they all knew it. Grash wasn't sure if he trembled out of excitement or fear, but he knew the others were shaking as well. It was his back, mostly, but it ran all through his limbs, and he wondered if he would actually be able to go through with it.

Up on the fence, the bird flapped its wings again. It wanted them to move quickly. It wouldn't need to lead them any farther, since the scent seemed even more "visible" than the bird was. Still, it flapped silently and gestured.

Now was the time. Now or never. Grash looked at the others and they all stared back, waiting for the order. He raised his left foot, and they broke into a straight dash for the gate.

The pack was going no farther. After picking up the puma scent Dropno had ordered them to stop, and no one had argued. They stood amazed, as the kribas gathered near the gate and contemplated going in. The bird still sat on top of the gate, urging them on.

It was almost dark, and the bird was nearly invisible.

Dropno wondered how well it would be able to fly in the dark. He had never noticed birds at night before.

Except for quiet panting the pack sat in silence, but only for a short time. They jumped to their feet immediately when the kribas broke for the gate.

Sarena extended her claws and gritted her teeth. She could smell the kribas and hear their shallow pants. Lanakila was up on the gate, flapping away, and Falanika was somewhere high above. Timing was everything.

It was almost dark, but she couldn't worry about it. Sarena could see fine, but she remembered Lanakila refusing to fly at night. She hoped her two feathered friends could see well enough, or she was in big trouble.

Either way, Sarena was safe for now. She sat on the roof of a tiny building, one where human children played in the daylight hours. She was completely surrounded by the fence. The entire area reeked of man, but there were none currently in the area. For this Sarena was glad. The men would return, however, and that left her jittery.

Sarena watched her friend on the gate, and nervously smiled. His plan was brilliant, even if in some ways flawed. Sarena had watched the two birds practicing their maneuver several times in the late afternoon. They had been awkward at first, but eventually got the timing perfect. But this had been in daylight, and now it was dark.

Sarena took another deep breath, trying to relax. The kriba scent brought back memories of the dreams. Her dreams had always left her in a tree, with the obnoxious animals howling below her. The reality was even more absurd, since she was sitting on the roof of a man-building instead of a branch.

If Lanakila's plan failed she could simply stay on this roof, and the kribas would never reach her. But men would arrive in the morning and they would have no problem catching her. The worst part was, she would have to listen to loud barking kribas all night.

Lanakila dropped his wings and Sarena heard the footsteps at the same instant. There were several of them, and they were loud and heavy. The kribas were on the way. She held her breath, and crouched as low as she could.

*   *   *

Grash cleared the gate first, and the scent hit him like a whip. The path to the puma was now a glaring bright scarlet, and he charged for it as fast as he could. The others bolted right at his heels, with Broed passing the gate last.

The scent was *everywhere*. Grash stopped suddenly, trying to decide which way to run. Grallus slammed into him hard, forcing out of both an involuntary yelp. Grash bit down hard, silently cursing himself.

The others, equally confused, stopped as well. They searched frantically in all directions, but saw no puma. They ran around the small yard in a frenzy, panting wildly and trying not to howl. The puma had been everywhere in the yard. Its scarlet blazed in every corner and even on the walls.

They were here. She had seen them rush through the gate. She wanted desperately to escape, to charge out at full speed, but she forced her paws to hold their place until the moment was absolutely perfect.

She saw them all. They were ugly and gross. Their stink was unbearable, and their eyes were cold and cruel.

Sarena dug her claws deep into the roof below her. Her tail was demanding to twitch, yet she held it motionless. She kept her teeth tightly together to prevent her system from gasping for air.

The kribas were all around her now. They could smell her and sensed her presence, but not one of them looked up. Fortunately, their noses were stuck to the places Sarena had marked with her scent.

They were big, and there were too many to face alone. She wanted desperately to rip the lungs out of at least one of the miserable creatures, but couldn't risk the potential injury. She couldn't even risk a fall. One slip could be fatal.

She saw Lanakila. His mate was on the way as well. Sarena held her breath, then looked to the sky for guidance from the Lady. It was time.

It was impossible to think. The scent was maddening, and the tribe was on the brink of hysteria. Grash was about to bark an order when suddenly a shrill screech rang out from above, dropping the already terrified tribe to a crouch. Grash quickly looked at the gate, and was stunned to see Lanakila still there. He looked to the sky but saw only darkness.

Before they could move, another bird was on the lower part of the gate. Grash tried to stand but dropped again when a thunderous growl ripped out from behind him. He started to turn, but froze instantly when he saw an airborne puma, heading straight for him.

There was no time to react. Grash closed his eyes and awaited the impact. He held his breath for what seemed like forever, but the puma landed beside him rather than on top of him. Grash turned and snapped instinctively, but found only air. The puma bounded only once, and was through the gate and gone. The tribe had never taken a single step.

The barking began the instant Sarena had cleared the fence. She made a beeline down the Canyon wall without once looking back. She heard the clink of the gate being closed, just as it had sounded when Lanakila and his mate had practiced successfully. The kribas were trapped.

Not slowing a single stride, Sarena continued her dash down the slope. She ran recklessly, fearing the possible escape of one or more of the kribas. She made a sharp turn around a huge clump of manzanita and suddenly found herself bounding directly into a pack of krahstas.

In full stride, she was unable to change course. She smashed directly into a large male, who was as startled to see her as she was to see the pack. Sarena stumbled slightly, but the krahsta was sent tumbling onto its back. The entire pack immediately broke out into terrified howls and scattered in every direction.

Sarena leaped over the fallen krahsta, who was now trying to regain his feet, and headed for the bottom of the ravine. She could still hear the barks of the kribas over those of their howling cousins, but they were getting no closer. The kribas were still at the top of the hill, and hopefully locked in the yard of men. With luck, the men would take them away and never set them free.

CHAPTER 38

The light breeze was cool and brisk as it lifted gently off of the waves. The ocean seemed to glow in the darkness, as its voice sang the eternal harmony of moving water. Sand crabs darted in and out of tiny holes as the waves reached farther with each pass.

Laura stood on the sand with Keith, watching Nature in the dark. She was pressed against him to keep warm, and he held her close. A wave stretched even higher on the sand, forcing them to take a step back with a laugh.

Dinner had gone well. They hadn't spoken much, but it was okay. It took a while for Laura to get used to the stares cast at Keith, and then at her, but she soon followed Keith's lead and simply ignored them.

Keith had looked at her all night, and as much as she had tried not to Laura looked back. They did little else but eat, and try not to make too much of a mess with the pasta sauce.

After dinner the limo driver took them for a ride, ending up on the sands of Solana Beach. At first Keith held her hand. This made her a little edgy, but the nerves gave way to the chill, which had led to her current position. She decided it wasn't such a bad position at all.

"So quiet tonight," said Keith. "Did you finally run out of questions?"

"No," said Laura. "It's just that the questions I have now are much harder to ask. And quite frankly, I don't think I'm ready for any answers."

"Will you ever be?" asked Keith.

"I don't know."

Keith nodded and held her a little tighter. Neither of

them looked at the other. Their eyes were somewhere out to sea.

"You never ask me questions," said Laura.

"I never get a chance," said Keith. "You're usually grilling me about various mountain lion issues."

"True."

"And besides, I'm not sure I'm ready for any answers."

"Goon," said Laura, with a raspberry.

They laughed for a moment, then stood in silence for several more. Laura let herself relax again as she listened to the rhythm of the waves. As far back as she could remember, the ocean had always been a source of calming for her soul.

"I know it's an incredibly inappropriate time to bring up business," said Keith, "but I'm sure you heard about the court ruling today."

"No," said Laura. "I was out on a stakeout all day. I didn't hear about anything."

"A court in San Francisco made the Fish and Game Commission cancel the hunt."

"That's great!" said Laura. "You must be really happy."

"I am. I guess it's the third year in a row."

"Are you still going ahead with the ballot initiative?"

"Of course," said Keith. "We'll kick it off with 'Sarena's Song,' just like we planned."

"Good for you," smiled Laura. "What about—"

"Enough about business," interrupted Keith. "Here we are, on a moonlit night, on a Southern California beach, watching the waves. This is too romantic a setting to waste on shop talk."

"Agreed," said Laura. "So what do you want to talk about?"

"You."

"I was afraid of that."

"I don't mean delving into your jaded past," Keith said with a smile.

"Oh. Thanks."

"We can talk about the present," said Keith. "And you don't have to talk if you don't want to. I'll do the talking if you'd like."

Laura shrugged. She was always uncomfortable talking

about herself, but if Keith was going to do the talking it was fine with her.

"Okay," said Keith. He took a deep breath and looked at the stars. "I've thought about you an awful lot since we've met. An awful lot. At first I was sure it was just because you were so gorgeous."

"Oh, come on," said Laura, instantly regretting it. She had thought she was finally getting Keith's come-on line, but the way he had tensed up proved her wrong.

"Anyway," said Keith, sounding determined to finish, "the more time I spent with you, the more time I spent thinking about you. I've had a blast every time we've been together. You make me forget about the life I've carved out for myself and think about other things. I've ended up doing juggling acts with other commitments just to be with you."

"Keith . . . I don't know, I don't know, I don't know. What do you want from me?"

"I don't know. I guess I just want to spend more time with you. I want to get to know you better, and maybe break down some of those walls. Maybe we can break down some of mine while we're at it."

"What about all of your girlfriends?" Laura asked.

"That's so unfair," said Keith. "If my sources are correct, *you're* the one who goes out with a different guy every night."

"Not every night," joked Laura. "There was one night a couple of years ago . . ."

"The rumors are wrong," said Keith. "I'd have died from exhaustion years ago if I'd messed around with even a quarter of the women the rumors say I have."

Laura nodded. She knew all about rumors.

"So what do you want from me?" Laura asked again.

"For starters, I'd like to see you again," said Keith. "That's all. I think asking for anything more at this point would be ridiculous."

Laura bit down hard and closed her eyes. "I'd love to see you again," she said, then reached up and gave him a kiss.

For once, she was smiling when she walked into the office so early in the morning. Laura hadn't slept much;

she'd thought about Keith all night. She was thinking about him still.

The evening had ended appropriately enough. Keith and his limo had dropped her off at the McDonald's where her car was parked. He kissed her goodnight, and she drove home alone in a cold, noisy RX-7. And for the first time in recent memory she went home with a smile after a first date.

There were no messages in her box for a change so she walked directly to her desk, where her phone was already ringing.

"Hi, it's Dennis."

"Where were you yesterday?" Laura asked. She had hoped to see him at the stakeout, but hadn't seen anyone she recognized at all.

"Out," said Dennis. "Anyway, I'm up in Carlsbad at a preschool next to a Canyon. You're never gonna believe this, but I think our attack dog friends are all locked up."

"They are?"

"Five of them, anyway. It's the most bizarre thing I've ever seen. I thought I'd call you first. I have to call Animal Reg to come and get them. If you hurry you should be able to beat them here."

"On my way," said Laura.

The sun was warm, and Sarena was positioned just right. She had been awake for several minutes, but she hadn't moved. The soft rye grass she used for a bed was padded down perfectly below her, and the thought of interrupting such a pleasure was obscene. She kept her eyes closed, hoping to nod off again.

The events of the night before seemed far-off and distant. Somehow, she knew it was over. The kribas were gone from the Canyon, and they were not coming back. The feeling was so certain that she had slept out in the open for the first time in quite a while.

A sudden jab at her tail jerked her to her feet. With claws extended she fluffed her fur and hissed with authority, but she stood alone. She was only momentarily perplexed. Lanakila landed on a rock beside her.

"It's time to get up!" demanded Lanakila.

"You feather-brained louse!" said Sarena. "Can't you see I was sleeping? You ruined it."

"Such nasty words for the genius who saved your fur-covered hide," said Lanakila. "The kribas are still locked up, and the yard is surrounded by men."

"You could have waited to tell me," said Sarena. "I was having a wonderful dream."

"Dream later," said Lanakila. "It's time to hunt."

"No. It's time to sleep. I'm not hungry."

"See where Falanika flies?" asked Lanakila, motioning to the eastern sky. "That's where we must hunt."

"No. I'm too worn out. We'll hunt tomorrow."

"We're both hungry now. There's a perfect opportunity over there. Let's go now, or we'll never let you sleep."

Sarena growled, but the bird didn't flinch.

"Come on," said Lanakila. "We need to teach Falanika how to hunt with us anyway."

"Okay," said Sarena, reluctantly. She could tell by her friend's eyes he was serious about not letting her sleep.

"This better be a big buck," said Sarena confidently. "Or else I'm going to pluck all of your feathers out."

"Promises, promises," said Lanakila, and launched himself into the air.

Laura beat the officers from County Animal Regulation, but just barely. Dennis was standing up against a chain-link fence, along with several small children and a few adults. Laura heard the dogs long before she got close enough to see them.

There were three German shepherds, a Doberman, and a pit bull. They were all barking wildly and running in circles. They looked ragged, hungry, and mean. Laura was glad they were on the other side of the fence.

"Those are the ones," said Dennis, talking loudly so as to be heard over the constant barking. "They're the ones that came up to me in the Canyon the other day. Sad, isn't it?"

"What's going to happen to them?" asked Laura.

"Animal Reg's on the way," said Dennis. "They'll catch them and bring them back to their yard for observation. Hopefully they'll be identified. I called Gordon's Dogs this morning, and the guy's gonna come down and see if they're his. We'll also have people who lost animals see if they can identify them."

"Do you think they'll be put to sleep?" asked Laura.

"I doubt it," said Dennis. "At least not if they belong to Gordon. If they're his he'll probably get them back. He's already said he'd pay for any damage they might have done."

"You're lucky they didn't come after you," said Laura.

"Yes, very lucky," nodded Dennis. "I'm really glad we finally got them. The whole area will be a lot safer."

"How did you catch them?" asked Laura.

"I don't know," said Dennis. "They were all locked up like this when the folks from the preschool showed up for work this morning. Beats me how they all got so neatly locked up like that."

CHAPTER 39

It was quite a hike for Sarena, and she was getting irritated. Both of her friends were hovering in a tight circle high above the bottom of the ravine. Sarena could see them easily, but looking at the brush beneath them couldn't see any antlers moving about.

There was no breeze. The brush was silent and unmoving as Sarena carefully crept along the hard dirt path. She could make a direct approach, since her scent would not be carried by the wind. Unfortunately she wouldn't be able to pick up the alleen's either.

Sarena glanced up at her friends, and they seemed even higher than before. They were almost too high for Sarena to get a good bearing on the alleen. She wanted to give them a sign to get lower, but couldn't figure out how.

This was strange. Lanakila had always flown low when they'd hunted in the past. Sarena wondered if she would be on her own this time, when it came time to chase the alleen. Perhaps Lanakila had tired of riding antlers.

When her tiny path crossed a smoother path she stopped, wondering if she should turn. She was about to continue forward when she noticed her own tracks on the crossing path. She stared at them for a moment, trying to remember the last time she had come this way. She thought about it, but couldn't recall. This wasn't surprising, since she'd had so much else to think about the past few days.

She suddenly remembered the task at hand and began to step forward, hopefully in the direction of the alleen. Her right paw came down directly beside one of the old tracks, and she froze before she took another step. Her back began to tense up, and fur began to tingle all over. She lowered her head for a closer look, but there could be no mistake. It was too big to be one of her tracks.

Sarena stared at the ground for several moments, and then she began to shake. Her foot remained next to the track, and it was difficult for her to look away. Finally she glanced to the sky, only to see the two birds flying west and almost out of sight.

Movement in the brush dropped her to an immediate crouch. She held her breath and extended her claws. She wanted to run, but couldn't move. She heard steps, and they were getting closer. She bit down hard, and her tail instinctively fluffed.

From behind the brush he stepped. He stared at Sarena, clearly as nervous as she. He was bigger than she was, with a tawny coat like hers and a white face with golden eyes.

Sarena thought he was the most beautiful animal she had ever seen.

EPILOGUE

Since returning from his business trip across the border, Jake Cotter had decided to play hooky and not even bother calling the store. He was certain the employees didn't miss him. They were probably glad the cat was away.

Jake had decided to go hunting instead, and possibly bring home some more business. Now, sitting in deep brush within a Carlsbad Canyon, he could see it was more probable than possible.

He couldn't believe his luck. It was rare enough to see one mountain lion in a lifetime, but now Jake was staring across the ravine at two. Two mountain lions, and within easy range. He had never been this lucky.

Concentration was the key. He needed to concentrate on the bigger one first, and then the smaller—presumably the female. His rifle was semiautomatic, and he was glad. If his luck held he would be able to take them both, without either of them having moved a step.

He stared at them through his scope. They were truly beautiful animals. He would have to raise his price. Beauty would cost money, just like everything else. He took in a deep breath, then let out half and held the rest. He began to feel for the tension on the trigger.

Dennis Jack also was feeling lucky. The attack dogs were gone, and life would be a lot easier for a while. Having seen them up close in their cages, he knew he would have been little more than uniformed stew if they had chosen to go after him that day in the Canyon. Yes, he was feeling very lucky.

The traps were no longer necessary. As he walked

through the brush looking for the last one, he was glad the dogs had been claimed by the guy from Gordon's. There was a good chance all of them would be spared as a result.

Dennis found the last trap and was relieved to find nothing inside. He had been certain at least one of the traps would be holding a skunk, but thankfully all of them were empty. He was just about to pick up the box when his eye caught the glare of something very shiny.

It was a man with a rifle. He was aiming at something across the ravine, but Dennis's view of the target was obstructed by high brush. They were outside the city limits so the man was legally clear to shoot, but Dennis decided to check it out anyway, since this was an area where there had been repeated poaching.

"Excuse me!" Dennis said loudly.

The man jerked and nearly fell over, at the sudden intrusion. He looked over at Dennis, startled and angry, until he saw the uniform. Then he only looked startled.

Obviously the man was hunting. He was dressed in camouflage fatigues, carried a knife on his belt, and looked like an infantry soldier from the Vietnam War. Men like these always made Dennis nervous, despite his badge and uniform. The man was holding an AK-47, and Dennis was armed only with a pistol.

"Fish and Game," said Dennis, as he approached. The man lowered his rifle and smiled.

"You scared the daylights out of me," the man said, beaming.

"Understood," said Dennis, returning a smile. "You looked pretty intense."

"Was scoping out a deer," said the man. "Took all my concentration. He's gone by now, I guess."

"Sorry," said Dennis. "Just needed to check up on you. You mind if I see your license and deer tag?"

"Not at all," said the man. He rested his rifle against a large rock and reached into his pocket. He pulled out a wallet, which held a valid license and deer tag. He handed it over to Dennis.

Dennis glanced at the expiration date and saw that everything was in order. He was about to hand it back when he saw the man's name. He stared at it for several moments and tried desperately to keep his hand from shaking.

What to do? The man was wanted for felony and federal offenses. He was also in possession of a serious rifle, which was capable of blowing several large holes in Dennis's body. The strange thing was, the man might not even know he was wanted. And even if he did, he probably assumed a game warden wouldn't know anything about it.

"Do you mind if I take a look at your rifle?" Dennis asked. He knew it would be in perfectly legal condition. They always were.

"Sure, have a look," said the hunter, handing it over to Dennis.

Dennis immediately unloaded it, then drew his revolver.

"Mr. Cotter, I'm placing you under arrest. Please put your hands above your head."

Author's Note

On June 5, 1990, California voters overwhelmingly passed Proposition 117, the California Wildlife Protection Act. This law requires the state to set aside $30 million a year for thirty years for wildlife habitat purchases and preservation.

The law also put mountain lions on the protected-species list, forever.

This initiative was put together and passed because of hard work by numerous environmental groups and thousands of volunteers. To my knowledge, there were no rock stars or newspaper reporters taking prominent roles in the campaign.

About the Author

Michael Peak is an Emmy Award-winning TV journalist based in San Diego, where he lives with a tabby named Lynxie. CATAMOUNT is his second novel.

PERILOUS DOMAINS

☐ **SHADOWRUN:** *NEVER DEAL WITH A DRAGON:* **Secrets of Power Volume I by Robert N. Charrette.** In the year 2050, the power of magic has returned to the earth. Elves, Mages and lethal Dragons find a home where technology and human flesh have melded into deadly urban predators. (450787—$4.50)

☐ **SHADOWRUN:** *CHOOSE YOUR ENEMIES CAREFULLY:* **Secrets of Power Volume II by Robert N. Charrette.** As Sam searches for his sister through the streets of 2050, he realizes that only when he accepts his destiny as a shaman can he embrace the power he needs for what waits for him in the final confrontation. . . . (450876—$4.50)

☐ **SHADOWRUN:** *FIND YOUR OWN TRUTH:* **Secrets of Power Volume III by Robert N. Charrette.** A young shaman unwittingly releases a terror from the ancient reign of magic. (450825—$4.50)

☐ **THE CHRONICLES OF GALEN SWORD, Volume I:** *Shifter* **by Garfield and Judith Reeves-Stevens.** Rich, New York City playboy Galen Sword is on a quest to recover his lost heritage—to return to a parallel universe where he had been heir to a powerful dynasty. (450183—$3.95)

☐ **THE CHRONICLES OF GALEN SWORD, Volume 2:** *Nightfeeder* **by Garfield and Judith Reeves-Stevens.** Galen Sword's search for the First World made him the focal point between warring clans . . . and his very survival rested with that most dreaded of legendary beings, an adept whose powers could only be fueled by the blood of the living. (450760—$3.99)

Buy them at your local bookstore or use this convenient coupon for ordering.

NEW AMERICAN LIBRARY
P.O. Box 999, Bergenfield, New Jersey 07621

Please send me the books I have checked above.
I am enclosing $_____ (please add $2.00 to cover postage and handling). Send check or money order (no cash or C.O.D.'s) or charge by Mastercard or VISA (with a $15.00 minimum). Prices and numbers are subject to change without notice.

Card #_____ Exp. Date _____
Signature_____
Name_____
Address_____
City _____ State _____ Zip Code _____

For faster service when ordering by credit card call **1-800-253-6476**

Allow a minimum of 4-6 weeks for delivery. This offer is subject to change without notice.